A deserted village. A dragon.
A damsel in distress.

The only ring of truth was the beautiful damsel's reaction to him, a jarring bit of reality in the fantasy. For who would want to dream of that kind of response?

Reynold did not know if Mistress Sexton had laid her hand upon his arm out of some attempt to lure him into staying or if it was an innocent gesture. But he was certain of what happened next. He had caught his breath at the lightness of her touch, at the warmth of her fingers and the simple sensation of gentle feminine contact, and then she had pulled away, repulsed.

It was a reminder not to let his guard down or let anyone get close to him, and as such it was welcome. Yet Reynold could not dismiss the incident as easily as he had others in the past. It was too fresh in his mind, too insulting, too much of a disappointment. For deep down inside, he had hoped that Mistress Sexton might be different....

* * *

Reynold de Burgh: The Dark Knight
Harlequin® Historical #958—August 2009

Author Note

It has been a long time since the last de Burgh book, and I want to thank all the readers who have written to me over the years, for their continued interest and enthusiasm. I really enjoyed stepping back into the medieval world of Campion and his sons.

Although firmly grounded in the past, these characters have a timeless quality. Certainly, they are strapping heroes, tall and handsome and great knights all. But I think much of their appeal lies in the sense of family that is at the heart of the series and transcends its setting. Campion's sons are proud of their heritage, honorable and loyal. Despite an awareness of the flaws and foibles of their siblings, they share an easy affection, even when roasting each other with good humor. To me, there's nothing more fun than getting all seven brothers together for a rousing, roisterous visit, and I hope you will feel the same.

DEBORAH SIMMONS

Reynold de Burgh:
the Dark Knight

TORONTO • NEW YORK • LONDON
AMSTERDAM • PARIS • SYDNEY • HAMBURG
STOCKHOLM • ATHENS • TOKYO • MILAN • MADRID
PRAGUE • WARSAW • BUDAPEST • AUCKLAND

Recycling programs
for this product may
not exist in your area.

ISBN-13: 978-0-373-29558-6

REYNOLD DE BURGH: THE DARK KNIGHT

www.eHarlequin.com

Printed in U.S.A.

For Bridget, Daisy, Irene, Ivy, Janet, Jo, Linda, Lori,
Mary Kay, Sandi, Siglinde, and all members, past and
future, of the Tuesday Night Tennis League.

Available from Harlequin® Historical and
DEBORAH SIMMONS

Other works include:

Chapter One

Reynold de Burgh stood on the castle battlements and looked out over his family's lands as the first faint light of dawn rose on the horizon. He had been planning to leave his home for some time, but now that the moment had arrived, the parting was more painful than he'd imagined. He loved Campion and its people, and he felt a traitorous urge to remain even though he had made his decision.

He could linger, but he knew that today would be no different. He had only to wait until his father, the Earl of Campion, led his new wife down to the hall to be reminded of the changes taking place at the castle. Although Reynold loved and revered his sire and had come to like Joy, their happiness was a bitter reminder of his own lack.

In the past few years five of his six brothers had wed, too, and Reynold was painfully aware that he was next in line. Although he felt no anger or regrets over the marriages that had led his siblings to wives and families of their own, he knew that the future did not hold the same for him.

Yet soon everyone at Campion would look to Reynold or his younger brother Nicholas, wondering and murmuring over who would be the last de Burgh to fall. Reynold had decided it was easier to go, to escape the questions and the pitying glances that would follow, as well as the happiness of others. By the time Campion began welcoming new sons, he hoped to be long gone.

The thought made him rue the precious moments he had wasted in this last goodbye, and he hurried back through the castle to the bailey where his destrier was waiting. He had spoken to no one of his plans, but he had left a message, telling his father that he was going on a pilgrimage.

Although he had no real destination in mind, that explanation would prevent his family from coming after him. A pilgrimage, whether to a local shrine or one further away, was a personal decision that should keep his father and brothers at bay. Reynold did not want them leaving their wives and children to comb the countryside for him—especially when he did not want to be found.

Mindful of the servants and freemen who were stirring with the dawn, Reynold was about to mount his destrier when he heard the jingle of bells coming from the shadows near the castle doors. The sound might have been anything, and yet, he had a sinking feeling that perhaps he had waited too long to make his escape. His suspicion was soon confirmed by the sight of a small plump woman hurrying towards him.

'Ah, there, you are!' she trilled, waving an arm that sent the tiny bells on her sleeve to tinkling.

Reynold stifled a groan. Ever since his brother

Stephen had married Bridgid l'Estrange, her aunts had felt welcome to come and go at Campion at their will. They were gentlewomen and provided good company for Joy in a household composed mostly of males, but there was something about the two that made their sudden appearance here at this hour unsurprising.

Reynold's eyes narrowed. 'I beg your pardon, Mistress Cafell, but I have no time to tarry.'

'Oh, we know you are leaving,' she said, waving a plump hand airily as her sister Armes emerged from the shadows to join her.

Reynold vowed they would not sway him with their wiles. In fact, he would tell them he was off to check the dam or the fields or any one of a number of tasks that he helped his father and the bailiff oversee, so that he would be rid of them. However, when he opened his mouth, he blurted out that which was uppermost in his mind instead.

'Don't try to stop me.'

'We wouldn't dream of it, my dear,' Cafell said, reaching out a hand to pat his sleeve.

'Of course, you must go,' Armes said. Taller than her sister, she lifted her chin to fix him with a serious gaze. 'It is your destiny to complete your quest.'

Her words were not only unexpected, but made no sense to Reynold. 'What quest?'

'Why, the usual one, I suppose,' Cafell said, with a smile. 'You must slay a dragon, rescue a damsel in distress, and recover her heritage.'

For a long moment, Reynold simply stared, dumbfounded by her speech. Then he snorted, a loud sound of disdain in the stillness of the early morning. 'You're confusing me with St George.'

'Oh, I think not,' Armes said, haughtily.

'Really, Lord Reynold, some might believe the de Burghs are saints, but after coming to know them personally, I must agree with Armes,' Cafell said. 'Though you all have many fine qualities.'

Reynold shook his head. He had no time for these women and their curious babbling, to which only a fool would give credence. He knew full well his brothers would have scoffed at the very notion of a quest right out of romantic legend. Indeed, the thought made him wonder if one of his siblings, probably Robin, had enlisted the old women to hoax him.

But Robin was gone, living at Baddersly, where he was holding the demesne for his eldest brother Dunstan's wife. None but Reynold's younger brother Nicholas could be blamed, and yet would he play such a jest? And how had Nick—or anyone—discovered that Reynold was leaving? He had kept his own council, and the only sign of his plans had been the packing he did this very morning.

'There is no time to waste in idle chatter, sister,' Armes said. Then she turned her attention back to Reynold. 'You must go, but do not go alone.' And with a lift of her hand, she summoned a young boy, leading a mount laden with its own pack. 'This is Peregrine, who will serve as your squire on the journey.'

Reynold frowned at the youth, who appeared unfazed by his grimace. Indeed, the lad flashed him a grin before nimbly swinging up into the saddle as though eager for a day's outing.

Reynold shook his head. If he wanted a companion, he would be better served by his own squire, who had done well for him these past two years. But he would not take Will away from his home, Campion, into danger, perhaps never to return. So why would this boy?

'We had better hurry, my lord,' Peregrine said, with a calm certainty. Those words, more than anything, made Reynold turn to mount his destrier. Now was not the time to argue; he would send the boy back later. As if as eager to be gone as he, Reynold's horse stamped restlessly, but Cafell moved toward him once more.

'Take this, too, my lord, for your protection,' she said, handing him a small cloth pouch.

At first Reynold refused. 'I am going on a pilgrimage, not a quest,' he said through gritted teeth. But a sound from somewhere in the bailey made him hesitate to linger, so he looped the gift around his belt. Then he looked down at the two eccentric females who were the only family to mark his departure and felt a sudden thickness in his throat. He eyed them for a long moment, knowing he had a final opportunity to leave a message for his sire, but in the end, he said only what was uppermost in his mind.

'Don't let them come after me.'

Tugging on the reins, he headed toward the gates of Campion without a backward glance.

'Reynold is gone?' Lady Joy de Burgh spoke without her usual composure as she stood at the head of the high table, holding the parchment that her husband had wordlessly passed to her. She read the words, but was unable to believe what was written there. Without waiting for a reply, she sank down into the intricately carved chair nearby.

'This is my doing,' she whispered, hardly daring to voice aloud the concerns that had plagued her after she impetuously married the Earl of Campion. 'He's left because of me,' she said, lifting her gaze to her husband, but afraid to see a confirmation in his own.

'No,' Campion said as he took his seat. 'This has been long in coming.'

Joy might have questioned her husband further, but for the appearance of his son Nicholas, who missed nothing of what was happening around him.

'Reynold's gone?' he asked. 'Where did he go?'

Campion picked up the parchment that had fallen from Joy's fingers and handed it to the youngest of the strapping de Burghs.

Nicholas read the missive quickly, then gave his father a questioning glance. 'But why didn't he tell me? Why wouldn't he take me along? I'm eager for an adventure.' That was obvious to anyone who took one look at the tall, dark-haired young man who was growing up—and growing restless.

'I don't think you're the pilgrimage type,' Campion said drily.

'But why would he go alone?' Nicholas said.

That worried Joy as well. Pilgrims, even knightly ones, travelling singly were prey to all manner of villains, from common thieves to murderous innkeepers. The de Burghs all thought themselves invincible, but one man could not best a host of attackers or foil kidnapping, piracy, injury, illness...

'He didn't go alone. Peregrine went with him.'

Joy looked up in surprise to see one of the l'Estrange sisters standing before them and glanced toward her husband. Peregrine? Was that the youngster the sisters had brought with them on this visit to Campion Castle? He seemed little more than a boy.

'He did, did he?' Campion asked, his expression thoughtful.

'I don't see what help a child will be,' Nicholas said, scoffing.

'You never know,' Cafell said with one of her mysterious smiles. She looked as though she would say more, but her sister Armes tugged at her arm, pulling her away from the high table, the tinkling of bells signalling their passage from the hall.

'Do we even know this Peregrine?' Nicholas demanded.

'Better a squire than no one,' Campion said, obviously unwilling to debate the merits of the youth. And what was the point? No matter who Reynold had taken with him, they were only two people travelling alone on often treacherous roads.

'What pilgrimage will he make?' Joy asked. Durham, Glastonbury, Walsingham and Canterbury were far away, Santiago de Compostela and Rome even further. 'Surely he isn't going to the Holy Land?' The thought of that longest and most dangerous of journeys stole her breath, for she remembered when King Edward, then a prince, had marched in a crusade on those foreign lands.

Silence reigned between the three de Burghs as Campion shook his head, unable to provide an answer.

Joy studied her husband, but he gave no outward signs of distress, only wore that thoughtful expression she knew so well.

'You can send someone after him,' she suggested.

'I'll go,' Nicholas said, eagerly.

But Campion shook his head.

'He must do what he must do.'

Joy knew that her husband wasn't infallible, but the certainty in his voice comforted her and she reached for his hand. Although Reynold was not as grim and bitter as she had once thought him, he was the unhappiest of Campion's seven sons, an anomaly in a household so prosperous and loving. Perhaps his father hoped that this journey, though perilous, might bring Reynold what had eluded him so far in life.

Joy silently wished it so.

Seeing the fork in the road ahead, Reynold slowed his mount, uncertain which route to follow. Where was he going?

'Where are we going?'

The sound of someone voicing his own silent question startled Reynold, and he turned his head to see the dark-haired youth the l'Estranges had pressed on him. Lost in his own thoughts, he had passed the hours since his departure in silence and had nearly forgotten about the boy. Peregrine, was it? Accustomed to the chatter of a train when travelling, Reynold wondered if his companion was mute, but then he remembered the words that had spurred him to leave.

With a frown, Reynold assessed the boy, who, though

dressed simply, was clean and neat. Reynold had no idea why the l'Estranges had decided this Peregrine was fit to be his squire, but he was accustomed to choosing his own.

A proper squire would be of a good family well known to him, courageous and honourable. Many squires began as pages, serving at table before being allowed to clean a knight's equipment. He must know about weapons, hunting and tournaments in addition to all that would be taken for granted, such as proper manners, music and dancing. And any squire to a de Burgh would have to be able to read, with wide-ranging interests and a thirst for knowledge.

Had Peregrine learned these things in the household of a pair of eccentric old women? Reynold doubted it. And even if the youth were well prepared, Reynold had no business leading him into the unknown, travelling to where he knew not.

'My destination does not concern you, for I am travelling on alone. You may ride back to Campion,' Reynold said.

'I can't, my lord.'

Was the fellow incapable of finding his way already? 'Just turn around and follow the road behind us,' Reynold said. ''Twill lead you back home.'

The boy shook his head. 'No, my lord, for the Mistresses l'Estrange told me not to return without you.'

Reynold grunted. Did the silly women think that young Peregrine was equipped to watch over a hardened knight? More likely, it would be the other way around, the lad becoming a nuisance the further they travelled.

'Then I release you from service. Find the nearest

village and present yourself to the manor's lord,' Reynold said.

Again, the boy shook his head. He appeared neither alarmed nor angry, just calmly insistent. 'I am bound to the l'Estranges.'

'Then make your way back to their manor and other duties there,' Reynold suggested. Although he had never been to the l'Estrange holding, he knew Bridgid's aunts lived on the edge of Campion lands, a journey that should not be too long or dangerous for the youth.

'I could not. I am bound by my vow, my lord.'

Annoyed as he was by the boy's refusals, Reynold had to respect such loyalty, especially coming from an untutored lad. He could insist, of course, but there was always the possibility that Peregrine would try to follow him, falling into some sort of mischief on his own. At least the youth wasn't the sort of companion who would chatter constantly along the road, Reynold mused, which brought him back to the original question.

Where were they going?

Although unwilling to admit as much to the boy, Reynold had no idea. When he had decided to leave Campion, he'd had a vague notion of joining Edward's army. But somehow fighting against the Welsh didn't seem right when his brother's wife had inherited a manor house there. And it was whispered that Bridgid possessed the kind of powers that you didn't want turned against you. The l'Estranges were all…strange, and Reynold frowned as he remembered their actions this morning.

'How did your mistresses know that I was leaving?' he asked.

'I don't know, my lord. However, it is rumoured that they hold the secrets of divination, so perhaps they became aware of your departure through such means. A quest, they called it,' Peregrine said.

Reynold snorted at such nonsense. 'I have no quest or mission of any kind to fulfil.' He slanted a glance at the boy. 'This journey bears no resemblance to the romances, if that is what you are thinking. We travel without the usual train and even pilgrims face dangers of which you know nothing. I will not be responsible for you undertaking such a trip, vow or no vow.'

But Peregrine did not appear daunted. In fact, the boy flashed a grin that made his eagerness obvious. 'Who would not seek adventure, if given the chance?' he asked, as though questioning Reynold's sanity.

Reynold's lips curved at the challenge, for he and his brothers would once have asked the same. And for the first time this day, his heart felt a little lighter. He had seen himself as a lone wanderer, an outcast even, though of his own choosing, but this youth might prove to be a welcome companion.

'Then let us be off,' Reynold said. He urged Sirius towards the right fork, away from the road that led to his brother Dunstan's holding. This route, as Peregrine had pointed out so cheerfully, led to something new, though unlike the boy, Reynold was not looking for adventure. Indeed, he hoped not to meet with any. Or anyone.

And yet, they had not gone far along the new track before they were hailed. Squinting into the distance, Reynold saw a horse standing ahead, alone with its rider. As they neared, Reynold realised it carried both a man and a young boy. They were neatly, if not richly dressed, and looked harmless, except for a sturdy wooden staff that protruded from their pack.

'Good morning, sire,' the man said, inclining his head. 'Where are you bound?'

'We are pilgrims,' Peregrine said, and Reynold realised he would have to have a word with the boy about the merits of discretion.

'We, too!' the man exclaimed, a pleased smile crossing his worn features. 'Where are you bound?'

Peregrine did not have an answer and so looked to Reynold, who said nothing.

'Ah. You are reticent. That is understandable. But may we ride with you? Fortune favours those who travel together.'

'I don't know if your horse can keep up,' Reynold said, reluctant to add more to what had begun as his own private excursion.

'Surely you are not in such a hurry?' the man asked, undeterred. 'Part of the journey is enjoying the sights and the good company of fellow pilgrims.'

It was the latter that put Reynold off, for he was not like one of his more gregarious brothers. He had always kept to himself and had no desire to lead a motley band across the country.

But the man was persistent. 'I beseech thee, as a fellow pilgrim, to allow us to travel with you for the increased safety in numbers. I ask not for myself, but for the boy, who would seek the healing well at Brentwyn. He is lame, you see.'

At the man's words, Reynold stiffened. His first

thought was that this fellow, too, was jesting, part of some vast scheme initiated by one of his brothers to turn his departure from Campion into a prank. But why, and how? Ultimately, Reynold rejected such notions as nonsense, and as much as he would have liked to reject the man's pleas, as well, he was a knight and bound to protect those weaker.

'Very well,' he said curtly.

Thanking Reynold many times over, the fellow introduced himself as Thebald and the boy, who nodded gravely, as Rowland.

'I am Reynold, and this is Peregrine,' Reynold said, hoping that his squire would adopt some discretion from his example. The name de Burgh was well known, at least in some areas, and he did not care to deal with whatever reactions it might bring. He had consented to ride alongside these people for a few miles, not share with them his background or his business.

To his credit, Peregrine appeared more circumspect when he next entered into conversation with the strangers. Still, he and Thebald chatted amiably, relating stories of the road and various shrines and sites. Reynold listened briefly, but having no patience for such chatter, he soon returned to his own thoughts, chiefly among them how his plans for a solitary sojourn had come to this.

Something woke him. Unlike his brother Dunstan, Reynold did not sleep upright against a tree when travelling, yet he would not be a de Burgh if he did not remain alert to the slightest sounds—and cautious. And so he came awake, but kept his eyes closed as he listened carefully.

What he heard was a rustling sound, but of man, not beast, as though someone were rifling through his pack. He lay still as stone and lifted his lids just enough to see what he might. They had made camp in the ruins of an old building off the road that provided some security, but the small fire had either died out or been doused.

The only light was that from a sliver of moon that shone through the roofless remains, but it was enough to illuminate the heavy walking stick that hovered above Reynold's head. Thebald loomed over him with the stout weapon at the ready, while the boy who had used it to hop about earlier was now standing upright without aid, going through Peregrine's supplies. Had they already knocked the youth senseless?

The thought of Peregrine's fate fuelled his strength, and Reynold leapt upwards with a roar. Although wiry and tenacious, Thebald was no match for a well-trained knight, and Reynold quickly wrested the cudgel from his hand even as the thief yelled for his companion. The boy, obviously no cripple, pulled a dagger and threw it with no little skill, a deadly missile carefully aimed at Reynold's chest.

Apparently asleep, Peregrine had awoken at the noise and shouted a warning as he rose to his feet. Reynold spared him a glance only to see him felled by the young brigand, who fought with the ferocity of a demon. The two rolled around the remains of the fire, stirring it back to life.

Snatching up the knife that now stuck from his chest, Reynold put it to Thebald's throat. 'Call off your dog, if you value your life.'

Eyes bulging, the would-be thief struggled for breath. 'Stop, Rowland. Stop!' he croaked.

The young miscreant showed no signs of hearing or heeding, so Reynold struck Thebald with the walking stick, hard enough to prevent any further mischief, and turned his attention to the brawl that was now perilously close to the fire. It was obvious that the devil was trying to roll Peregrine into the embers in hopes of burning him or even setting him alight.

With a grunt, Reynold grabbed Rowland by the back of the neck and threw him on to the ground. Before he could rise, Reynold had put his own dagger to his throat.

'Listen carefully, *faux* cripple, lest you lose your life. I *am* lame, and yet I can gullet you like a fish.'

Even when presented with the sight of his injured master, Rowland remained difficult. He would admit nothing, and struggled so that Reynold was forced to tie him up with a length of rope in his pack. And after Peregrine and Reynold had gathered up their belongings and mounted, taking the thieves' horse with them, the youth railed at them, screaming curses into the night.

'I cannot believe it,' Peregrine murmured, obviously shaken by the encounter. 'He seemed so gentle and kind this afternoon.'

'Let that be a lesson to you, boy. Appearances can be deceiving.'

'They could have killed us while we slept!'

'You perhaps, but not I.' When Peregrine ducked his head in embarrassment, Reynold softened his tone. 'I think they are nothing more than common robbers who make a living by preying on pilgrims. Murder is probably only a last resort for them, else they would have killed us first and then picked our pockets.'

Peregrine did not look comforted. 'But what about that knife? I saw it strike you in the chest! Are you not wounded, my lord?'

Reynold shook his head. 'I would not go upon the roads without mail, though I've covered the short coat with my tunic so I don't draw attention.'

'But you will always draw attention.'

Dare the boy refer to his leg? Reynold slanted him a glance, and Peregrine stammered. 'I—I mean… It's only that you've got that big sword and, well, you're a de Burgh. Who could mistake you?'

Reynold snorted. 'I was unremarkable enough for Thebald and Rowland to think they could master, if those were their names.'

'Was it true, what you told him?' Peregrine asked. At Reynold's sharp look, he stammered again. 'I—I just wondered because you can't tell, by looking at you, I mean.'

'Yes, I have a bad leg,' Reynold said.

'Were you injured in battle?'

Reynold shook his head. 'I've had it since birth,' he said with a carelessness he didn't feel. But the pose came easily to him, for he was accustomed to hiding his feelings, whether it be his resentment when his brothers urged him on, making light of his affliction, his jealousy at the abilities they took for granted, or his bitterness at his place as the runt of the litter that was the grand de Burgh family.

'Was it the midwife's doing?'

Lost in his own thoughts, Reynold was surprised to hear the question, for no one ever asked him about his leg. He never discussed the subject. Although he could hardly reprimand the boy for simple curiosity, Reynold could not bring himself to comment, especially when the question was one none could answer. He gave a tense shrug.

'I—I only asked because my sister helped the midwife at home, and she says sometimes the baby isn't in the right position to come out properly. The women try to move it as best they can, but who knows what injury they might do? And some come out not at all or feet first. Is that what happened to you?'

Again Reynold shrugged. There was no use speculating since everyone involved was dead.

'Or it could have been the swaddling,' Peregrine said, as though thinking aloud. 'They're supposed to stretch and straighten the baby's limbs, but carefully. The midwife told my sister that bad swaddling has caused men to grow up to be—'

The boy must have realised what he was saying, for he stopped abruptly, leaving his final word unspoken.

It hung in the air between them, an appellation that Reynold rarely heard, but was painful none the less. He drew in a deep breath and spoke in a tone intended to put an end to the conversation.

'I am not a cripple.'

Chapter Two

They kept along the same road. Wide enough for a cart, it was probably designed for market traffic. After their experience the night before, Peregrine suggested a smaller track, which led to a manor house where they could rest in safety and comfort. But Reynold was not eager to proclaim his whereabouts, and he reminded the youth that danger was part of travel.

Frowning, Peregrine didn't appear quite as eager for adventure as he had a day earlier, but 'twas a good lesson for him, Reynold knew. Better that he learn now rather than later when they were even further into the wilds.

'Are we going to Walsingham or Bury St Edmunds?' Peregrine asked.

Reynold slanted the boy a glance, for he had given a pilgrimage no thought beyond using it as an excuse to leave his home. But now he considered the idea more carefully. They could hardly continue wandering aimlessly through the land, and a pilgrimage would give them a destination and a worthy one. Indeed, had he been alone,

Reynold might have headed to the healing well that the thieves had mentioned—just for curiosity's sake.

But Peregrine's presence stopped him.

Reynold had learned to keep his private yearnings to himself long ago—when his father had caught his brother trying to sell him the tooth of Gilbert of Sempringham, the patron saint of cripples. There was nothing personal in the deceit; Stephen had quite a busy trade in dubious relics going among his brothers and other gullible parties. But, Campion, horrified by Reynold's duping, had put an end to it.

And, Reynold, young as he had been, understood it was better to hide his feelings, along with any trace of vulnerability. His family preferred to ignore his bad leg, and so he did his best to oblige them. By now, he was so well practised in the art that he would not let anyone see himself, not even a strange lad who already knew far too much about him. So where else would they head?

'What made you think we are going to Walsingham or Bury St Edmunds?' Reynold asked.

'We are heading east, my lord.'

Reynold was impressed. 'And how can you tell that, by the sun?'

'I've got a chilinder, my lord.'

Reynold looked at the lad in surprise. Not many travellers possessed the small sundial. Just how well had the l'Estranges supplied the would-be squire?

'I looked at all the maps, too. Glastonbury is south, and Durham is north.'

Reynold began to wonder how long the l'Estranges had suspected he was leaving. He was tempted to ask

Peregrine, but thought better of it. Did he really want to know the answer?

'You obviously have your heart set on a longer journey than our thief Thebald had in mind,' Reynold said. 'But maps are usually of little use.'

Geoffrey, the most learned of the de Burghs, had complained that most were vague and ill made. In fact, on the map of the world, the Holy Land was at the centre, with various places of the ancient world boldly marked, while other countries were depicted only by fantastic beasts. England was at the edge of the world, as though marking the end of it, when sailors knew that was not true.

What Peregrine referred to was probably one of the routes written down that showed little or no drawings, but placed the larger towns on a line of travel and estimated the distances between them. 'Twas a little better, but still… 'I'd put my faith in a good reckoning by the sky, the tolling of the church bells to guide me or your chilinder,' Reynold said.

Peregrine grinned at that, and Reynold felt his own lips curve in response. 'Where would you like to go?' he asked, surprising both himself and the boy. He expected that the youth would say London, for who would not want to see that great city?

Instead, Peregrine shrugged. 'It doesn't really matter, does it, my lord?'

Reynold slanted him a sharp glance. Had last night's misadventure stolen all of the boy's enthusiasm?

But Peregrine did not appear to be unhappy. 'I just mean that where we head is not quite as important as what happens, is it?' he said. 'Since we are on a quest, I mean.'

Reynold snorted. Surely the boy was not hanging on to that bit of nonsense? What had the l'Estranges said? That he was to slay a dragon and rescue a damsel in distress? It sounded like one of the stories about Perceval, whose mother enjoined him to be ready to aid any damsel in distress he should encounter as a knight.

'I hate to disappoint you, Peregrine, but I think the l'Estranges have heard too many romantic tales. I have been on many journeys and have never encountered a damsel in distress.'

'But what of the Lady Marion?' Peregrine asked.

Reynold frowned. Marion had been in trouble, having been waylaid upon the road, but it was his brothers Geoffrey and Simon who found her, not Reynold or Dunstan, the de Burgh who married her.

'In fact, weren't all the de Burgh wives once damsels in distress?'

Reynold choked back a laugh. A few of his brothers' wives he barely considered damsels, let alone distressed ones. One or two were as fierce as their husbands, and he said as much to Peregrine. 'If you dared suggest to Simon's wife that he rescued her, she would have you dangling by the throat in less time than you could blink.'

'Still, they were all in need of aid.'

'Some, perhaps,' Reynold said. 'But none were menaced by a dragon. Did the l'Estranges mention to you that they enjoined me to slay one?'

That silenced the lad. When Reynold glanced his way, Peregrine was looking straight ahead, his face red. Perhaps the boy still believed in such things, and though some might have taken the opportunity to mock the youth, Reynold did not. There had been too many times when he wanted to believe himself—in the romantic tales, in the healing wells, in the possibility of making himself whole…

But he drew the line at dragons.

'I think we've missed it somehow,' Peregrine said.

The boy's disappointed expression reminded Reynold of Nicholas, the youngest of the de Burghs, and he felt a twinge of wistful longing. Had he ever been that young and eager? He felt far older than Peregrine—and his own years.

They had been travelling for more than a week, swallowing dust, fording streams and avoiding forested areas and the brigands that frequented them. They had given away the thieves' mount to those in need. And at Reynold's insistence, they had kept off the old wide roads to the smaller tracks and byways, which meant they had taken a meandering route that might have led them astray.

Yet Reynold could muster no concern. While an interesting destination, Bury St Edmunds inspired no urgency, perhaps because he couldn't help wondering what would follow their visit there. For now they were pilgrims. What would they become afterwards? Eventually, his coin would run out. And he had no wish to join the rabble of the road—outlaws, former outlaws who were sentenced to wander abroad, bondsmen who had fled their service and vagabonds who kept to unpopulated areas in order to avoid arrest.

The thought gave him pause. As a knight and a de

Burgh, he was a man of discipline, ill suited to an existence without goal or purpose. He had set out to escape
the happiness and expectations of his relatives, but
leaving behind his family had not given him the satisfaction he had sought. Had he had hoped that once
away…? But, no. He had trained himself not to hope.

'Perhaps we should turn around,' Peregrine suggested, rousing him from his thoughts.

Reynold shook his head. He did not like the idea of
retracing their steps, making no progress, going back…
'There's a village ahead. We can right ourselves there.'

But when they reached the outlying buildings of the
settlement, they saw no one about to question concern-
ing their whereabouts or the direction of Bury St
Edmunds. Indeed, the village was eerily devoid of life.
Reynold slowed his massive mount, as did Peregrine his
smaller horse, and the sound of the hooves were loud
in the silence. Too loud. Around them, Reynold heard
none of the typical noises—of animals, screaming
babies, shouting children, bustling villagers, creaking
wheels and banging tools.

The hair on the back of Reynold's neck rose, and
he tried to dismiss the notion that someone was
watching them.

'What is this place?' Peregrine asked, his voice
hushed with apprehension.

'It looks deserted,' Reynold said. In his travels with
his brothers, he had come across the remains of abandoned buildings and even villages. 'Sometimes the land
just isn't good enough to sustain the residents, so they
move to richer soil. Sometimes repeated floods cause

them to move.' Reynold paused to clear his throat. 'And sometimes death is responsible.'

Reynold heard Peregrine's swift intake of breath. 'Do you mean someone killed them?'

'Not someone, something,' Reynold said. 'Sickness can strike and spread, wiping out all but a few who flee for their lives.' His words hung in the air, and he tried not to shudder. Unlike his brothers, who carelessly considered themselves invincible, Reynold was aware of his own imperfections and mortality, and he felt a trickle of unease.

'Then maybe we should turn around.'

'No.' Reynold spoke softly, but plainly. This place did not hold the stink of death, and yet it seemed that something was not right. What was it?

'So there's nothing to be afraid of?' Peregrine asked. His question, hardly more than a whisper, was followed by the sudden sharp sound of something flapping in the breeze, and Reynold saw the boy flinch.

'No,' Reynold said, even as he wondered how long the village had stood empty. The roof thatching had not deteriorated, and the buildings were well kept. Instead of ruins and weeds, he saw homes that appeared inhabited, except there was no one. No people. No animals. No life.

'It looks like they just left, doesn't it?' Peregrine asked in a shaky voice.

The situation was peculiar enough to make a grown man wary, but Reynold found no signs that the place had been attacked—by man or disease. There were no corpses to be seen—or smelled—and no evidence of recent graves. The residents were just…gone.

'Maybe they are off to a fair or festival elsewhere or were called up to their lord's manor,' Peregrine said.

Reynold shook his head. He could think of no instance in which every person, able or not, man, woman or child, would be commanded to leave their homes. And the huts were neatly closed, animals and possessions gone, as far as he could tell.

'My lord, we are headed in the wrong direction. Let us go back,' Peregrine said, and there was no mistaking his anxiety.

Again Reynold shook his head, and this time he held up a hand to silence the lad. Had he heard faint footsteps, or was that simply the same piece of leather flapping in the breeze? Although he could perceive no threat, Reynold still felt as though eyes were upon him, taking in their every move. If so, constant chatter was a distraction, as well as providing information to the enemy.

Reynold was aware that the seemingly deserted structures could hide brigands nearly as well as a wooded area, but he had no intention of turning tail and fleeing. He had never walked away from a fight and was not about to start now, even if he and the boy were outnumbered.

But as they moved forwards, nothing stirred except the tall grasses that surrounded a pond, where the mill was quiet, its wheel still. A small manor house stood apart, further from the road, its doors and shutters closed. Ahead lay the ruins of a stone building, and then the road veered round an odd hill. Opposite a small church was situated, unremarkable except for some kind of decoration on its side. Reynold slowed his mount further in order to take a better look, only to draw in a sharp breath of recognition.

'Is that a dragon?' Peregrine whispered. Again, the words had barely left his mouth when a sound echoed in the silence. But this time it was no errant noise produced by the wind, but the loud and unmistakable ringing of bells. *Church bells.*

Sabina Sexton stood in the shadows of the chapel as the echoes died away and watched the two strangers in the roadway.

'This will surely be the death of us!' Ursula said, dropping the bell ropes as though they burned her.

'Even brigands would not kill us in a church, surely,' Sabina said, hoping it were true. She had run out of options, and these two were the first people they had seen in weeks. When young Alec had alerted her to their arrival, she had hurried to the church, hoping that a meeting here would offer more protection than the roadway.

'And these two do not resemble robbers. Perhaps they are pilgrims,' Sabina said.

'Then how are they to help us? They will likely run away and spread the tale of Grim's End even further afield.'

Sabina hoped not, for already they were cut off, their small corner of the world avoided by any who knew of its troubles. Outside, the man dismounted, and Sabina stepped to the window for a better view. 'He does not have the look of a pilgrim, nor does his horse. That is a mighty steed, the kind a knight would ride.'

Ursula hurried over to join her, but Sabina kept her attention on the stranger. There was something about the way he held himself that made him different from any man she had ever seen. Straight and tall, wide-shouldered, with dark hair falling to his shoulders, he wasn't dressed as a knight, and yet he had not fled the village. Nor did he seem fearful, just wary. And confident.

'He wears no mail or helmet or gauntlets,' Ursula said.

'Yes, but look at his sword,' Sabina whispered. The scabbard was too large to hold the sort of weapon a pilgrim would carry or handle with ease, unless that pilgrim were a knight…

'He has a harsh visage,' Ursula said, and Sabina finally turned to face her attendant.

'He does not,' Sabina whispered. She was about to vow that she thought him handsome, but Ursula's worried expression stopped her. As did the realisation that she should not be focusing on such unimportant details when so much was at stake.

'Very well. Then let me speak to them, mistress, while you hide in the cupboard,' Ursula said.

'Nay. You hide, and I will treat with him.'

'Mistress, you do not understand! You are a young, beautiful woman. We know nothing of this man, except that he looks dangerous. At least wait until Urban arrives.'

'I cannot wait,' Sabina said heatedly, though she kept her voice to a whisper. 'If we dally, these two will be gone, and our last chances for aid gone with them.'

Ursula started wringing her hands. 'Mistress, please, we can leave ourselves. We have but to—'

Sabina cut her off with a sharp shake of her head. The argument was a familiar one, which she did not intend to resume here and now. Quickly, she glanced out the window to see that the boy had dismounted as well, but it was the man who held her interest.

Large, muscular and formidable, he seemed the answer to her prayers. Drawing a moaning Ursula to her side, Sabina stepped back into the shadows, her hand on a small dagger that was hardly more than an eating utensil.

It would be little use against the strength of the stranger, but Sabina did not fear for her safety. Instead, despite Ursula's warnings and the man's grim expression, for the first time in months she felt a glimmer of hope.

Motioning the pale-faced Peregrine towards the door of the building, Reynold drew his sword. He had never stepped so armed into a place of worship, but this was no ordinary church. Those bells had not rung themselves, and he did not wish to be cut down by robbers intent upon luring their victims inside. At his nod, Peregrine pulled open the door, and Reynold peered into the darkness. But he saw no movement within.

'Maybe the wind struck the bells,' Peregrine whispered.

Holding up a hand for silence, Reynold slipped into the building, but the shadowed interior appeared empty, and he heard nothing except what sounded suspiciously like a whimper from Peregrine.

'Who is there? Show yourself.'

'Don't kill us! Have mercy!' a female voice rang out, and an older woman fell before him, quaking with fear.

Reynold stepped back, startled, for she was no beggar, dressed in rags. Nor did she appear to be ill or hurt, a victim abandoned by her fellows. But she could be in league with robbers, who, as he had already discovered, went to great lengths for any spoils.

'Who else is here?' Reynold called, refusing to let down his guard.

'Only I.' It was a woman's voice, but unlike the shrill screech of the other's, this one was low and smooth and made Reynold think of honey. The figure that emerged from the shadows was different, too. Definitely not a cutpurse or any sort of mean female, she was dressed in the finer clothes of a lady and held herself thusly, with grace and composure.

And she was beautiful, like an image from a book or a tapestry. Golden hair fell about her shoulders, and her skin was flawless and pale. Although she was slender, her dark green gown revealed a woman's form, and Reynold had never seen any who so approached the romantic ideal. For a long moment he simply stared, wondering whether she was some sort of vision. But Peregrine's gasp told Reynold that he had seen her, too.

'I am Sabina Sexton of Sexton Hall here in Grim's End, and this is Ursula,' she said, helping the older woman, who was still shaking, to her feet.

'Grim's End?' Peregrine's voice was little more than a squeak.

'Yes. May I not know your name?'

'Peregrine,' he answered. Then he stepped into the light, so as to make a better target of himself. But before Reynold could reprimand him, he spoke again. 'And this is Lord Reynold de Burgh.'

Reynold frowned. Had the boy not learned to keep his confidences? If they were outnumbered, they might well be held for ransom and Reynold would wring the cost out of his squire's hide. But a few strides around the inside of the church revealed no one else. Yet why would these two be here, alone in a deserted village? Had they survived some illness that had killed the other inhabitants?

'We are pilgrims, on our way to Bury St Edmunds,' Peregrine said, and Reynold shot him a quelling look. But the boy appeared to be totally enthralled by the woman, and who could blame him? Fleetingly, Reynold wondered whether she was some kind of siren, luring travellers to their death in this empty place called, fittingly, Grim's End.

'My Lord de Burgh.' If she was intent upon mischief or murder, it was not apparent, for Mistress Sexton called his name with a mixture of urgency and entreaty. She even moved towards him, only to step back, away from his outstretched sword. With a frown, he sheathed it, though he remained alert.

'Obviously, you are no simple pilgrim, but a lord, and a knight as well?'

'All the de Burghs are knights,' Peregrine piped up, with a giddy smile that Reynold longed to wipe from his face.

'Quiet, you,' Reynold admonished. Although the women appeared to present no threat, the situation was hardly normal.

'I am not familiar with these de Burghs of whom you speak, yet I am in most dire need of a knight,' Mistress Sexton said.

Reynold slanted her a glance of surprise. Although he did not expect everyone in the country to know of Campion and his seven sons, still her reaction made him uneasy, as if she were not of this world. Dismissing such a fancy, Reynold turned towards the other woman, who looked ordinary enough, if frightened. 'What happened here? Where are the rest of the villagers? Did some sickness kill them all?'

'Nay, my lord,' the one called Ursula said. She drew in a shaky breath and began ringing her hands in agitation. ''Tis worse than that, more horrifying and deadly than any illness.'

Again, Reynold felt the hairs on the back of his neck rise.

'But no challenge to a man such as this! Knights fear nothing,' Mistress Sexton said, with a certainty that Reynold could not share.

He feared plenty, but he was not about to go into the details with these two. Were they being menaced by outlaws or brigands? Had there been a kidnapping? Murder?

'Perhaps you should explain the situation more fully,' Reynold said, returning his attention to Mistress Sexton. She appeared the more lucid of the two, though neither made much sense. 'Are you and this woman all who live in the village?'

'Nearly,' Mistress Sexton said. 'There are a few stalwarts who remain with us.'

Reynold frowned. Had he and Peregrine stumbled into some kind of local conflict, a battle between neighbouring landowners? He walked towards the window and glanced out, but all was still and quiet. 'Where are the others now?'

'Hiding! We are always hiding!' Ursula wailed. 'I beg you, my lord, take us away from this place.'

Reynold glanced sharply at Mistress Sexton, but she shook her head in disagreement. Still, if only a few people were here, they could hardly survive for long. Maybe the older woman *was* the more lucid of the two.

'What are you hiding from?' Peregrine asked, wide-eyed.

'Yes, if sickness didn't kill the others, what did?' Reynold asked.

'Nothing! They fled like cowards, rather than face our foe,' Mistress Sexton said, with obvious contempt.

'What of your family? Your father? Your liege lord? Surely he would send soldiers to aid you,' Reynold said.

'My parents are dead,' Mistress Sexton said. 'And our lord's only concern is greed. It matters little to him where he gets his labour, whether here or Sandborn or elsewhere.'

'Yea, let us all be eaten, for he cares not!' Ursula wailed.

'*Eaten?*' Peregrine's question was little more than a whisper, but it echoed Reynold's thoughts. Was some kind of wild beast attacking the villagers?

'Yes, eaten!' Ursula said. 'Swallowed whole, roasted on a spit of fiery breath!'

'You cannot be certain of that.' Mistress Sexton turned to reprove her companion, as though their discussion was not one bit peculiar. 'And 'tis no matter because a knight does not fear such things. Nor can he refuse a plea for help.'

'*Swallowed whole?*' Peregrine's voice rose, and Reynold wondered if *either* of the women was lucid. Perhaps they had been left here to wander witless, abandoned by those who feared the insane.

For the first time since leaving Campion, Reynold wished that one of his brothers were with him. Surely Geoffrey, who had handled his lunatic of a wife, would know what to do with these two. Simon would probably have taken them to the nearest convent, but Reynold was reluctant to remove them against their will, though the older one seemed eager for an escape. Perhaps she was held in the thrall of Mistress Sexton.

Reynold could certainly understand that, for when she turned toward him, it was hard for him to focus on anything except her beauty, which was enough to seize one's breath.

'I am a damsel much distressed, my lord,' she said in an earnest tone. 'And I charge you to honour your vow to aid any such as me, to rescue me and my people by slaying the great beast that is menacing this village.'

Reynold heard Peregrine's gasp, but he ignored it to study Mistress Sexton with a more jaundiced eye. Although her entreaty seemed serious enough, her words sounded far too familiar for his comfort. 'And just what great beast am I supposed to slay?' he asked.

Mistress Sexton lifted her delicate blonde brows as though surprised by the question. But her lovely face wore a serious expression when she gave him the answer he both dreaded and expected.

''Tis a dragon, my lord.'

Chapter Three

'It's just as the l'Estranges said!' Peregrine's voice, laced with awe, rang out in the silence, but Reynold was not so gullible.

'Yes, it does seem very familiar, doesn't it?' he asked, his voice lowering to a harsh whisper. Stepping closer to Mistress Sexton, he bearded her with a pointed look. 'And I'm curious as to who is responsible.'

To her credit, the woman appeared bewildered by his attitude. No doubt she had been chosen with an eye towards her charms, which were intended to dazzle him into witlessness, and he felt the sharp sting of insult. 'Was it Stephen? Or Robin? Whoever it was went to some trouble to involve you, considering how far you are from Campion.'

He turned to Peregrine. 'Is that why you led me here?'

'I—I? I did not lead you here!' Peregrine stammered. 'You chose the roadways, my lord.'

'Yet I recall you suggesting Bury St Edmunds.'

'But that's just because you were heading east, my

lord.' The boy's face flamed, and he acted indignant, yet Reynold had seen mummers and such who could appear convincing in some sham. And there was no denying that Peregrine was allied with the l'Estranges, a family that both Stephen and Robin had married into.

Reynold opened his mouth to demand some answers, but everyone started talking at once, and it was all he could do to sort them all out. As far as he could tell, Peregrine was denying any involvement in the so-called quest, Mistress Sexton claimed to know nothing of the boy or Campion, and Ursula wailed unintelligibly.

'Silence!' he said.

Everyone looked to him, even Ursula, who finally ceased her moaning. And in the ensuing quiet, Reynold heard something, an odd roar that was faint yet discernible in the stillness of the deserted village. Curious, he cocked his head to listen, but the noise was replaced by that of footsteps. Just how deserted was this village? Reynold put his hand on his sword as a man ran into the church carrying a pitchfork.

'Get below!' the fellow said, rushing toward the rear of the room, and the women, white-faced, turned to follow.

'Hurry,' Mistress Sexton said, putting a hand out as if to take Reynold's arm just as something shot past him.

'Alec! I told you to return to your mother,' Mistress Sexton said to the blur that revealed itself to be a young boy. 'Where is she?'

'At the manor, mistress. I can run there.'

'No, you cannot!' Reaching for his arm, Mistress Sexton dragged the youth towards the back of the building, where shadows hid a narrow door and a spiral stair that led into a small cellar. Although Reynold did not share his brother Simon's abhorrence for underground spaces, he was reluctant to join these strangers, especially if it was part of some prank being played upon him.

But he had been raised to respect women, no matter what their manner, and the urgency of these people made him follow, if more slowly than Peregrine. He did not shut the door completely and halted on the steps, where he could keep both the area below and the door in view. He could probably kick it in, if necessary, but would rather prevent it being shut—or locked—against him.

The two women huddled together, Ursula whimpering softly, and the man took up a stance next to Mistress Sexton. Although his pitchfork pointed toward the ceiling, there was no mistaking his defensive posture. Surely he was not her husband? Reynold tensed at the thought. He had assumed she was unmarried because she wore her hair down and, well, she was so beautiful… Reynold frowned at such reasoning. But hadn't she called herself a damsel? Reynold felt a certain tautness in his chest ease.

Besides, the man's clothes were not as fine as hers, nor was his manner, for he said nothing, only looked frightened. Indeed, everyone was still and silent, as though awaiting something, though Reynold had no idea what. Perhaps Stephen was arriving to personally witness the havoc wrought by his jest.

The thought annoyed him. 'All right, I have followed you here like a trained monkey. Now what?' he asked.

'Shh! He'll hear you,' the boy Alec said, his face ashen.

'Who?'

'The dragon,' the man whispered in a fierce tone.

Reynold snorted. 'So it is here now? I admit I'd like to see the creature for myself.' He turned to go up the stair, but a squeak from Alec stopped him. The stark terror on the boy's face made him hesitate.

'He can hear really well,' Alec whispered. 'Or else he sniffs us out.'

'What makes you say that?'

'Because sometimes he'll burn the places where people are hiding with his fiery breath.'

Reynold tried to remember if he had seen any charred areas when riding through the village, but thatched roofs were prone to fire, as were the flimsy structures of most village homes. What would make these people think a dragon was responsible? Reynold's eyes narrowed and then he shook his head as if to clear it. This was only a jest, some nonsense concocted by his brothers, and though the players were convincing, he would not be mocked as a fool. He turned once more to go.

'Don't move.' The man spoke in a nervous high-pitched voice, but his words made Reynold swing toward him. Although the fellow still appeared frightened, he was holding the pitchfork in front of him, as if intending to run Reynold through with it. *Let him try*, Reynold thought, his hand on his sword hilt.

'No, Urban, stop!' Mistress Sexton said, grabbing at the man's arm. 'What are you doing?'

'I am protecting us all from this stranger and his actions,' the man said, though he seemed to possess more bravado than bravery.

'This stranger is a lord and a knight who is here to

save us,' Mistress Sexton said, and the pitchfork dipped, as though its owner faltered in surprise.

'Perhaps your weapon might be better used against the dragon,' Reynold said, wryly. 'You are welcome to join me above.'

Without waiting for a reply, Reynold was up the stair and through the narrow door in a moment and heard no sound of pursuit. Indeed, he heard no sound at all. Whatever had driven the group to the cellar had stopped, and the building was eerily quiet once more. Reynold moved to the exterior door and scanned the area outside, but nothing stirred. Thankfully, his destrier and Peregrine's mount remained where they were tied, Sirius idly flicking his tail at a fly, with no sign of distress.

Reynold glanced upwards, but the only thing in the sky was a bird or two. Leaning against the doorframe, looking out over the oddly empty village, he tried not to wonder why his brothers had concocted this elaborate scheme. In their younger days, boredom, restlessness and a competitive streak might have driven them, but to these lengths? And now they all were occupied with new responsibilities, except for Nicholas, who usually was not one for such silliness. Had Reynold once expressed some yearning to Geoff over a romantic tale long forgotten? To slay a dragon? His wish for a damsel, or a lady of his own, he hoped he had kept well to himself.

Reynold shook his head. There would be time for such musings later. Now he just wanted to get away from a place that, fraud or not, was too strange for his taste. And then what? And then where? Again, Reynold pushed such thoughts aside, focusing solely on Bury St Edmunds. Hearing footsteps behind him, he straightened, but it was only a rather shame-faced Peregrine who approached.

'You would think that a hungry beast such as a dragon would make short work of such tasty morsels, wouldn't you?' Reynold asked, inclining his head toward the horses.

'My lord, I swear I had no hand in this,' Peregrine said. 'All I know is what the l'Estranges told me about your quest.'

'The seers,' Reynold said, with a low sound of dismissal.

''Tis true! They can foretell the future, my lord! Why, I've heard that—'

Reynold cut the boy off with a raised hand. 'Do you see a dragon?'

'No, my lord.'

'Then let us cease this nonsense and be gone.'

'My lord, I…' Peregrine's words trailed off as though reluctant to voice his opinion. *That had to be a first*, Reynold thought wryly.

'Well, what is it?'

Wearing a worried expression, Peregrine faced Reynold directly. 'I think they are serious.'

'What?'

'About the beast, my lord. I know you believe the l'Estranges had something to do with it, but I don't see how. And those people seem really frightened.'

'What makes you say that?'

'I didn't follow you up the stairs right away, a

cowardly act that I'm sorry for, but the man with the pitchfork was right by me,' Peregrine explained in a rush. 'And after you left, they were arguing.'

'Who?'

'That man Urban and Mistress Sexton. I think he's her servant or inferior, but he still tries to tell her what to do.' Peregrine glanced behind him and lowered his voice. 'I fear he's a bully.'

Reynold almost laughed aloud. They were standing among empty buildings in an abandoned village inhabited only by a couple of people who were raving about a dragon. And Pergrine was concerned that one of them, a fellow who looked ill at ease wielding even a pitchfork, might act the petty tyrant? It didn't take his brother Geoff's intelligence to figure out just why the boy was concerned. Mistress Sexton had made at least one conquest, though not, perhaps, the one intended.

'I don't think we should leave her here with him,' Peregrine said.

Reynold shrugged. 'She is welcome to go with us to Bury St Edmunds.' *Or wherever she makes her true home.*

Peregrine shook his head. 'She won't go. I think she's pretty stubborn since she wouldn't listen to that man.' The boy gazed up at Reynold with a look of expectation, as if waiting for him to fix everything with a wave of his sword.

Reynold frowned. As the runt of the de Burgh litter, he was used to seeing such blind faith directed at his brothers, not himself. 'What would you have me do?'

'Listen to me.' Mistress Sexton's voice rang out behind him with a strength and determination not evident before, and Reynold turned towards her. She stood alone, lovelier than ever in a shaft of light from the doorway, her hands clasped in front of her, and he could see why his young squire was so taken with her. But Reynold told himself he was older and wiser—and far more cynical.

'You cannot abandon us,' she said, with a fierce expression that did not lessen her beauty. 'I charge you upon your vow as a knight to hear me out. Let us go to my home, where you can eat, and we can talk.'

'Why should we open our pitiful stores to those who may rob us?' Urban asked, appearing behind her.

'There is precious little to steal, should they be so inclined,' Mistress Sexton said, without even turning towards the man. She kept her attention upon Reynold, and such was the force of it that his own will wavered. What if she wasn't lying? He could almost hear his father's admonition not to turn his back on a woman in trouble.

'You don't know this stranger,' Urban protested. 'And you have only their word that he is a lord or a knight.'

Reynold gave Urban a long, assessing look, trying to determine what part he played in the scheme. The fellow appeared both frightened and belligerent, but one thing was clear: Peregrine wasn't the only one taken with Mistress Sexton. Was Urban simply covetous of the damsel, or was he the bully Peregrine thought? Reynold had an obligation to aid those in need, as Mistress Sexton liked to point out. But was there a need, and, if so, just what was it?

If he could get her alone, Reynold thought he might be able to discover the truth, but that idea led his mind in another, more tantalising direction until he put a stop to it. He needed to keep a clear head, lest he become just another addled admirer of Mistress Sexton. Even if she wasn't a liar, experience had taught him to be wary of women, especially beautiful ones, for they had no interest in a man like him.

'Very well,' Reynold said. 'I shall hear you out.'

The look of relief on her face made Reynold uncomfortable, and he stayed well back when she led the way out of the church. From that position, he could keep a wary eye on the pitchfork, lest it find its way into his back.

Gathering the reins of their horses, Reynold and Peregrine retraced their route round the curve in the road, then followed a short track to the small manor. It looked like any to be found in a little village, solidly built of stone and slate, except for the forlorn aspect and the grass that was growing too tall around, proclaiming its neglect.

Inside, the hairs on the back of Reynold's neck stood up again, for he had never seen a hall such as this: empty, lifeless and silent except for their own footsteps. Mistress Sexton's voice, when it rang out, nearly made him flinch.

'Adele,' she called. 'Come out, for it is safe now. And we have guests.' A woman hurried in from the kitchens, fright etched upon her worn features, but at the sight of the boy she cried out and ran forwards.

'Alec!'

Throwing her arms around the lad, she wept with apparent relief, and for the first time this day, Reynold began to wonder whether he was in the wrong, for who would pretend such fear and joy? The words of the l'Estrange sisters might be coincidence or otherwise, but these people did not seem capable of perpetrating so enormous a hoax. Indeed, Reynold felt a bit ashamed of his assumption that even here, so far from Campion, the de Burghs would hold sway.

With a glance, he took in the small band that appeared to be the only inhabitants of the village: one sullen fellow who looked unable to defend himself, let alone others; a boy younger than Peregrine; the boy's mother, obviously a servant; and the two other women.

As if divining his thoughts, Mistress Sexton turned towards him. 'This is all that is left of Grim's End,' she said, her bearing proud none the less. 'Will you hear our story?'

Over a simple meal of cheese, dried apples, and some kind of egg dish, Mistress Sexton spoke. 'It began even before spring, so that few proper crops were put in, and the winter seed was destroyed. Animals were killed and their owners were run off.'

'People were afraid. They would rather start anew than face the beast,' Urban said, and Reynold couldn't tell whether he was disgusted with those who fled or wished he had joined them.

'We learned to hide when we heard it coming,' the boy Alec said.

'We have little growing except small, scattered gardens, and no cows or pigs or oxen. And what food we have stored cannot last indefinitely,' Mistress Sexton said.

Obviously, they were frightened of something, but

any beast might kill animals or attack humans, and fires were usually the result of dry thatch and sparks, not burning breath. 'Why a dragon?' Reynold asked.

'Someone woke it!' Alec said, wide-eyed.

It had been sleeping? Before Reynold could comment, Mistress Sexton spoke. 'Our village, Grim's End, was founded by a dragon-slayer. You must have seen the mound across from the church.'

The odd hill. Reynold nodded.

''Tis said that the dragon is buried there, and when the attacks began, the villagers thought it had reawakened, though there were no disturbances in the earth.'

Reynold studied the small group carefully. No mummers these, but people who were definitely afraid of something. Of what, Reynold was less sure. Although he did not have personal knowledge of every animal, a dragon seemed more otherworldly than natural, no matter what the local lore might say.

Dragons or worms were giant serpents with wings, a tail and clawed feet with which they could grasp their prey. They could swallow animals and people whole, spit fire or poison, and lash a victim with their heavy tails. And they were difficult to kill because of the nearly impervious scales that covered them.

Although Reynold kept his expression impassive, he knew what Stephen would say in a mocking tone. *Have you ever seen a dragon? Do you know anyone who has ever seen a dragon?* There were always tales from travellers and sailors of wild beasts and those who claimed to have seen them, and St Perpetua, St Martha and many others besides St George were revered as dragon-slayers. Geoff's books had pictures of the creatures, some drawn in intricate detail.

But Reynold had never come face to face with one. 'Who has seen it?' he asked.

For a moment they were all silent, then Alec began chattering about this person and that person, young Jem and Henry the miller's son. He was joined by Urban, who seemed to take umbrage at the question, launching into a long, involved display of indignation.

Reynold held up his hand for silence. 'But who among the five of you has seen it, personally, with your own eyes?'

The question set off another outburst from Urban, culminating in, 'Are you calling us liars?'

It was Mistress Sexton who quietly and gracefully took control of the conversation before things became too heated. 'I admit I was sceptical at first,' she said, 'but there is no denying its roar and the damage it leaves in its wake. What else could be responsible?'

Reynold could not comment on the sound since he had heard very little of it, but he knew that the poor animals used in bear-baiting roared loudly. Perhaps one had escaped its owners. More likely a wolf or wild boar was responsible for any attacks, while the fires were nothing more than a coincidence, attributed to an awakened creature by ignorant people weaned on village traditions.

When Urban would have protested again, Mistress Sexton stopped him with a glance. 'It matters not,' she said, leaning forwards, to eye Reynold sombrely. 'What matters is that you, Lord de Burgh, are bound to help us.'

The hall was hushed as everyone awaited his reply, but Reynold knew he could not deny such an entreaty. Knightly honour, as well as his de Burgh blood, demanded that he aid those in need. And Grim's End was plagued by something, even if it was only an especially vicious wolf that carried off livestock.

Although there were many things here that did not make sense, including why the liege lord had not sent men to dispatch such an animal long ago, Reynold's duty was clear. And he need only kill the beast to be on his way again. It was hardly a challenge, though a raging boar might be a bit more difficult to handle.

As for the other possibility, Reynold preferred not to consider it. For now, at least, he still drew the line at dragons.

'Mark my words, there will be trouble between those two,' Ursula said, as the two women prepared for bed. '"Tis like bringing another rooster into the henhouse.'

'Ursula!' Sabina felt her face flame. A rooster was brought in to breed with the hens, hardly a similar circumstance since she was a maiden and had no intention of breeding with Lord de Burgh. The very thought made her catch her breath, and she deliberately turned her mind from it. 'The situations are not at all alike.'

Ursula eyed her cannily, and Sabina was forced to acknowledge, if only to herself, that Urban was being difficult. Her father's man, he was fiercely loyal to the Sextons; she knew he had her best interests at heart. After her father's death, he had urged her to leave Grim's End, promising to take her anywhere that would offer her refuge. But she had refused to abandon her home and her family's heritage. The Sextons, descendents of the church's original warden, were said to be related to the founder of the village, as well. How could she abandon it?

''Tis your own fault, Mistress,' Ursula said, in her usual plain speech.

Sabina frowned. Perhaps the older woman was right. Sabina probably had leaned too heavily upon the servant after her father's death, subtly allowing him more input into her decisions. But what else was she to do? Eventually, there were none left in Grim's End except three women and a boy. As the only adult male, Urban had naturally assumed a more prominent position.

'Once you give a man mastery over you, you can never get your own back,' Ursula warned, as if privy to her thoughts.

'I would hardly call Urban my master,' Sabina said.

'No, but what does he call himself? That's the question.'

'I cannot conceive of him calling himself my master,' Sabina said. Nor could she imagine any man except her father in that role, although Lord de Burgh would appear to be master of just about anything he wanted. Again, her breath caught, and she veered away from such thoughts.

'Urban has simply become accustomed to being the only man in the village, sole counsellor, protector and provider of sorts. It has nothing to do with me.'

'As you say, mistress.' Ursula bowed her head in apparent agreement, but that phrase always proclaimed the opposite. 'Still, you can see why he might not take kindly to this stranger's usurpation of his place.'

'Lord de Burgh is not replacing him. Lord de Burgh is doing us a service, and once that service is done, all will return to normal again,' Sabina said, hoping it was true. Perhaps Urban could travel to the nearby villages, urging the former inhabitants to return to their homes and bringing new families, as well, so Grim's End could grow and thrive once more.

'As you say, mistress.'

Sabina gave her companion a sharp look. 'And just what would you advise?' Although Urban had been right to be suspicious of strangers, Sabina was desperate for aid, and this knight seemed the answer to her prayers.

'I would advise us to leave, mistress,' Ursula said, as always.

'And where should I go, an unmarried woman with little except the land you would have me abandon?'

'There is one who would still have you, if you but knew how to contact him,' Ursula said.

Sabina's head jerked up at this new suggestion, and her fingers tightened upon the brush she was running through her hair. 'Julian Fabre is dead.'

'You don't know that for certain,' Ursula said softly. 'His own father did not know.'

'He is dead,' Sabina repeated. She set her brush aside and rose to her feet, signalling an end to that conversation.

Ursula sighed, but did not comment.

'Our hope now is Lord de Burgh, and I would ask that you treat him with respect,' Sabina said as she slipped into bed. She could understand why Ursula and Urban were leery of the man, for Lord de Burgh was tall, strong, assured and, well, rather grim. He would make a fitting foe for the beast, but a dangerous adversary for any person at odds with him. Sabina shivered at the realisation.

Seeming to guess her thoughts, Ursula slanted her a wary glance. 'Let us hope that you have not unleashed upon us something more perilous than the dragon.'

Chapter Four

Reynold lay on his back, put his arms behind his head, and tried to appreciate his comfortable berth. He was at Sexton Manor, in a soft bed with clean linens, a sliver of moonlight shining through the window to cast a pale glow on the small, tidy room. But he could not relax. Certainly, the eerie emptiness of the village and its peculiarities was enough to give even a hardened warrior pause. Would he wake up to discover it was all a dream or find himself roasted like meat on a spit?

When showing him to his room, the servant Adele admitted that the remaining villagers often slept in the cellar, fearful of night-time attacks. But this evening they would seek their beds, as if Reynold's very presence would protect them. That sort of faith sat poorly upon him. In truth, he had never shouldered such responsibility by himself. He had been involved in rescues, battles and skirmishes of various sorts, but always with one or more of his brothers. Never alone.

Reynold shifted uncomfortably under the weight of

their expectations. Here in the darkness, distanced from those involved, he realised that he should have tried to convince Mistress Sexton and her companions to leave Grim's End. But if there was some beast preying on the people here, it might simply move on to the next place.

Reynold frowned as he mulled over his options, the safety of the villagers his upmost concern. Perhaps tomorrow he should insist that the others go, while he stayed to concentrate fully upon his task. Not only would he prefer that they be removed from any danger, but he had a feeling that Mistress Sexton would present a distraction even to the most hard-hearted of men.

Shying away from that subject, Reynold looked to where Peregrine had made his pallet by the door. The youth had been sunk in silence for some time. Was he languishing over Mistress Sexton, or was he having second thoughts about urging Reynold to listen to her?

'Are you regretting our stay already, squire?'

'No, my lord,' Peregrine said. 'I'm just wondering how you're going to fight it.'

Fight it? Did his squire know how attracted he was to the beautiful damsel? Then, with a start of surprise, Reynold realised that Peregrine was talking about the worm. Reynold loosed a low breath. 'I don't think there is one to fight.'

'Still and all, we might be prepared.'

Reynold could not argue with that, a good idea in any situation. 'All right,' he said, sensing that his squire wanted to discuss their course of action, should a dragon swoop down upon them. 'What would you suggest?'

'Well, the saints just cast them out, usually to the desert.'

'I think we've agreed that I'm not a saint,' Reynold said, drily. Nor did he understand how a mere mortal would communicate with the beast. He paused to think. 'But didn't St George shove a spear down its throat?'

'Yes…' Peregrine's words trailed off as though he were reluctant to speak further.

'What?' Reynold asked. Although he didn't do any tourneying, he could handle a lance and a sword.

'That would require really good aim and an awful lot of strength. And who's to say the thing wouldn't burn the spear with its fiery breath?'

Reynold squinted into the gloom. He had never really concerned himself with the techniques needed to kill a worm, but he supposed that any mistakes would be costly, if not fatal. In the hushed silence of the room, he found himself wishing for his brothers' counsel. This was just the sort of question they would argue over for hours, whether they really believed a dragon posed a danger or not.

Geoffrey would propose a variety of clever and unusual solutions, while Simon would advocate brute force, and Stephen would proclaim uninterest. Suddenly, Reynold missed them all. For the first time since leaving Campion, he wondered whether he ought to return home, but then what? Nothing would have changed.

'Do you know any more of the stories?' Peregrine asked, and Reynold searched his memory. His family thought Geoff was the romantic, always ready for a chivalrous story, but that was because Reynold kept his opinions to himself. He had not cared to be mocked as the moonstruck one, pining for adventures he would never have, living out the lives of heroes bold and whole while knowing he was not.

Once in a while, his shrewd father would give him a book or suggest a tale, but he had avoided his brothers' taunts. And yet now that small victory seemed petty. Perhaps if he had let his interest be known, he would not be struggling so hard to remember dragon lore. 'Didn't someone just beat it with a club?' he finally asked.

A long silence followed while Peregrine presumably mulled over that idea before ultimately rejecting it. 'I don't see how the creature would sit still for that. What's to stop it from flying away, and what about its tail and breath?'

Reynold agreed with a grunt. And who knew if any of the accounts were based upon fact? How many dragon-slayers lived to tell the tale? And how many such valiant acts were witnessed?

'I know I've heard stories where the hero digs a trench and hides in it in order to smite the beast's belly,' Peregrine said. 'But that would take a lot of time and labour, especially with no one else to help. Do you think a hole would work just as well?'

Reynold could not picture crouching in a freshly dug hollow waiting for an opportunity to poke the underside of anything, let alone a ferocious beast. But it was just the sort of tactic Geoff might suggest and Simon would dismiss as faint-hearted.

'That's if the belly really is vulnerable. Some say it is, and others say it isn't,' Peregrine said. 'And, you'll need some protective garments, of course.'

Protective garments? Reynold had his short mail coat and some gauntlets, but no shield or helmet. If he had planned on going into battle, he would have brought Will and all his gear.

'But it shouldn't be too hard to make some fur breeches and soak them in tar,' Peregrine said.

Fur breeches? The day he donned such things would be the day his brothers all laughed themselves to death, worm or no worm. 'I don't think we need to go that far,' Reynold said in a tone that brooked no argument.

'There are several stories like that of the founding of Grim's End, where a local hero slayed the dragon and was rewarded with rich lands,' Peregrine said. 'One such fellow pushed a big stone into its mouth.'

'And how did he get it to hold still for that?' Reynold asked.

Peregrine had no ready answer. 'Others used poison,' he suggested.

Although that sounded more feasible, it would require a significant amount of a deadly substance, of which Reynold knew nothing. However, his squire certainly seemed well versed in a variety of subjects. 'Where did you hear all these tales? Can you read?' Reynold asked.

'Of course, my lord. The mistresses l'Estrange have been training me up for knighthood.'

Ah. That might explain why they had sent him off with Reynold, hoping that the opportunity might come for a sudden elevation in status.

'And, of course, there might be magic involved.'

'Of course,' Reynold said in a voice heavily laden

with sarcasm. At least the sisters weren't here, exhorting him with various strategies. He could just imagine facing the great beast while they shrilly called out instructions.

'I'm afraid we'll have to do without the magic,' Reynold said. So far, their conversation had only made him more aware of the main problem with the task: there were simply no hard-and-fast rules, as there were for tourneying or hunting. All he and his squire had were conflicting reports and half-remembered legends, some more famous than others. 'What did Beowulf do?' Reynold asked.

'Well, he didn't come out of that too well, did he?' Peregrine asked, subtly reminding Reynold that the hero was mortally wounded in his battle. 'But I know that he couldn't have killed the dragon without the help of his faithful squire.'

So that was it, Reynold thought, as the reason for the discussion became clear at last. Poor Peregrine probably thought he'd be called upon for heroic feats during an epic battle with the beast. Reynold slanted a glance at his squire and tried for a reassuring tone. 'I really don't think it will come to that.'

At least, he hoped not.

Closing his eyes, Reynold effectively put an end to a conversation that would have seemed ludicrous only a day ago. Next he would be expected to ride into battle on a unicorn, he thought, swallowing a snort. In order to accomplish that, according to the bestiaries, he would have to find out where one lived and bait the place with a virgin. He nearly laughed aloud at the likelihood of that…although Mistress Sexton might volunteer.

Reynold sucked in a harsh breath as he pictured her lying on a green bower, long strands of her golden hair flowing about her, smooth and bright as ribbons. For a moment, his chest ached with the beauty of the vision, but he pushed it aside firmly. There was no point in taunting himself, a lesson that he had learned the hard way.

Lest he forget himself and fall prey to Mistress Sexton's charms, Reynold forced himself to remember the visit to Longacre years ago when he had realised the depth of his difference.

The de Burghs had been visiting a noble family with several daughters and fostered girls, probably in a misguided attempt by Campion to expose his sons to a female household. But the earl was not pleased with the outcome, as the young women fluttered around the boys and Stephen was caught in a compromising situation that enraged their host and curtailed future stays at noble homes.

In his mind's eye Reynold could see each one of the girls. Pale and soft, with high voices and flashing smiles, they had been more exotic and enticing than the finest sweets. But it was Amice who had enthralled Reynold. He had thought her beautiful, perhaps as beautiful as he now thought Mistress Sexton.

Indeed, probably more so, because his young heart had not yet been hardened. He had trailed after her like a lovesick puppy, and she had tolerated him, no doubt in order to gain access to his brothers. For good or ill, the older de Burghs did not notice or else did not care to share the obvious: that Amice did not return his admiration.

Reynold had had to find that out for himself. He had come upon a gaggle of the girls giggling and whispering, only to stop short when he heard his name mentioned in her company.

'He is quite taken with you, as everyone can tell. What say you?'

'Reynold? Why should I be stuck with the lame one?' Amice asked in a petulant voice. 'Let one of the fostered girls have him. I've my eye on another de Burgh.'

And that was the way of it, then and always, as the boys grew into men. If they chanced to meet a well-born woman, she preferred one of his brothers—or even his father.

In the back of Reynold's mind, he might have thought that by leaving them behind, he would no longer suffer in comparison. But he could not leave behind his leg, which soon gave evidence to all that he was the de Burgh who was different, the lame one.

The next morning, Sabina sat at the head of the manor's table for the first time in a long while. For years she had taken her place beside her father, looking out over a hall bustling with residents and servants. But those few who remained in Grim's End these days usually gathered elsewhere, in the kitchens or cellars or a villager's empty home, to eat. They varied their movements and their sanctuaries, so as to avoid attack. And that lack of routine and comfort had become their lives—until now.

Sabina hoped that sort of existence was over, yet she sorely felt the lack of her household, knowing that she could not present her guest with all that she would have in the past. Although Lord de Burgh did not look like the type who would be impressed by much, he was probably accustomed to far more than she could provide.

She told herself that he was just a man, like any other, and not the first knight she had known. But when he entered the hall, Sabina realised just how wrong she was. Reynold de Burgh was not like anyone else she had ever seen. Tall, dark, lean and handsome, he might have been excused for some conceit, but he did not even appear to be aware of his own good looks.

As he slowly made his way across the tiled hall, Sabina decided it was the way he held himself that struck her. Although he had none of the arrogance of the vain, he possessed a quiet confidence that inspired trust. She knew that this man would not quake in the face of danger or dither over any decision. Steady strength and a cool, casual assurance had been bred into him and were evident in his every move.

Sabina loosed the breath she had been holding as her body relaxed, perhaps for the first time in months. Maybe now she would not jump at each sound, fighting against the panic that seemed to assail her at every turn. For surely, if anyone could vanquish their foe and return their lives to normal, it was this man.

As he drew nearer, Sabina saw he wore that rather grim expression Ursula had described as harsh. It wasn't, of course, though neither was it open and friendly. Yet even his grimness was heartening, a sign that he was no light-hearted jester, but a serious warrior. Sabina wondered what had shaped him, for he was young, certainly younger than Urban, and maybe even younger than herself. And yet he must have a wealth of experiences beyond the small realm of Grim's End.

Yesterday, he had seemed nothing more than a figure of legend, a hero who appeared just when she needed him. But now Sabina found herself curious about the man himself. Had he fought in battles, knowing death and destruction such that a dragon was trifling in comparison? Sabina wanted to know, but he was no common visitor and she sensed that he would not welcome her intrusion.

Indeed, his greeting was clipped, and when Sabina gestured toward her father's chair, empty beside her own, he shook his head. Instead, he sat on the bench at the side of the table, as far away from her as possible.

Ignoring the slight, Sabina called for Adele to bring some ale and food. Ursula had gone into the kitchens to help, but Urban appeared, as if he had been waiting behind the wooden screen at the end of the hall for Lord de Burgh's arrival. Sabina gave him a nod, grateful, as always, for his sharp eyes and constant protection.

'Mistress Sexton,' Lord de Burgh said, recalling her attention.

His sombre expression did not bode well, and Sabina felt a sudden fear that he would not hold to his word. Had he partaken of their hospitality only to go on his way, leaving them to their fate? 'Yes?' she asked, tension filling her once more.

'I would like to take you away from here. I'll be happy to escort you to the nearest village, to relatives you may have elsewhere, to your liege lord's manor, or even to my own home,' he said, looking as surprised by that last offer as Sabina felt. She might have questioned him about his residence, if she were not so distressed by his advice to leave her own.

'She is not going anywhere with you.' Urban spoke up from his position nearby, but Lord de Burgh did not bother to acknowledge him.

The knight kept his gaze on Sabina as he made clear his intent. 'I would like to take you *all* away from here.'

Urban quieted at that, and why wouldn't he? He had been trying to talk her into leaving for months. Apparently, he had found some common ground with the stranger, but Sabina could not join them. Instead, she felt an overwhelming sense of betrayal. Lord de Burgh had agreed to help them. Would he now abandon them, as had so many before him?

'You have a duty to do, sir knight, and that is to slay the dragon. Have you thought better of the task over the night?' Sabina spoke sharply, hoping to wound or shame him, but he gave no sign of feeling either.

'I would only that you and the others be safely away while I dispatch the…beast.'

Sabina felt a small measure of hope return, yet long months of frustration and broken promises made her weary and suspicious. She wanted to believe this man, just as she wanted to believe that a knight's word was good. But she knew that was not always the case. How could she be sure of his success, if she were not here to witness the deed? And, even if she did trust him to complete his task, how could she flee as so many others had done and leave her village in the hands of a stranger?

'No,' Sabina said, quietly. 'You are welcome to escort the others where they will, but I am staying.'

'I'm not leaving you here with him!' Urban sputtered.

'That is your choice,' Sabina said.

Adele appeared, bringing some apples and cheese and ale, and Sabina ate silently, trying not to stare at the knight in their midst. She regretted the sharpness of her words, brought on by her own fear and panic, and she realised that she would do better to tread softly around the stranger. 'Twould be wise to remember that she needed him and not the other way around.

When she had finished her meagre meal, Sabina rose to her feet and addressed her visitor. 'Come, my lord, let me show you my home, and perhaps you will see why I care so much for Grim's End.'

For a moment, Sabina thought he might argue, but a flicker of something, perhaps resignation, passed over his features. Then he downed his cider, picked up an apple and stood. 'Very well,' he said, with a nod.

'Where do you think you're going?' Urban asked.

Sabina glanced towards him, surprised by his sharp tone. For a moment, she could find no cause for it, and then she realised just how far removed she was from the niceties that once had ruled her life.

Those who stayed in Grim's End had clung together, their numbers dwindling, until the remaining few had become like a wandering family, making camp where they would. No one paid heed to who was with whom, where or when. Indeed, Sabina often had been alone with Urban, who had made no objection at the time. But she could understand the need to keep up appearances for their guest.

'Perhaps Ursula can walk with us,' Sabina said, heading toward the kitchens to call for her attendant.

Urban made some sort of sputtering noise again, as if protesting, and Sabina eyed him curiously. As her father's man, he was well accustomed to protecting her, but she saw no need for it now. Everything about Lord de Burgh spoke of honesty and courage. And if he were up to mischief, he could have robbed and murdered them in their beds.

And since he could easily overpower the older man, there was no sense in Urban following her every movement. The thought had barely crossed her mind when Sabina realised how much she longed to escape his company, and she immediately felt a pang of guilt. They were all grateful to Urban, for how could they have remained here without him? Yet his gloom and fear were a palatable presence. Sabina could not remember the last time she had been outside without the threat of attack dogging her steps. Nor could she remember the last time she had a conversation that did not revolve around the survival of their small band.

Selfishly, Sabina longed for both, away from Urban's sullen presence. Yet she might have invited him to join them had not Ursula appeared at that moment to say that Adele had need of him. Sending them all a chary look, Urban disappeared into the kitchens, while Ursula hurried to accompany them.

Without Urban to remind her, Sabina did not even peek out the doors before exiting, warily listening for roars and watching for streams of fire. She simply stepped outside, and it felt wonderful. The sky was clear, the clouds wisps of white and the air fresh and warm. Sabina took a deep breath and smiled with pure pleasure.

Her feet easily found the familiar paths, taking the one that led to the rear of the manor, where the ground sloped gently upwards. 'We try to keep up the garden as best we can, as well as others scattered throughout the village,' she said, though the area looked sadly depleted and overgrown. There were so few of them and so much to do…

Sabina drew in a sharp breath. But she would not think about that now. In fact, as they walked quietly through the orchard, she tried to imagine this stroll taking place another day, another time when her heart was lighter. She might even pretend that the man beside her was here of his own volition.

But one glance at her companion made her dismiss such fancies, for Reynold de Burgh was not a figure of romance. She could not see him dropping on one knee or prosing lyrical about a lady's charms. In fact, the very thought made her smile. Lord de Burgh was a man's man, and if not for her predicament, he would have no use for Sabina Sexton.

Yet Sabina felt no dismay at that truth, for the taciturn figure at her side kept her fears at bay, while she basked in the day's warmth. It was more than she had dreamed of in these past hard months, and she would ask for nothing else. Turning away from the deserted barn and dairy, Sabina led her companion toward the stone stable.

'What happened to your cattle? Your horses? Your sheep?' he asked, peering into the dark interior, where only his horses stood among the shadows of carts and harnesses.

'Killed, driven away, disappeared,' Sabina said.

'Perhaps they were eaten, or maybe they are still wandering.'

Refusing to dwell on the past, Sabina walked on, skirting the tall grasses at the edge of the pond where she had played as a child. They were headed towards the road when Ursula called to them from behind. Sabina turned to see the older woman seated upon the Marking Stone.

'You go on, and I will watch you from here,' she said.

Sabina lifted her brows in surprise, for Ursula was always frightened to go out, and now she would sit in the open? Mindful of her attendant's fears, Sabina did not venture far, but paused in the dust of the track to point out the baker's and the blacksmith's. Then they crossed the road to wind their way through the scattered plots and abandoned homes that had once teemed with life, and Sabina felt her pleasure dim.

As much as she might like to pretend differently, the changes in Grim's End could not be ignored. The bustling village now stood empty and so silent that she felt her nerves stretch taut. It was not the place she had once known, but something eerie and frightening, and Sabina moved a little closer to the warrior who walked beside her.

'What was there?' Lord de Burgh asked, pointing across the road.

Sabina lifted a hand to shade her eyes and blinked at the tumble of stones. 'That's all that remains of the original church, although it's said to have been built on the site of one that was even older.' The manor had replaced an earlier one, as well, though all traces of that building were gone.

'You've seen the new church, of course,' Sabina said, leading him toward the structure with a small measure of pride. 'The Sextons have always been associated with the sanctuaries of Grim's End. Long ago, my ancestors tended the first, and later, they helped build this one,' Sabina said. She always felt a connection here, even now.

Lord de Burgh walked around the exterior, stopping to look at the fine carving on the wall that faced the road. 'Rather unusual depiction for a church, isn't it?' he asked, with a nod toward the dragon.

'I'm sure there are others of saints slaying the beasts, especially George,' Sabina said.

'But this shows only the dragon, not the slayer.'

Sabina shrugged. 'I've heard that grim can mean worm or beast, so I think it represents our history, the founding of our village upon a great deed.' What better place to remind its residents of their good fortune and the need for vigilance against evil? But had their vigilance grown slack? Sabina could think of no real reason for the dragon to awake, except perhaps… She shook her head.

Lost in her thoughts, Sabina did not stir until she remembered her company. Then she glanced up to see Lord de Burgh standing not far away, waiting patiently. The man was sparing, of movement, of speech, of himself. But Sabina needed no reassurance of words or posturing, for she felt a security she had never known before, basking in the quiet strength of her companion. And the silence between them was comfortable, unlike the unnatural hush that had haunted her days for so long.

Motioning for him to join her, Sabina led the way inside the building, cool after the heat of the sun. She walked around the interior, its familiarity soothing, though the priest had long since fled to a less dangerous place of worship. According to him, one or more of the villagers was responsible for their troubles, someone in league with evil, perhaps even a demon. His alarming words had neighbours eyeing each other warily, so Sabina was glad to see him go.

She turned to find Lord de Burgh studying the wall where a smaller depiction echoed the one outside. He seemed deep in thought, and Sabina felt a surge of affection for him. The man was on his way to Bury St Edmunds to see the great abbey, and no doubt he had been to other cathedrals that soared into the sky, laden with riches. And, yet, he appeared to appreciate even this small work of art.

'Repent and seek your reward,' he read in that deep voice of his. It was gravelly and yet acted like liquid warmth seeping into her bones. He turned his head to give her a questioning look. 'Is that advice for the dragon or the worshippers?'

Sabina laughed and then went still. How long had it been since her heart was light enough for laughter? For one giddy moment, she felt like throwing herself into this knight's arms in gratitude. But his expression became shuttered, and he turned away. She had already discovered he had a dry wit. But did he ever laugh himself?

There was something melancholy at the core of Reynold de Burgh, a weight that Sabina wished she could lift. But what could she, a mere female in dire straits herself, offer a man such as this?

Chapter Five

The woman called Ursula was waiting for them when they approached the manor, and Reynold was surprised he had been so long alone with a beautiful woman. At the time, he had not realised it. For once, he had been at ease in such company, probably because Mistress Sexton made it very clear what she wanted from him, and Reynold knew, as well. He had a job to do. Nothing more.

When they entered the hall, Reynold nearly laughed at the sight of Urban and Peregrine, who were wearing matching disgruntled expressions. It was evident that they would rather have accompanied Mistress Sexton, and Reynold was glad that he had learned to hide his own emotions rather than parade them for all to see—and mock.

'Come, squire, make yourself useful,' Reynold said to the lad in voice a bit gruffer than usual.

'Where are you going?' Urban asked.

'I'll just have a look around.'

'I thought that's what you already did,' the man said. His speech sounded a challenge, more often than not, as though he were suspicious of Reynold's every move. Simon, the most hot-headed of the de Burghs, would have already slammed him against a wall a time or two.

Luckily for Urban, Reynold was not his brother, so he only shook his head. 'Mistress Sexton kindly showed me parts of the village, but I would have a closer look myself, for signs of the dragon.'

Mistress Sexton's head jerked up at his words. 'I'm sorry,' she said. 'I did not think of that. How foolish of me to simply…' She did not finish, but gazed at him, her eyes wide, and Reynold realised they were blue. Of course, they were blue. What other colour would they be?

Reynold held up a hand to stop her apology. 'Now that I know my way around, I would rather search the area myself.'

'I'll come with you,' Urban said, though he did not appear happy about the prospect.

Reynold shook his head. He didn't want anyone telling him what had happened where, preferring to observe for himself and draw his own conclusions. 'I'll just take the boy here, and we'll see what we can find.'

No one seemed pleased at that pronouncement. Both Urban and Mistress Sexton looked like they would rather go with him, for whatever reason, while Peregrine eyed the damsel longingly.

'Come along, squire,' Reynold said, in a tone that brooked no argument. From anyone.

Once outside, they walked first to the road, then weaved among the buildings, searching for signs of attack. There were a few blackened areas, but they were small, as though well contained. Still, Reynold studied the sites, running his hands over the burned edges, bending low to the ground to sift through the ash.

'What is it?' Peregrine asked.

'Sand,' Reynold said, with a glance toward the ocean that lay some distance from Grim's End.

On the outskirts of the village, they found fields that had been scorched, just as Mistress Sexton had said. Yet, further out, they found nothing. No rotting carcasses, no bleached bones, no unusual fur or feathers or excrement. Deep in thickets, they stirred up hares and some good game birds, including a few doves that might have once belonged to Grim's End. He would have to ask Mistress Sexton if she had kept a dovecot.

Reynold shook his head at the thought. He had met some strong women in his brothers' wives, but surely none like Mistress Sexton, who not only held her manor, but an entire village on her own, while radiating a beauty that eclipsed any other.

Reynold frowned. Better he not dwell on Mistress Sexton's attributes, for she already had enough admirers, he thought, slanting a glance at young Peregrine. Who she was or what she did or how she looked was not important, as long as it did not impede his task, which was to find out what was menacing her and her people.

But so far Reynold was having no luck. He had paused frequently to study the tall grasses, the undergrowth and coppices, often bending down to the earth. Although he could not track as well as his brother Dunstan, he still sought footprints and marks of passage.

But he found few prints, owing to the dry weather, and only the usual broken twigs and stems. There was no sign of bear or boar or wolf. Was he missing something?

The land sloped gently, except for the odd hill across from the church, and from one spot that stood a bit higher, Reynold could even catch a glimpse of the sea, past the village and through some trees. Perhaps they should search that area, too, though it was even further, and his leg was already bothering him. Tomorrow, he thought, for he needed to be able to move as quickly as possible. His decision certainly had nothing to do with keeping his limp in check in the presence of others, such as his hostess.

As much as he wished to ignore Mistress Sexton, she was the only thing that seemed solid in the curious muddle that was Grim's End. Putting a hand up to shield his gaze, Reynold looked upwards as if he would find the answer there, but all was clear and blue as her eyes.

'What is it?' Peregrine asked, lifting his head as well.

'Not what, but where,' Reynold muttered as he searched the skies, just as he had searched the earth below. 'Where is the worm?'

Lord de Burgh was growing impatient. Sabina could see it in the set of his jaw, in the way he moved, with a stiff gait, and she felt her body tense in reaction. Ursula, seated nearby at the hall's trestle table, reached over to nudge her.

'He looks better every day, doesn't he?' she whispered under her breath.

The older woman's remark drew Sabina's attention to his appearance, and she acknowledged that he did look better every day, though she was not about to admit as much to her companion. Tall, dark-haired, wide-shouldered, his face more familiar now, but no less handsome, Lord de Burgh was not the most beautiful man Sabina had ever seen, yet he was the most compelling. There was no softness in his chiselled features; they were the hard planes of a man. And yet he was not arrogant or cruel, but kind and gentle, a combination that was more appealing than mere beauty.

In truth, Sabina had not expected to like the knight. When she had first caught sight of him in the road, she had thought of him foremost as a possible saviour. He had been more hero than person, larger than life, untouchable. But as the days passed, she had come to know him a little and like him even more.

'Lord de Burgh,' Ursula called, rising to her feet. The older woman certainly had changed her tune. At first wary and full of warnings about him, Ursula doted on him now. And who could blame her, for when had they seen the likes of such a man? Even his voice was seductive, a hint of hoarseness making it exotic and compelling, as he answered her greeting.

Unfortunately, Ursula did not stop there.

'Come sit by Sabina,' she urged. 'I have found a cushion to make the chair more comfortable.' Walking to the seat next to Sabina's, Ursula patted the thin pillow invitingly, and Sabina cringed.

Lord de Burgh shook his head, moving past the chair that had belonged to her father to the long bench on the side of the table. No amount of cajoling could entice him to take the seat that stood beside her own, one of a pair intended for the master and mistress of the hall. And when Sabina saw a muscle leap in his jaw, she was moved to action.

'Lord de Burgh is our guest, Ursula, and may sit wherever he likes,' she said in a tone that put a stop to her attendant's nonsense.

Sabina was going to have to speak to the woman about what could only be interpreted as increasingly clumsy efforts at matchmaking. At first Sabina had let it go because she was glad to see Ursula acting like her old self, a giddier version of the frightened creature her attendant had become. But it had gone too far and for too long. Not only did all that flittering and flirting make Sabina uncomfortable, but Lord de Burgh's expression became even more shuttered.

For Ursula could not be more misguided. During the week since his arrival Reynold de Burgh had been unfailingly polite, but cool and distant. He showed no interest in Sabina whatsoever, and why should he? He might be married or pledged to a high-born lady with more riches and lands than Sabina could imagine. He was doing a duty here, nothing else, and obviously longed to return to his home and his life, where he was not thrust into awkward situations by a foolish old woman.

Trying to ignore her own embarrassment, Sabina cleared her throat again. 'Good morning, my lord,' she said. 'Will you break your fast?' Although she gestured toward the table, Sabina knew there was little there to tempt him. He was probably used to fine dishes, a variety of meats and exotic spices that Sexton Hall could not have offered in the best of times. Now, they were living off what little stores were left.

'Just some ale, perhaps,' he said, with an eye to the limited provisions, and Sabina flushed. Yesterday, their guest had scouted the area around the village and returned with some hares for their dinner.

'You must eat more, to keep up your strength, my lord,' Ursula said, with a sly look.

Sabina sent her attendant a quelling glance. Was the woman intent upon driving him away? His expression was not encouraging, and Sabina tried to think of a way to divert him, to change his grim features, to prevent him from saying something she did not want to hear.

'Adele, please bring some cheese and ale. No, is there any wine?' Sabina asked, as Urban and Alec entered the hall, Peregrine the squire not far behind.

Lord de Burgh shook his head, and Sabina's heart sank as he gazed directly at her. 'Mistress Sexton, I need to speak with you.'

Sabina's pulse began pounding even as a protest rose to her lips. But she swallowed it and met his gaze, for he deserved no less. 'Yes, my lord, what is it?'

Before he could answer, Ursula spoke, drawing Sabina's attention. 'Come, Urban, I have need of you,' the older woman said, motioning to her father's man as if to lead him away. Sabina could only eye her attendant askance. Did Ursula think Lord de Burgh wanted private speech of a personal nature? Any fool could see he had grown weary of his task. This was no silly conjured romance, but serious business, for he held their very survival in his hands.

'Stay,' Sabina said. Turning back to Lord de Burgh, she nodded, though she dreaded what he would say.

'Mistress Sexton, my squire and I have been through the entire village and all along the perimeter, and we can find no evidence of any beast, let alone something the size of a dragon.'

There it was, that which she did not want to hear, and Sabina had no answer for it. A kind of hushed silence fell upon the small band as they all realised just what Lord de Burgh was saying.

The quiet was broken by Alec. 'Perhaps it hides in caves along the coastline.'

Ursula gasped. 'Alec, you haven't been wandering around the cliffs, have you?'

'No, I'll not go looking for it, but if Lord de Burgh is, maybe he should look there.'

'Perhaps Lord de Burgh is reluctant to look further,' Urban said, 'without being compensated for his time.'

Ursula gasped again, but Sabina's sharp look kept her from commenting further. Urban had simply given voice to a concern that had never been addressed, and there was no point in protesting it. Lord de Burgh was the only one who could answer such an accusation, and Sabina turned towards the great knight.

Like Ursula, Sabina was unwilling to believe he would be driven by greed, but perhaps the much-vaunted knightly code could only be bought with coin. 'I could promise you a tithe, a yearly gift from the manor once my people have returned,' she said. Having no personal wealth, that was all she could offer, and to give him that, she would need the village to thrive again, as it once had.

'Will that be enough?' Urban asked, caustically.

'Perhaps he wants more, especially if has heard of the Sexton hoard.'

Sabina shot Urban a startled glance. Rarely did anyone speak of that long-forgotten rumour, so how would a travelling knight learn of it? And should he be aware of the story, he was bound to be disappointed. 'Urban, you know as well as I that there is nothing to that old tale.'

Urban shrugged, and Sabina frowned in annoyance. Why would he bring up such nonsense? Now she owed Lord de Burgh an explanation, and she looked at the knight, though she could tell nothing from his carefully closed expression. Surely he did not imagine she had some hidden wealth?

'My lord, that is nothing but talk that has been around for years. One of my ancestors gave the church a gift of a gold coin, and the story grew that the Sextons had a cache of them, to be doled out when the village was in need. But we have always lived simply, as you can see,' Sabina said, gesturing toward the small hall. She glanced sharply towards her father's man. 'And if I had such money, I would have used it to buy the services of a dragon-slayer months ago.'

'I want no payment,' Lord de Burgh said, drawing Sabina's attention back to him. She would have been relieved, but for the still-sombre set of his face. 'However, I cannot stay here indefinitely. It has been a week, and I have seen or heard nothing of the creature.'

'Perhaps it has moved on,' Alec suggested.

Sabina felt a small spark of hope. 'If the dragon is no longer threatening the village, then we should convince those who left to return,' she said.

'How would we find them all?' Urban asked. 'And what evidence do we give that the beast is gone except that it has not appeared recently? That is no assurance.'

'Those who left, where did they go?' Lord de Burgh asked.

'Who can know for certain?' Sabina asked. 'But probably to nearby villages. North is Sandborn, south is Baderton, east is Ballinghoo and still further Bury St Edmunds.'

'How do you know they moved and were not killed on their way elsewhere?' Peregrine, the squire, asked. His question sent a shiver up Sabina's spine, for she had long wondered how many of her people lived. The dragon usually left no remains.

'Urban went to Sandborn and spoke to several who left, trying to convince them to return,' Sabina said. 'Twas at her urging, but it came to nothing.

'They didn't listen,' Urban said. 'They were too afraid of the worm.'

'They saw it?' Lord de Burgh asked, suddenly intent.

'Some did. Some didn't,' Urban said with a shrug. 'It doesn't matter. They are cowards all.'

'But some actually saw it?'

'Of course,' Urban said, with an angry scowl.

Alec went even further and began naming those villagers who had survived an attack, while Sabina eyed Lord de Burgh with a measure of curiosity and dread. Although she could tell little from his expression, she realised that he was more than impatient. *He doesn't believe us*, she realised.

A protest rose to her lips, only to be swallowed up in

the sound of the others' conversation. She had thought him convinced; now he would doubt them again. And how could she persuade him? If she hadn't lived through this, would she accept the truth? If she hadn't heard the sounds, seen the dead animals, felt the blast of heat, and seen the scorched remains, her own father struck down…

'I would speak with those who saw the creature,' Lord de Burgh said, effectively silencing the others. 'Do you know where they are?'

Urban shook his head. 'They could be anywhere.'

'Well, I'll begin with Sandborn.'

The way he rose to his feet, his expression and his stance all told Sabina there would be no argument, but still Ursula begged him not to go. 'Please, my lord, we are not safe here without you,' she said, her voice rising to a wail.

Sabina kept silent, refusing to waste her breath lest she become short of it. But, in truth, she, too, had only felt secure since his arrival. Such was the strength of Lord de Burgh's presence, inspiring confidence and hope and other, unwelcome thoughts…

Sabina watched in dismay as Lord de Burgh ignored Ursula's entreaties to stride towards the doors, Peregrine at his side. 'We should be able to ride to the next village and be back before nightfall,' he said. But his words were not reassuring. What would they do until then? What would they do if he did not return?

Belatedly rising to her feet, Sabina following, stopping him with one final injunction. 'Remember, you are all that stands between Grim's End and destruction,' she said, reaching out to touch his arm.

It was an automatic gesture meant to give force to her

admonition, and yet, as soon as her fingers made contact with his sleeve, Sabina felt a jolt. Heat rushed through her, inviting her to linger, to close her hand upon his muscles, to move into the warmth of his body. Her heart began to pound, and her breath came fast and low, a most alarming sensation that made her jerk away. She glanced upwards only to see Lord de Burgh flinch, as well, before his face became a hard mask.

With a nod of dismissal, he turned to go, and Sabina stood, trembling, upon the doorstep. Still shaken by the encounter, she watched the two visitors leave Grim's End, just as she had watched so many others, her father's servants, the freemen, those who made the ale and ground the grain and did all the work that was necessary for the village to survive. They were all gone, and now she wondered whether her last hope was vanishing, as well.

It was Urban who voiced her fears aloud as he moved to stand beside her.

'Mark my words,' he said. 'They won't return.'

Reynold shut down his thoughts, concentrating only upon Sirius. Once mounted, he wanted to kick the destrier to a gallop, leaving the dust of Grim's End and all it entailed behind. Refusing to give in to such impulses, he made his way slowly to the road, keeping an eye out for anything unusual, just in case an animal should show itself. But he saw nothing, even though he again had the sensation that he was being watched. It was eerie, for he knew the place was deserted, having looked through every building himself for signs of life.

When they reached the church, Reynold half-expected the bells to begin ringing as they had the last time he had ridden this way. But all was silent. Still, he was uneasy as they reached the outer boundaries of the village. He had once heard a tale of a phantom community that came and went in the blink of an eye, trapping travellers inside, and he wondered whether they would encounter some kind of barrier upon their departure.

Although there was none, he turned to look back at the familiar buildings clustered around the track that wove between them, just to make sure he had not imagined them. Reynold shook his head at such fancies, but now that he was leaving, it seemed as though he had dreamed the whole business. A deserted village. A dragon. A beautiful damsel.

The only ring of truth was the beautiful damsel's reaction to him, a jarring bit of reality in the fantasy. For who would want to dream of that kind of response? Reynold did not know if she laid her hand upon his arm out of some attempt to lure him into staying or if it was an innocent gesture. But he was certain of what happened next. He had caught his breath at the lightness of her touch, at the warmth of her fingers and the simple sensation of gentle feminine contact, and then she had pulled away, repulsed.

'Twas a reminder not to let down his guard or let anyone get close to him, and as such it was welcome. Yet Reynold could not dismiss the incident as easily as he had others in his past. It was too fresh in his mind, too insulting, too much of a disappointment. For deep down inside, he had hoped that Mistress Sexton might be different.

The more beautiful the woman, the more spoiled, selfish and deceitful, Reynold told himself, and Mistress Sexton was the most beautiful, by far. Although she had seemed like a saint, valiantly holding her people together, what did he actually know of her? What did he know of any of them except their bizarre tale of attacks, for which there was little evidence beyond a few scorched spots? Reynold's tightly coiled emotions threatened to spill forth, and as his anger grew, so did the temptation never to go back, to continue on to Bury St Edmunds and further, perhaps across the ocean…

Reynold slanted a glance at his companion, who would not approve of any such oath breaking. Indeed, Peregrine looked unhappy just to be leaving the village. Was he languishing after Mistress Sexton already? Reynold felt an unreasoning annoyance at the boy's devotion to the woman. And he had to fight an urge to enlighten the lad on the subject of females and their perfidies.

'Do you intend to sulk throughout our journey?' Reynold asked. He spoke more sharply than he intended and could almost hear his father's admonition in his head: *Don't take it out on the boy. 'Tis not his fault you are what you are.*

'Forgive me, my lord, but I don't see why we are leaving at all,' Peregrine said.

'I seek information,' Reynold said. 'We need to know more about our enemy.' He spoke the truth. For although Mistress Sexton and her small band obviously feared attack, Reynold was no closer to discovering the cause than he was on the day he had arrived in Grim's End. He might be the runt of the de Burghs, but he had the family's sure sense, and it told him that something wasn't right.

Peregrine said nothing, and Reynold frowned. 'What would you have me do?' he asked. 'Remain there until supplies run out?'

The look Peregrine shot him told Reynold that the boy could see no reason not to linger. They had nothing awaiting them in Bury St Edmunds, no one to visit, no business that required tending. And yet Reynold could not see kicking his heels in Grim's End for ever, no matter how lovely and appealing the Mistress Sexton. *Especially* considering how lovely and appealing the Mistress Sexton.

'Why don't you trust her?'

The words, so close to his own thoughts, startled Reynold. 'What?'

'You don't trust Mistress Sexton, do you?'

'I don't give my faith as easily as you do,' Reynold said, with a sidelong glance at his companion. Peregrine flushed, no doubt remembering his easy acceptance of the fellow pilgrims who had tried to rob them.

'It has been my experience that most ladies are spoiled, selfish and deceitful, and the more beautiful they are, the worse they are,' Reynold said. 'Perhaps that is the way high-born women are raised, but my father does not approve of intrigues. He prefers honest dealings and simple pleasures, and his sons a strong sword arm and a good horse.'

'But Lady Joy and Lady Marion aren't like that,' Peregrine protested.

'No,' Reynold acknowledged. The women who

married de Burghs were not the pampered ladies of court. And he supposed they were pretty, though he had never felt an ache at the sight of them. Mistress Sexton, on the other hand, was so beautiful that sometimes he had to blink. It was like looking at the sun, for his eyes stung from the effort. And over the past week, he had looked far too often. He caught himself noticing little things about her, such as the curve of her wrist, the slender column of her neck, the golden ribbons of her hair, like a work of art…

'And, anyway, Mistress Sexton isn't high born,' Peregrine said. 'She might be to the manor born, but she's not nobility.'

No, but she is more beautiful than any of them, Reynold thought.

'And she's not spoiled or selfish. She's always thinking of the others, always helping out. Why, she even works in the garden,' Peregrine said.

Reynold gave a stiff nod. Mistress Sexton was certainly accustomed to doing for herself. And when he searched his mind for her flaws, he could find little enough to present to Peregrine, for she appeared kind and generous, courteous and courageous, never complaining, always encouraging.

'I think she would make a good wife,' Peregrine said, startling Reynold from his thoughts.

'She's too old for you, lad,' Reynold snapped.

Peregrine blanched and opened his mouth as though to argue, but Reynold stopped him with a glance. He'd had a bellyful of this discussion.

Lovely, strong and capable, Mistress Sexton was certainly well suited to be a de Burgh bride. And perhaps if he were one of his brothers, Reynold might even let his thoughts drift in that direction. But her reaction this morning had been a bitter reminder that he was not one of his brothers and would never be.

He was what he was: a man who would never marry.

Chapter Six

Although Reynold had looked forward to a respite from the eeriness of Grim's End, the sensation lingered even as they travelled, for the road they took was just as deserted as the village had been. They saw no one, not a man, not a cart, not a sheep, and though Reynold said nothing to his squire, his uneasiness grew. He began to suspect that nothing existed except for the few people of Grim's End, and the track would lead them back to its empty buildings.

When they finally caught a glimpse of movement ahead and heard the noises of life, Reynold grunted in relief. As if released from a dream, he welcomed the sights and sounds of Sandborn, a bustling village that appeared to be crowded, perhaps with new residents. Although not much larger than Grim's End, Sandborn was situated right on the coast, and he and Peregrine enjoyed a hearty meal of fresh fish in a small ale house.

The proprietors were friendly and talkative until Reynold mentioned Grim's End. He had hoped to find someone to deliver supplies there, but the man and woman shook their heads and grew silent, obviously eager for their guests to exit.

'See, everyone knows about the dragon,' Peregrine whispered as they left the tiny building.

'Everyone knows something,' Reynold said, squinting at the sky above them, clear and blue as a certain pair of eyes. 'But what?'

Luckily, they had asked about one of Grim's End's former inhabitants before mentioning the village itself, and now they made their way to a small hut that had been pointed out to them as the couple's home. They found the woman tending the small croft in the back of the house.

'Githa? Githa Smalle?' Reynold asked. The old woman straightened and eyed them warily.

'I would ask you some questions about Grim's End,' he said.

But at the mention of the village, the woman turned pale and glanced about, as if to find some way to escape.

'We mean you no harm,' Reynold said. 'I only wish to know why you left the village.'

'I do not speak of it!' she said, hurrying into her house and shutting the door behind her.

Peregrine wanted to follow the woman, but Reynold shook his head. 'Just as you would, these people protect their own, and I would not care to have a mob wishing us ill.'

Eyes wide, Peregrine nodded, and they went in search of the woman's husband. They found him in the fields, so he could hardly flee, but he was not much more informative.

'You must know why we left, else you would not be here,' he said, his face brown from the sun and lined with age. 'We are entitled to our lives and a safe place to live them.' He lifted his head, as if expecting an argument, but Reynold nodded.

'Of course. But what drove you away?'

The man leaned upon a long staff. 'It was the beast, as well you know.'

'What kind of beast?' Reynold asked. 'Did you see it yourself?'

'No. But a man doesn't have to see the devil to know he's there.' He turned and went back to his work, shaking his head at any further questions.

'If you will say no more, then who else can I talk to?'

The man hesitated, as though unwilling to name his fellows, but finally he pointed a bony finger toward another hut, recently built, its wattle and daub obviously fresh. A cow and a pig were penned in front of the structure, and Reynold walked past them in order to rap on the door.

The man who opened it was short and stout, with the look of someone who fears little, giving Reynold hope that he might at last learn something.

'Yes?'

'I come seeking information about Grim's End.'

But even this hardened fellow blanched. 'If you are thinking of making your home there, taking our old land, filling our old homes, beware the ancient evil,' he said, then he moved as if to close the door.

'Why did you leave?'

'We do not speak of it,' the man said in a low voice. 'Do you want to draw it here?'

'Draw *what* here?' Reynold asked. This time he held up a small coin, and the man took it with a wary glance.

'You would do better to spend your money elsewhere, settle here in Sandborn or further east, where the land is good.'

But Reynold had not paid for advice. 'What do you fear?' he asked.

The man leaned closer to whisper his reply. 'It flies through the air. It destroys all in its path. That is all I can tell you.'

'Did you see it yourself?'

'No.'

'Then how can you say what it is?'

The fellow shook his head angrily. 'A man does not have to stare death in the face to recognise it. I heard its awful roar! I saw its fiery breath! It set my house alight! I did not stay around to get a closer look at the inside of its belly.'

He slammed the thin wood of his door in their faces, and Reynold felt the sting of conscience. Perhaps he deserved such treatment. Just because no one had seen the attacker did not mean that they had not suffered…something. And he would do well to remember that.

Reynold looked up at the sky, but it was empty, as always, and the sun had passed its zenith. 'We should go back,' he mused aloud. Although he hated to admit it, this trip had been a waste of time. He had learned nothing except that those who had left Grim's End were just as frightened as those who remained.

'Perhaps we should try another village,' Peregrine suggested, as though unwilling to admit defeat.

But Reynold shook his head. 'It will be the same there, the same everywhere.' Whatever attacked Grim's End was like a lone wolf, a rogue that slinked in and stole the chickens and more, but went unseen and uncaught. Yet how could a dragon remain hidden? Just how big was the beast?

'Hello! Sire!'

Reynold turned at the sound of the hail to see an old man hobbling toward them, waving an arm. He limped, and Reynold felt himself flinch, as he always did, at the sight.

'Yes?'

'You seek the beast?' the man asked. He had a wild look in his eyes and stank of ale, but he grinned, revealing a couple of missing teeth.

'What do you mean?'

'I heard you talking. You're interested in Grim's End?'

Reynold nodded.

'I'm Gamel. I lived there for many a year and can tell you anything you wish to know, for a decent meal.'

'Who holds the village?' Reynold asked. Unwilling to throw good coins after bad, he was not about to pay some wanderer to conjure tales of some fanciful place.

The fellow cackled, as though pleased by the test. 'Mistress Sexton, as last I knew.'

Reynold nodded stiffly and paid him. 'Now, tell us why you left your home. And I would hear enough to have my money's worth.'

The old man nodded vigorously. 'Of course, sire, of course. 'Twas the dragon that sent us all running. Someone woke it from its sleep,' he said, leaning close.

''Twas Cyneric the Grim who killed it, you know, the first worm, the great one.'

Reynold squinted at the fellow. 'I thought "grim" was a name for the beast.'

Gamel shrugged. ''Tis said that it was such a sight that people came from all around for the burial. And then they stayed, settling there by the burial mound. 'Twas Cyneric's descendants who had the first manor house, too, though 'tis long gone now.'

Reynold frowned, confused, but the old man kept talking.

'Sexton Hall stands there now, like a guardian of the mound. The church on one side, the hall on the other,' he said, pointing a gnarled hand. 'But nothing on the other sides except grass and trees. So maybe that's where someone poked him and woke him.'

'How?' Reynold asked.

Gamel shrugged and cackled. 'Who knows? But 'tis awake now. We heard its roar and smelled its breath that soon lay waste to all around.'

'But did you see it?' Reynold asked, reaching out to grasp the man's arm. 'Did you see the worm yourself?'

Gamel grinned. 'Didn't I promise to tell you all you wished to know?' he asked. 'A rare creature it is, something between a lizard and a bird, with that demon fire in its belly. It can swallow you whole or whip you to death with its tail.'

Reynold felt a chill dance up his spine. Was the old man telling the truth or embellishing upon a sighting from a distance? Or was the ale talking?

'How big is it?' Peregrine asked, wide-eyed.

'As big as that there,' Gamel said. He gestured to a building the size of the church in Grim's End, certainly far larger than any animal Reynold had ever seen.

Reynold studied the grinning fellow, unsure of what else to ask. He had sought only to find someone who had seen the dragon, and, apparently, he had finally met his man. Gamel had certainly given him a description, but could he trust it?

'Have you heard enough? Can I get my supper?'

Reynold hesitated, then released him with a nod. The old man whooped and hurried off, limping as he went. Still, Reynold watched him go, trying to make sense of what he had said.

Was Gamel mad? Or was there really such a beast? Reynold felt a sort of stunned shock at the thought. For, if so, how on earth would he kill it?

The sun was dipping low as they neared the village. 'Will we reach Grim's End before nightfall?' Peregrine asked, with an anxious look at the horizon.

'Yes, we aren't too far away now,' Reynold said, sending the boy a sidelong glance. 'Are you eager to get back to Mistress Sexton?'

Peregrine appeared flustered, and Reynold grunted, urging his mount forwards. They had been travelling at a good pace, even though they were loaded down with supplies, and he was glad now that he had not brought back a cow, which would have made for a much slower, though perhaps livelier trip.

Even the bawling of cattle would be welcome along this stretch of road, for it was as empty as before. Obviously, the people of Sandborn, and perhaps everyone in the area, avoided Grim's End, going so far as to abandon the road that led to and from it. In fact, the silence was such that when Reynold heard a sound in the brush nearby, it startled him. He glanced up, seeing nothing in the dark copse of trees.

'Is it the worm?' Peregrine asked, his voice little more than a squeak.

Before Reynold could answer, something burst from the shadowed cover of leaves, hurtling directly towards him. It was no dragon, but an attack none the less, by a hooded horseman, and Reynold cursed himself for his lack of alertness. The deserted track had lulled him into inattention when he should have known better. Although superstitious villagers might avoid this area, travelling ruffians and robbers could not be counted upon to do the same.

It was too late now to do anything except draw his sword. Although Sirius could outrace nearly any other horse, Peregrine on his smaller mount would be left in the dust, easy pickings if the villain did not follow Reynold.

'Hold,' Reynold shouted, but a sword came slashing towards him. He knocked it aside with his own, steadying himself as the horse and its rider swung around for another charge. Sirius was well trained and moved with just a nudge of Reynold's knee, dancing out of the way, and again Reynold blocked the assailant's weapon. He tried to get a good look at his foe, but the light was fading, and the hood shadowed the man's face.

His horse was smaller, as was his sword, but he was quick, competent, and perhaps desperate, which gave strength to even the weakest opponent. Reynold needed all of his skill and wits about him. Sending Sirius dancing away, he tried to get behind the fellow, but suddenly Peregrine was there, tugging at the man's cloak.

What the devil?

Reynold heard a groan and a shout, and then Peregrine was knocked to the ground, where he could easily be trampled under the hooves of any of the three horses that were clustered together. Instead of running the attacker through, Reynold grabbed at the man's reins, pulling the other horse away with his own, while trying to avoid the weapon that sliced through the air.

When it came perilously close, Reynold loosed the horse's reins and sent Sirius around to the opposite flank. Peregrine's mount, the smallest of the three, fled in the face of the stamping and whinnying of the larger beasts. Reynold could only hope he had moved the battle far enough away to save the boy, for he could waste no more attention upon his fallen squire.

He swung his sword in a high arc towards his assailant, but even before it made contact, the man howled in pain. Instead of fighting off Reynold, the fellow swung backwards, as though attacked from behind. Reynold heard a thud, and then the rider turned and fled, his mount eating up the ground to disappear into the darkness of the woods.

For an instant, Reynold thought of giving chase, despite the gathering twilight and his unfamiliarity with the area. The dark horse was no match for Sirius, and few men could best a de Burgh. Although his pride called for satisfaction, Reynold resisted the urge, for he had more important concerns. His squire had fallen in the fray.

Dismounting quickly, Reynold kept his reins in hand. Peregrine's horse was gone, but who knows what might have happened to the boy while he was down? Reynold found him lying in the road, unmoving. Stepping close, he knelt to the ground, looking for injuries, but there were no visibly broken bones and no blood.

Foolhardy boy. Courageous, but foolhardy.

'Peregrine,' Reynold said, cursing his solitary state. He knew little of healing and had no way to summon help. All he could do was throw the boy over the back of a horse and hope that their attacker was not summoning companions from a camp in the forest.

'Peregrine,' Reynold said, his tone more urgent. He put a hand to his squire's head, feeling for lumps, and the boy stirred.

'M-my lord,' he said, opening his eyes. He blinked and started to rise, but Reynold stopped him.

'Hold, squire. Are you hurt?'

Peregrine frowned. 'No,' he said, as though testing himself. Then he surged upwards. 'He knocked me down!'

'I thought you fell,' Reynold said. Relieved to see the boy's outrage, Reynold held out a hand to help him to his feet.

'Well, I guess I did fall, at first,' the boy said. He reached down to dust himself off, then bent to retrieve the long knife they had taken from the thieves. 'I pricked him, right in his leg,' he said, with a grin.

Reynold saw the blood on the blade. 'Good work, but let us not tarry in case he has friends.'

Peregrine's triumphant smile vanished. 'My horse!' he said, glancing around the deserted track.

Reynold whistled, and the black came trotting back. They hurriedly mounted and put some distance between themselves and the wood though it was nearly full dark now.

'I wish I could throw a knife like that crippled boy,' Peregrine said. 'I mean the boy who wasn't really crippled,' he added. 'But I knew I couldn't, so I tried to get close enough to bury it in his chest.'

'By pulling on his cloak?'

'Well, yes, but I did strike him, my lord, and just like when the knife hit you, it was turned away. He must have been wearing a mail shirt, just like you do.'

Reynold found that hard to believe, and yet, the boy would not lie. He had struck at the villain, fallen from his horse, and risen to try again, this time thrusting his blade into the rider's leg, only to be knocked down once more.

'Maybe he's a knight, too,' Peregrine said. He paused, as if mulling over his words. 'But he couldn't be, not when he's a brigand attacking travellers.'

'Knights go bad, like everybody else,' Reynold said. He slanted a glance at the boy. 'It is expensive to maintain a good destrier, proper equipment and a squire, as well as pay the scutage or days owed to one's lord. Unless you come from a wealthy family, capture others in battle, or are successful on the tournament field, it is a hard life, a fact that is conveniently missing from the romances.'

'Perhaps he was an outlaw.'

'Perhaps,' Reynold said, but he was more concerned with the two of them than their assailant. The roads were always prey to attacks, especially along a wooded stretch, and Reynold thought himself equal to any fight.

Now he wasn't so sure. If not for the boy, he could have managed, yet his squire was lucky to have escaped serious injury or death. And what if there had been more than one assailant? Reynold shook his head, his de Burgh confidence shaken, as they neared the outskirts of the village.

And that's when he heard it, a faint noise that could be called a roar, if closer. Already uneasy, Reynold felt the shock of full-blown fear for perhaps the first time in his life. For he had not yet reached the outskirts of the village, and Mistress Sexton might be in danger, with nothing except Urban and his pitchfork to protect her from the kind of monster Gamel had described.

Too late, Reynold regretted his hasty departure, and with a low curse, he urged his weary mount onwards to Grim's End.

It was growing late, Sabina knew, for she kept glancing at the tall windows, where the light was fading. The hall was cast in shadows, an eerie reminder that things were not as they should be, and without the presence of Lord de Burgh, even the familiar turned sinister, frightening…

Ursula had suggested they do their mending, and Sabina had welcomed the task to keep her mind occupied, but it wasn't working. And Urban was no help. For the past hour he had been pacing the room, predicting doom.

He was certain that Lord de Burgh would not return, and though Sabina tried not to let his words sway her, she was becoming concerned. It was nearly dark, and still there was no sign of the knight, yet Sabina was sure he was the one she had waited for during the bleak months that Grim's End had been under siege. His arrival seemed no accident, but the answer to her prayers, and she would have sworn his word was good. Surely he would not abandon them to their fate?

'If he's a lord, as he says, he's got better things to do than stay here,' Urban said. 'Some nobles live in castles the size of the abbey at Bury St Edmunds, with servants to attend their every need. They have elegant garments, fine food and wine, hunting, hawking and entertainments to rival the king's own.'

Urban did not have to gesture to the small, dim hall for Sabina to realise the difference between such a household and her own. Here, they hid from the dragon in the shadows, while the de Burgh home probably blazed with light and sound, candles and torches, music and dancing. Sabina tried to picture such a place, but what she saw more clearly was a high-born woman wearing rich clothes, furs and jewels, waiting for a certain knight…

'I've heard that noblemen don't even bathe themselves, but are washed by the lady of the house,' Ursula said, slyly.

Sabina jerked up her head at the words. Had Lord de Burgh been expecting such treatment here? They didn't have enough servants to fill even the smallest tub with hot water, and as for bathing him… Sabina swallowed hard at the thought of such a duty. She had seen no male naked since she was a child and had come across the village boys swimming in the pond.

But Lord de Burgh was no boy. He was a man, the biggest man she had ever met, and she couldn't imagine those wide shoulders, the breadth of that chest, that amount of skin... She drew in a sharp breath at the thought of the water, the warmth, the feel... And then, like a bubble of soap, the vision burst as she remembered his reaction this morning.

'Lord de Burgh doesn't like to be touched,' Sabina said.

'*What?*' Urban's voice rose, loud in the stillness.

'*What?*' Ursula echoed, though her version was more like a shriek.

Sabina shook her head to dispel their suspicions. 'This morning when I touched his arm, he flinched.'

Urban appeared mollified by the explanation, while Ursula looked more disappointed than anything else. *Or perhaps he doesn't like to be touched by me*, Sabina thought with a twinge of disappointment. Or perhaps he was faithful to whoever waited for him, longing only for that woman's hand, that woman's bath, Sabina thought, wistfully.

'If he is a knight, he will have plenty of females dallying after him,' Urban said, 'especially at the tournaments, where they try to kill each other in order to impress the ladies of the court.'

Sabina frowned, for the sort of man Urban described was not Lord de Burgh. He didn't flaunt his skills or brag about them. He didn't dress like a peacock, and he didn't expect to be waited on. He and his squire had brought small game for the Sexton table and helped, rather than stand by, watching the others work.

'Mark my words, he's halfway home by now,' Urban said.

Home. Sabina wondered where that was. Was it the tall castle Urban described, or something smaller, more intimate? Did it look out over the sea or a valley? More important, who else lived there? Lord de Burgh spoke little and offered less about himself, while Sabina found her own curiosity about the mysterious knight growing.

'Why would he go home?' Ursula asked. 'They were on a pilgrimage to Bury St Edmunds.'

'Yes,' Sabina said, seizing upon that information with new hope. 'I hardly think such a knight would deny his vow.'

'Not all pilgrims are motivated by their faith,' Urban said, scoffing. 'In fact, most travel to see the sights and enjoy the company of others, rather than seek aid from the saint. Though I suppose this fellow might be headed there for his leg.'

Sabina jerked her head up again. She glanced at Urban, but his back was turned as he stared out the window and Ursula was bent over her sewing, strangely quiet.

'What do you mean?' Sabina asked. 'What's wrong with his leg?'

'How would I know?' Urban asked, turning to scowl at her. 'He does not take me into his confidence. But 'tis obvious that there's something wrong. Haven't you seen him limp, especially at the end of the day?'

Sabina gaped in astonishment. She had noticed that Lord de Burgh walked stiffly sometimes, but surely that did not mean that he suffered any affliction.

'Perhaps that's why he left,' Urban said, as if enjoying her discomfiture. 'He knew he wasn't up to the task, but did not want to admit it.'

Sabina heard Ursula's low gasp, and she, too, was shocked by Urban's careless condemnation. No matter what ailed him, Lord de Burgh was more of a man than this village had ever seen and capable of accomplishing anything. Perhaps she had blindly viewed him as a hero out of legend, invulnerable and impersonal, but even Sabina could see that nothing slowed him down, nothing stopped him. Never had he turned away from a chore or complained in any way.

'No,' she said, with certainty. She met Urban's gaze with her own steady one, waiting for him to argue the point with her. Although they had disagreed more than once since her father's death, she had never felt so angry and disgusted with him. Whatever his personal feelings and beliefs, there was no reason for him to lose all manner of discretion or simple courtesy.

Whatever Urban was going to do, whether dispute her or turn away, Sabina would never know, for in that instant, a sound rent the stillness and the small gathering was thrown into chaos.

'Get down! Let us go down below!' Urban shouted, looking more terrified than ever before. And who could blame him? They had all been lulled into complacency these last few days by the presence of a knight and the absence of the beast he would protect them against. They had stopped hiding in cellars and resumed some semblance of their former lives, pausing less often to look over their shoulder or to listen for the dragon's roar.

And now they paid the price. Ursula dropped her

sewing and surged to her feet, while Adele grabbed
Alec by the hand and hurried towards the stair that led
underneath the hall. But Sabina rushed to the window
instead. On the way, she passed Urban, who reached for
her, but she pulled from his grasp, looking out to see the
flash of fire nearby.

'It struck not far from the pond,' Sabina said. 'If we
hurry, we can put out the blaze before it spreads.'

'The worm could still be out there,' Ursula wailed,
but Sabina paid no heed and ran for the doors.

'The buckets,' Alec cried, breaking away from his
mother. He hurried to the nearby wagon that held all the
water containers, pulling it outside after Sabina.

Soon they had taken up their usual positions to fight
the flames, and although Sabina's heart pounded, she
did not fail. She was determined to hold the village in
Lord de Burgh's absence, not to lose all that she would
have him fight for, and more. The weight of the buckets
made her arms hurt, but she kept going, her gown
sodden and dragging in the dirt, concentrating only on
lifting each one in turn.

Sabina didn't know how long they had been working
when, above the crackling of the fire and the sound of
their efforts, she heard a shout. And then he was there,
his great destrier dancing to a halt as he slid from the
saddle, both horse and rider unmistakable even in the
near darkness. Such was her joy at the sight that Sabina
could not contain it.

'My lord!' Dropping her empty bucket, she ran to
him, throwing herself at his tall figure. And when he

caught her to him, his strong arms closing around her, Sabina could have wept with relief. She pressed her face against his hard chest, the links of mail beneath the cloth a welcome reminder that this was a warrior.

'You are here,' she whispered. 'You came back.'

Did he answer? Sabina thought she heard a hushed voice against her ear, before another shout and the thud of hooves echoed around her. The arms that encircled her fell away, Lord de Burgh stepped back, and Sabina drew in a deep, shaky breath at the sense of loss that surged through her. She told herself it was the night's events, the danger, the tension, and yet she searched his face, hoping for an invitation back into his arms. But it was not to be. He turned to greet his squire, who was running towards them.

Soon, it was all over, Lord de Burgh using the last of the dying embers to light a thick piece of wood that had fallen from the hut. He held it aloft as he walked round the building and burned thatch, as if to learn something from the dragon's deadly fumes. He even sniffed the air, but Sabina could smell nothing except the acrid scent of smoke and a hint of salt breeze, off the sea.

Then he turned to face the bedraggled band. 'So this is how you've contained the fires.'

'Yes,' Sabina said, feeling a small spark of pride. 'We collected the buckets months ago, those that were left behind, small tubs, anything watertight.'

'We brought a cart of sand back from beside the sea!' Alec said.

'Water, dirt, sand,' Sabina said. 'We throw on whatever is handy.'

'That explains the sand you found at the site of some of the fires,' Peregrine said, with a pointed look at his master, and Lord de Burgh nodded. Then the boy turned back to the dripping remains with a frown. 'It strikes at night?' he asked. 'When does it sleep?'

It was Alec who answered, with the matter-of-factness of youth. 'It has been sleeping for days.'

At those fateful words, Lord de Burgh's makeshift torch flickered out. But he gathered the reins of his great horse and led them back to Sexton Hall as if he had been born there. He feared neither the darkness nor the beast, and Sabina found herself wishing that she were walking alongside him, one of his strong arms draped over her shoulders, his tall form pressed against hers, keeping her safe and warming her with his heat. The yearning was so sharp it startled her, yet what right had she to want such a thing?

Lord de Burgh had returned to Grim's End, despite what might await him elsewhere, and that was enough. She could not ask for more.

Chapter Seven

Reynold couldn't sleep. Unlike his brothers, who often lay like stones, propped against trees snoring—or, in the case of Stephen, drank himself insensate—Reynold had never found it easy to drift off. Sometimes his leg bothered him. Less frequently, his thoughts were the culprit. But tonight he suffered from both.

As a child, he was concerned with keeping up with his brothers, ignoring his aches, or garnering his father's approval. In recent years, only his decision to leave his home had kept him awake. But now, it was Mistress Sexton's safety that weighed upon him. He had failed her once; he did not intend to do so again.

As he lay there in the dark, it all came back to him: the terrible pounding of his heart when he saw the orange glow in the distance and the frantic urgency that drove him to push his mount on. He had been in dangerous situations before. He had fought in battles, had suffered when his family was at risk, but he had never felt anything like the horror he had known racing towards Grim's End.

And he had only himself to blame. The uneventful days since their initial arrival had dragged, making it easy to dismiss the claims of the inhabitants. And the eerie atmosphere of the empty village had pressed down on him until he longed for a respite from the abandoned buildings, the same small company, the dwindling food and the beautiful damsel who captured his thoughts too often for comfort. Had he really been seeking information at Sandborn or just an opportunity to escape from his growing distraction…attraction?

Now his trip seemed an excuse, a dangerous tempting of fate that could have gone far more awry. Reynold's heart pounded anew at the thought of what might have happened to Mistress Sexton in his absence. Her beauty might make him wary, but it was no defence against the beast.

As much as Reynold disliked Urban, he could appreciate how the man always had a careful eye upon her, protecting her, hurrying her to safety. What had seemed like the jealous actions of the besotted now appeared more sensible. But Urban was no help against the worm, a realisation that made Reynold uneasy. Perhaps Reynold would not prevail in such a contest, either, but at least he could handle a sword.

That simple truth made Reynold determined to guard Mistress Sexton himself. Originally, he had planned to return to the spot where he and Peregrine were attacked and search for signs of the brigands in the woods. But now he dismissed such a journey as unimportant. The lone rider could well be an outlaw who would strike and move on, especially when he found that stretch of deserted road would provide few victims.

He had more pressing concerns here in Grim's End. Indeed, the more he contemplated the danger, the more Reynold wondered whether he should be keeping closer watch upon Mistress Sexton, sleeping outside her door, or perhaps even inside… Such treacherous thoughts led him where he did not want to go until, despite his best intentions, he remembered that moment when he had seen her in the firelight.

His already-hammering heart had skipped a beat at the sight of her, alive and unharmed. With one look at him, she ran towards him, and without conscious thought, Reynold caught her up, drawing her so close that the golden ribbons of her hair slid against his cheek. And instead of the acrid smell of smoke, he was enveloped in a soft sweet scent and something so powerful he had been overwhelmed. Never had a woman been so elated to see him.

Because of what he must do, not because of who he was, Reynold reminded himself as he stared at the ceiling above him. He would do well to remember that. 'Twas the dragon-slayer she greeted, not Reynold de Burgh. And yet, like some tantalising dream, he could not dismiss the images, the memories, the feelings…

'My lord, are you awake?' Peregrine's voice was barely a whisper.

'Yes,' Reynold answered, grateful to be drawn from his own restless musings. He was not surprised that his squire did not sleep, either, for the possibility of another attack probably weighed on the youngster. The description the old man in Sandborn gave them was enough to concern anyone, even a knight. And Reynold's mind had not been idle.

'What are we going to do?' Peregrine asked. 'About the worm, I mean.'

'I've had enough of sitting and waiting for it to strike,' Reynold said, with sudden determination. 'We must find a way to entrap it.'

'How?'

Reynold squinted into the darkness. 'Perhaps a net like the fishermen in Sandborn used.'

'But surely it could just burn through the ropes.'

'Perhaps,' Reynold admitted. But would it become entrapped enough for them to hold it and somehow kill it?

'If only we could make the net out of something like your mail coat, then the dragon couldn't escape,' Peregrine said.

''Twould take too long to craft, and who would lift it?' Reynold asked. 'A chain might work, though, especially if we could wrap the lengths around its neck and choke it to death. It has to breathe, doesn't it, like every other animal?'

'I don't know,' Peregrine whispered, as if he thought the beast too supernatural to be vulnerable. 'But we would need a big chain. And who is going to throw it?'

'Maybe we could string it up and then just pull it tight, snapping the worm's neck,' Reynold said, warming to his idea.

'But that would require such force, especially if the beast is flailing around, trying to escape. Who would be able to do it?'

The de Burghs. His family could do it, Reynold knew. He and his brothers had often tested each other's strength by pulling on ropes, sometimes stretched across a hog wallow or some equally unappealing spot. But his brothers were not here, and Reynold had no way to get a message to them unless he sent his squire, *his courageous, but foolhardy squire, who trusted far too readily.*

'We could rig it up like a noose, and hang the creature,' Reynold said.

Peregrine remained silent for a long moment as though mulling over such a plan, but when he spoke, he did not dispute the idea. 'What are we going to use for bait?'

Reynold squinted into the darkness. 'We'll have to buy an animal, something the worm has a taste for, such as a cow or a pig. A sheep from some nearby flock would be easiest, especially if we can obtain it closer than at Sandborn.' He slanted a glance at the boy, barely visible in the glow of moonlight through the window. 'What say you, squire?'

Although he did not argue, Peregrine's tone made his reservations clear. 'I think we're going to need all the help we can get, including the furry breeches.'

Sabina turned at the sound of footsteps and was surprised to see Lord de Burgh, his squire not far behind. She had only just arrived in the hall herself this morn and had not expected his early appearance. Although she eyed him curiously, his face revealed nothing and she glanced away, flustered.

Lord de Burgh's closed expression had once been a comfort to her, a symbol of his calm competency, but now Sabina found herself resenting it. She wanted to see more, to know more, to have more… Although never prone to whims or wishes, Sabina felt a sudden impatience, which she swiftly dismissed. What had she sworn last night? He was here. That was enough.

So why should she yearn for something else? Because somehow he had become more to her than just a stranger who would do her a service, a knight, a dragon-slayer. Sabina frowned at this unanticipated development as she moved towards the head of the table. She took her seat, only to see Lord de Burgh walk past the other chair to sit on the furthest bench.

His position took on new meaning this morning as the night's events returned to Sabina's mind. Flushing at the memory of her boldness, she realised that he probably didn't want her throwing herself at him again, and she cringed at the thought. What had come over her? She had been so overjoyed to see him that she had gone beyond the bounds of propriety. And he had let her.

Had she given him any choice? All kindness and strength, Lord de Burgh would never turn away from a need. He had given her comfort because she had asked for it, taking on yet another onerous duty at her request without complaint. No wonder his expression was shuttered.

'I don't suppose Urban is a blacksmith,' he said, suddenly.

'Urban?' Sabina had to bite back a smile, for she could not imagine anyone less suited for such a life. 'No, he was my father's steward.'

'We had a blacksmith,' Alec said, between huge bites of apple. 'John Fabre, but he is gone now.'

Sabina frowned at the reminder. The Fabres always had been blacksmiths and loyal to her father, yet John was one of the first to leave Grim's End. Unhappy after his son went missing and disgruntled at the subsequent talk around the village, he seemed to seize upon the dragon as an excuse to go elsewhere and serve another.

'We have need of a smith to make a large chain,' Lord de Burgh said. 'Though I can do simple repairs, I have neither the tools nor the materials for such a heavy piece of work.'

'A chain?' Sabina echoed.

'For the dragon?' Alec asked, brimming with excitement.

'It is only an idea at this point,' Lord de Burgh said, as though to quell the boy's enthusiasm. But it did not work. Alec fairly danced in his seat as the three males discussed the possibility of snapping the dragon's neck with strong metal links.

Sabina said little, for the plan was not what she had expected. Although she had blind faith in Lord de Burgh's ability to dispatch the worm, she had never considered exactly how he would do so. Vaguely, she imagined him pulling a mighty sword from a jewelled scabbard to slay the beast single-handedly, like the heroes of lore. But now she realised just how difficult that would be.

And this talk of bait and tricks added to her discomfort. Sabina had been content in her ignorance, but the conversation made her aware of the harsh realities of any battle with the beast. And for the first time since she begged Lord de Burgh to rescue her, Sabina wondered at what kind of danger she would put him in.

She knew how deadly the creature could be, and yet, she had felt no qualm asking for this knight's help. Now she looked across the table at the man who would risk his life for her and felt a pang, of guilt and something else. Fear for him.

At that moment, the rest of the small band arrived, Adele with their food, Ursula to take a seat near her, and Urban to stand, as if on guard. Sabina tried to concentrate on them, their safety and the future of Grim's End. But doubt pricked at her, where none had been before, and she picked at her food as Urban made some rude comment about Lord de Burgh's absence during the dragon's attack.

'Yet my trip to Sandborn was not wholly wasted, for we did speak with a man from Grim's End who saw the beast,' Lord de Burgh said. He proceeded to describe something even more horrible than Sabina's imaginings, and her heart began to pound. Ursula gasped, and even Alec's eyes grew round as saucers.

'So at last you believe,' Urban said, smugly.

'Who was it? Who told you this?' Sabina demanded.

'His name was Gamel,' Peregrine answered.

'Gamel? Gamel Cyneric?' Alec said. 'Why, he's just a mad old man.'

'Alec!' Adele admonished the boy. And Sabina felt her tension ease, for Gamel was hardly a trustworthy source of information.

'He's not a bad man,' Alec said. 'The children all

liked him because he told stories. But they were wild tales of pirates and tall marauders who came over the sea and old kings buried with their riches.'

Ursula appeared startled, and Sabina turned toward her attendant. 'Do you not share kinship with Gamel?' she asked.

''Tis a feeble tie at best,' Ursula answered, with a sniff.

'I can show you where the blacksmith used to work,' Alec offered, obviously dismissing Gamel's claims. And soon all the males trooped from the hall, except for Urban, who snatched up a hunk of the cheese from the new supplies and walked towards the window, as though to keep an eye upon the others from the protection of the manor.

As soon as the steward stepped away from the table, Ursula leaned close. 'I heard Lord de Burgh's footsteps outside our door this morn,' she whispered.

'What?' Sabina asked, flustered.

'He was standing outside our room. He must have been waiting for you and then followed you down to the hall.' Ursula leaned back as though she had made an astounding pronouncement, but Sabina did not grasp the significance.

As if exasperated with her, Ursula leaned close again. 'That is why I waited to follow you. I wanted to give you a few moments alone together.' She gave Sabina a sly smile. 'Well? What happened?'

Nothing happened. And nothing would happen, Sabina thought, flushing. It was time she put an end to her attendant's matchmaking.

'Ursula, you must stop this nonsense. Whether Lord

de Burgh rises early or late means naught. And there is no need for your machinations. I have no wish to speak privately with him.' Had Ursula seen her run to him last night? Had they all? Sabina tried to remember who was next to her in the darkness, but there had been too much confusion.

To Sabina's relief, Ursula made no mention of the fire or what had transpired there. But she refused to drop the subject of Lord de Burgh. 'He is a handsome man, a knight and a lord, and you are a beautiful young woman. I can be forgiven for trying to help things along, that is all.'

Sabina shook her head. 'Your actions are making me uncomfortable and disturbing our guest, too, a man who is under no obligation to help us.'

Ursula sniffed, offended. 'Bah! You have not seen how he eyes you, like a starving man might.'

Sabina felt a jolt of surprise, but ignored the temptation to hear more. She had seen no such hungry looks from Lord de Burgh, and Ursula was known to twist a tale to suit her listener's desires, though not as much as her kinsman Gamel.

Rather than argue, Sabina sought a conciliatory tone. 'For all we know, he has a betrothed waiting for him, or a wife, or even a child,' she said, though the words stuck in her throat.

'Bah! I don't believe it, but I shall ask his squire.'

'Ursula! Don't you dare,' Sabina warned. All she needed was for word to get back to Lord de Burgh of Ursula's continued meddling.

'As you say, mistress,' Ursula said, ducking in her

head. 'But you are no longer young, and Julian Fabre has been gone for a long time.'

Sabina drew in a sharp breath at the mention of the name she had forbidden her attendant to speak. 'He is dead,' she said, unwilling to continue the discussion.

'Either way, it is time you took an interest in someone else,' Ursula said.

With a fierce glance, Sabina effectively silenced her attendant, but her thoughts were not so easily stilled. In truth, though Sabina was not about to admit it to Ursula, she had never taken an interest in anyone…until Lord de Burgh arrived.

Reynold did not like the errand that was upon him this morn. Yesterday, they had gone to the blacksmith's to find the forge still in place, but no iron to work. And Reynold knew the size of the task required someone with skill, else it would take too long to make and might not hold when the time came.

He had no choice but to commission a chain from a blacksmith, which meant leaving Grim's End, a mission he was loathe to undertake. How could he guard Mistress Sexton when she was not with him? Yet it made no sense for her to accompany him, especially since he did not have the men to protect her on the road.

For an instant, Reynold had considered taking them *all* with him, but he had dismissed the notion as unfeasible and risky. It would be just his luck to return to find the village burned to the ground while they were away.

He could send Peregrine, but even if able to bargain with the smith, the brave lad could easily be waylaid, his purse stolen, or worse. Unpalatable as it might be, Reynold could see only one solution: he must go alone, leaving Peregrine to act in his stead. And he would go now, at dawn, in order to avoid any arguments and goodbyes.

Shaking Peregrine awake, he spoke softly of his intentions to the wide-eyed boy, who rose up from his pallet, protesting valiantly. 'But my vow! I swore to the l'Estranges that I would accompany you always.'

'And you shall, my squire, but not today,' Reynold said. 'I need someone trustworthy to watch over Mistress Sexton, should the dragon appear in my absence.'

That silenced the boy, who nodded gravely.

'There is no need to reveal my whereabouts immediately, lest you worry the women,' Reynold added. 'However, do not let them search the village for me either. Your concern is with them.'

Peregrine nodded again, and Reynold slipped out the door and through the silent manor far easier than he had Campion. For here there were no servants stirring in the hall, nor stablemen to notice him taking his horse.

He had thought to return to Sandborn since he had become familiar with the small village, but the attack along the road made him hesitate. No doubt the brigand had moved on, but Reynold had no time to waste with a petty villain. Not when he had something far more dangerous to fight.

Heading south instead, he reached Baderton more quickly than Sandborn and easily found the blacksmith's. There he was able to purchase a helmet and a shield, though smaller than he liked, from the man's meagre stock, along with some items for his squire. He commissioned another, larger shield, in addition to the chain, which required some haggling.

The blacksmith, a quiet sort who was well pleased with Reynold's coin, did not question the intended use of so large a shackle, though he did advise Reynold to have a strong cart ready when he came to pick it up. And who would lift it? That question lay between them both, unspoken. Although Reynold knew one possible answer, he was not sure whether he wanted to pursue it.

Loading Sirius up with his goods, Reynold stood in the roadway, uncertain. No one here knew that he was from Grim's End, so he received no suspicious or fearful looks. And as a de Burgh, he could inquire at the manor house, talk with the master of the hall, and find out about the politics of the area, including why the liege lord was not doing his duty by the people of Grim's End. He might even be able to garner support from the local leader. And perhaps someone in that household would take a message home…to Campion.

He could ask for help.

Reynold had thought long and hard about whether he should contact his family. And if so, what he should say—that his pilgrimage had been interrupted by a dragon? His lips curved at the thought of the reaction that might bring. While some might think he had lost his mind, Simon would be here in an instant, hoping to fight it himself. Indeed, Reynold would do better to contact Robin or Stephen, those brothers least likely to come haring after him.

Reynold followed the track to the manor house, squinting at the old-fashioned stone building until Sirius grew restless beneath him, and still he had not made a decision. Here in this strange village, he felt a sharp yearning for his brothers, for their company, their wisdom and their aid. And there was no doubt in his mind that with the might of the de Burghs behind him, he could slay any beast, accomplish anything. None had yet bested them.

Still, he hesitated. He had left Campion for a reason. If he called upon them now, he would not so easily escape a second time. And he did not want them to leave their families in order to take on a dangerous task that was solely his responsibility. The l'Estranges had deemed this his quest, and though Reynold would not term it such, he was loathe to involve others.

In the end it did not matter, for he was turned away from the manor, one of several owned by a Lord Cyppe, a baron who could not be bothered with the petty concerns of the villagers. And, as Reynold headed toward Grim's End, he felt a sense of relief that he would continue this undertaking himself.

Still, he missed Peregrine's cheering presence, for this track, too, was deserted, especially when he neared the empty village. Perhaps Peregrine was not as versed in battle as Will, his former squire, but Reynold appreciated the boy far more. Had Reynold once thought him mute? More often than not, Peregrine chattered like a magpie, full of questions and opinions that Reynold's former squire would never have voiced.

As Reynold reached the outskirts of the village, a deathly quiet seemed to descend, as though the dragon drove away all other birds and beasts. But Reynold knew that wasn't true, especially when a hare skittered from beneath some bushes to cross his path. Still, there was no denying the eeriness, and Reynold knew the familiar feeling of being watched. This time, instead of shaking it off, he looked carefully about.

Behind him the road was empty, and ahead lay Grim's End. To the right he could glimpse the sea in the distance, and meadows rose to his left. Searching out the source of the sensation, Reynold abandoned the pathway, moving around the village and the tall grasses that marked the pond, keeping alert for any movement. But he saw no sign of man or beast. He even squinted into the sky lest the worm be watching him from above. But all he saw was the clear blue of Mistress Sexton's eyes, and he urged his mount towards the stables, back to her.

Leaving Sirius to wait for Peregrine's grooming, Reynold strode towards the manor. At first glance, nothing appeared to be amiss, for he heard no roars, saw no fires and smelled no smoke. Yet he realised he would not be at ease until he saw her, whole and well. He slipped through the kitchens silently, pausing before the hall, relaxing only when he saw the glimmer of her golden hair.

They were all gathered together in the eerie quiet of the hall. Urban was standing at the window, looking out, the boys were huddled in a corner, in conversation, and the women were seated near the table.

'He's back!' Alec's voice rang out. But as Reynold

stepped into the room, his attention was focused solely on the mistress of the household. Upon seeing him, she half-rose from her chair, a cry upon her lips. Then, as though collecting herself, she sank back into her seat.

Reynold's pleasure at finding her safe was tempered by her greeting, far different from the one he had received upon his last return to Grim's End. But what did he expect? That she would throw herself into his arms again? That night she had been besieged. Now all was quiet, and she could see clearly in the light of day who—and what—he was.

Although Reynold wanted nothing more than to hold out his arms for a more welcome greeting, he did not. While Urban and Alec pelted him with questions, Mistress Sexton said nothing, only watched him with huge eyes, her hands clasped in her lap. And Reynold could not complain, for this was what he expected, what he knew, and far preferable to some unusual favour that meant nothing. Yet his heart felt heavy. Answering little, he signalled for Peregrine to join him as he headed back towards the kitchens.

'Where are you going?' Mistress Sexton finally spoke, though it was a whisper.

'To the stables to tend to my horse,' Reynold said. He did not wait for further comment, but turned on his heel to stride back the way he had come. All this long day he had been eager to return, yet now he wanted only to escape the eerie atmosphere of the hall and its few inhabitants.

'What is it?' Peregrine asked, hurrying to keep up with Reynold's long strides. 'Were you attacked again?'

'No, I went to Baderton, and the journey was uneventful. I commissioned the chain and picked up a few other items that you may help me unload.'

Peregrine nodded, though he still gave Reynold a questioning glance. Indeed, the squire might have said more, but his thoughts were soon diverted by what Reynold withdrew from his pack.

'For you,' Reynold said. 'It is high time you learned how to handle yourself.'

'But, my lord,' Peregrine protested, his voice full of wonder, 'this is a fine sword, fit for a knight.' He looked up at Reynold, his dark eyes filling, and Reynold felt his own throat tighten.

'And how am I to fend off all manner of attack upon Grim's End by myself?' Reynold asked. 'I trust not to Master Urban and his pitchfork.'

Peregrine laughed, but the sound was shaky, and Reynold slapped him on the back. 'Now put on your new helm, and you shall learn a thing or two.'

Blinking, Peregrine nodded, apparently struck speechless for the first time in weeks. And as he taught the boy how to hold the weapon, Reynold remembered his own tutoring from his brothers, often couched in goading and taunts, but treasured none the less. How old had Nick, the last of them, been when he'd handled his first sword? They had all been young, getting an early start and benefiting from the skills of the older de Burghs.

Now Reynold welcomed the familiar heft in his hand of a weapon that was nearly an extension of himself. And as he wielded it with expertise, slicing through the gathering twilight with precision, all thoughts of Mistress Sexton and even food were forgotten.

For this was what he knew. This was his life.

Chapter Eight

Reynold knelt beside Mistress Sexton, trying not to breathe in her sweet perfume above the scents of the garden, and wondered how he had ended up alone with her here in a leafy bower hidden by tall plants. But he knew there was no help for it.

Ursula and Adele were tending the garden behind the hall, the boys were setting a fish trap in the pond, and he had not seen Urban for some time. Had the man grown annoyed with Reynold's constant presence? Although Reynold was weary of Urban's biting remarks, they served a purpose, often preventing private conversation with Mistress Sexton.

Now Reynold had that in abundance. But when she wanted to work another small patch of garden among the abandoned homes of the village, Reynold could hardly let her go alone. And so he listened as she spoke of the villagers she had held dear, her childhood and the father she had loved. And he found himself wishing to be a part of that group, someone who caused her voice to dip lower and softer with affection. Then, realising his foolishness, he wanted to block out the very sound of her, to prevent himself from learning any more about Mistress Sexton.

For this kind of closeness was dangerous. It fostered hopes and wishes that he had no business dwelling upon, dreams he had long abandoned, desires he had long denied. When she was so near, speaking to him easily, Reynold found himself relaxing, weakening, succumbing to her charms. Having no wish to join his squire and her man in languishing after Mistress Sexton, Reynold tried to harden himself against her. But the cool façade he had cultivated in order to keep his distance from others seemed to crumble in her presence.

Although Reynold turned his attention to the task she had set him to, that was no easier. First, she had showed him how to tell the difference between the shoots of plants and the weeds that must be removed, then how to tell what was ripe and ready to be picked. She had demonstrated gently, with her own pale hands, which drew Reynold's gaze like honey a bee.

Leaning back on his heels, Reynold squinted up at the sky, but it only reminded him of the blue of her eyes, and he grunted in annoyance. If only she would do something to prove his theory, by shouting at her servants, wasting food, telling lies… But she did not. Still, Reynold refused to reconsider his life lesson that all beautiful women were spoiled, selfish and deceitful. Mistress Sexton might appear to be none of those things, yet why was she here alone, with none to defend her except a passing knight?

Suddenly, he turned toward her. 'How is it that as an unmarried female, you serve as head of your household and the village?'

Obviously startled by his bold question, Mistress Sexton flushed. 'The Sextons have held the manor for a long time, my father receiving it from his father. But my father had no siblings who lived beyond infancy, and he took as wife a gently born woman who was orphaned. I was their only child.'

'But surely your father made some provisions for you?' *To be married*, Reynold did not add, *to be under the protection of a man with the power to provide for you and to keep you safe.*

'I am his heir, yes, though I'm sure he expected, and deserved, to live much longer. But the dragon had other plans,' Mistress Sexton said, frowning fiercely at the soil beneath her hands.

'The dragon? The dragon killed him?' Reynold asked, with sudden interest. How was it that he had never been told this?

'The dragon struck him down,' Mistress Sexton said. 'We heard the roar, and Urban advised everyone to go below, but Father would not. He ran out of the hall, shaking his fist at the sky, and then he fell. I was inside, so I don't know exactly what happened, whether he saw the beast or it breathed upon him, but when I went to him, he was clutching his chest, barely alive. He spoke some words before he died, but nothing that made sense. Perhaps he died of fright.'

'I am sorry,' Reynold whispered, wishing that there was some way he could take away that horror, that pain.

He had been so young when his mother passed away that he had never really felt the loss, though he had been aware of the lack of a nurturing female as he grew older. Sometimes he wished that his father had married again, not now, when he was grown, but when a woman like Joy might have made a difference in his life.

Mistress Sexton acknowledged his words with a nod, and for a long time they both were silent, until Reynold realised she had never really answered his question. Was there no one in the area deemed worthy, or had her father valued her too much to part with her? 'Did he not wish you to marry?'

Mistress Sexton started, as though surprised by the question, and for a moment Reynold thought she would not answer. 'There was talk of an alliance, but he is…dead,' she said.

'Again, I am sorry for your loss.'

'Don't be,' she said, in a tone of dismissal. 'It was long ago.'

And that, Reynold decided, was another reason why he hadn't wanted to know more about Mistress Sexton. For now he was racked with curiosity about this proposed alliance and what it had meant to her. But even had he dared ask her more, Mistress Sexton effectively put an end to the conversation.

'I think that's enough for now,' she said. Rising to her feet, she brushed the dirt off her hands, still pale and beautiful, despite the use she put them to. Were her fingers trembling? Reynold nearly took them in his own, but she leaned down to retrieve her basket, and he could only do the same. Had the mere mention of the dead man so upset her?

Reynold frowned as he followed her from the garden, but the gentle sway of the hips in front of him and the warmth of the day soon chased such thoughts from his mind. The breeze was fresh with the tang of salt air from the sea, and a bright sun shone upon them as they wove their way toward the manor.

When they reached the pond, Mistress Sexton called to the boys, and they stopped to admire the morning's catch. It was a far cry from the bounty Reynold had once taken for granted, and yet he found himself enjoying these simple pleasures far more than others he had known. Glancing at the woman who laughed and teased with Alec and Peregrine, Reynold realised that he did not want these days to end.

But end they would once he accomplished his task here. Reynold wondered, suddenly, if his brothers had shared this feeling. Simon had taken it upon himself to undermine his future wife's manor. Stephen had been given the task of escorting Bridgid to her family home. Dunstan had been assigned to deliver Marion to her home, as well. When had they decided to linger, to wed?

Startled by the direction of his thoughts, Reynold told himself it did not matter what they had felt or done. For the first time in his life, he was so at ease with a woman that he could almost pretend that he was one of his brothers. But he was not.

Although some of their adventures might have ended in marriage, his own set of circumstances prevented any such romantic ending. He was to slay the dragon, that was all. And if he survived, there would be no reward and no damsel to wed.

* * *

As Reynold squinted into the sky, he decided there was no comparison. Even on a day like this, without a cloud within view, Mistress Sexton's eyes were bluer. And he could tell. He had only to glance over to her, perched upon Peregrine's black, alongside Sirius, to see for himself.

This morning, he had intended to ride the perimeter of the village, as he often did, while Mistress Sexton was still abed, but she had caught him in the hall and begged to join him. Her eagerness for the exercise had been difficult to resist, and Reynold could guard her nearly as well horsed as not. But somehow his familiar task of searching for anything unusual on the outskirts of Grim's End had turned into a pleasure ride.

His first.

Reynold had seen his father and Joy out surveying their lands, laughing and smiling as they did so. And sometimes, they returned with their garments awry, as though they had ridden more than their mounts. His brothers and their wives, too, would go off together, sometimes leisurely seeking out the banks of the pond, sometimes racing full out upon a stretch of level ground. And although they had often invited Reynold to join them, he had seen no point in riding for leisure.

Until today.

It was his companion who made the difference, for Mistress Sexton took a simple pleasure in the boundaries of her world, in pointing out to him her favourite spots, where flowers grew and birds nested and the ocean could be seen between the trees, where broom and heather stretched off into the distance and the cries of gull and heron could be heard.

And in that moment, Reynold wished that they could go on for ever like this, even though he knew they could not. When the chain was finished, he would set his trap, and even if he caught nothing, they could not survive the winter without meat and other provisions. Nor was there much sense in buying supplies. A community had to be self-sustaining to survive, and soon his own coin would run out.

Perhaps he should take her to Campion, where she would be safe, where they would all be safe, Reynold thought suddenly. But then what? Would he leave, or would he stand by and watch another take her hand? She could not be that much older than his brother Nicholas. Was that his fate, to provide the youngest de Burgh with a wife? Reynold shuddered. He did not know if he had the strength to do that, even if Mistress Sexton would be willing to go.

Slanting a glance at her lovely profile, he saw that her gaze was fixed on the lands she loved and Reynold knew that he could never convince her. And would she ever be happy elsewhere? Would her eyes light up when discussing some other patch of coastline, another copse of birch? Reynold shook his head.

'We should be getting back,' he said gruffly.

'Oh, yes,' she said, though her expression fell. 'We have dallied too long. Why, the others will be wondering where we are! And you have had nothing to break your fast.' She babbled, as though apologising for her brief happiness, and he felt churlish for cutting short a time when she seemed to have forgotten her woes.

She was quiet as they reached the stable, and Reynold wondered why he had even suggested they return. What awaited them here, but an empty hall, Urban with his biting tongue, and Ursula, who nattered incessantly about nothing? For an instant, he almost suggested that they ride away, but where? There was no avoiding the situation, no escaping himself no matter how far from Campion he might run.

Dismounting, he turned to see her eyeing him with concern. 'What is it?' she asked.

Reynold shook his head. It was nothing. It was everything. He felt a stranger to himself, assailed by too much when he had always made do with too little. And because he had no answer for what ailed him, he could only return to the one thing they had in common.

'Where is it?' he asked, squinting at the horizon once more. 'Where is the worm? How can something so big hide itself so well? And why does it strike so infrequently?'

Mistress Sexton shook her head. 'The pickings are slim here now. There are no animals, no villagers, little movement to attract its attention. Perhaps it has found better feeding elsewhere.'

Reynold had heard that refrain before, so put little faith in it as he stepped forwards to help her from the saddle. He moved automatically, but when his hands closed about her waist, he was seized by a yearning so strong that he shuddered with the force of it. His fingers tightened around her, and he glanced toward her face, only to see a startled expression on her lovely features.

Hurriedly, he set her on her feet, then turned and walked away, determined to fetch Peregrine, rub down the horses, and forget everything about this morning. Absently, he rubbed the leg that ached from his ride as he tried not to think of what else pained him: a body that he usually kept under tight control and a heart that he had thought long dead.

Reynold had not waited for her, so she was a few steps behind him when the deafening roar shook the air. Without conscious thought, he leapt towards her, taking her with him to the ground and covering her. For a long moment, he lay there, protecting her with himself even as he expected licks of fire upon his back. But when he felt nothing, he lifted his head and looked upwards.

The sky was just as clear and empty as before, perhaps more so, for this time, he did not even see the flash of a bird's wing. Still, Reynold knew better than to linger when he should get Mistress Sexton inside and below as quickly as possible. He turned his face towards her to tell her just that, but found himself staring into eyes that put the heavens to shame. Her flawless skin was barely inches from his own, and her rosy lips were parted in surprise.

Although he had knocked her to the earth in haste, Mistress Sexton showed no sign of fear of the beast and made no move to rise. She simply gazed into his eyes, and then her attention dropped lower, to his mouth. And, once again, Reynold did not pause to consider his actions. Without thought, he dipped his head and took her mouth with his own, seizing what he could, for this moment, at least.

When he felt her start beneath him, he pulled back, shocked at his behaviour. Had he learned nothing these past days? But before he could loose her, Mistress Sexton's arms slid around his neck and she lifted her mouth to his, kissing him just as boldly. And then he was lost, sinking into sensation, revelling in softness, warmed throughout. She tasted as heady as fine wine, not too tart and not too sweet.

A fine strand of her hair caught against his cheek, and Reynold welcomed it. Beneath him, her lithe form curved against his own, as if moulded to him, and he felt his body stir to life. He gasped, burying his face against the smoothness of her pale neck, where the delicate scent of her golden hair enveloped him, as though calling him home.

'Mistress? Lord de Burgh?'

At the sound of Alec's voice, Reynold jerked away, rolling to his feet as though roused by a weapon. Indeed, such was his state of mind that his hand went to the hilt of his sword. Thankfully, the boy was not yet upon them, but was approaching from the entrance to the kitchens. By the time he saw them, Reynold was already standing, and Mistress Sexton was rising to her feet.

'Are you hurt?' Alec asked, running towards them.

'No,' Reynold said. 'We fell to the ground when we heard the roar.'

'Why are you outside?' Mistress Sexton asked. 'Adele will be worried.'

'Peregrine and I were going to check our traps when it sounded,' he said. And, as if hearing his name, Peregrine burst upon the scene, sword drawn.

'Was it here? Did you see it?' the squire asked, his eyes wide.

At the boy's simple question, the full import of his actions struck Reynold like a blow. As if struggling from a dream, he came awake to realise that he had not gone after the beast. He had not even seen it. He had been too busy making love to Mistress Sexton.

'No,' he muttered.

'Lord de Burgh was concerned with protecting me,' Mistress Sexton said, in a breathless whisper.

But Reynold knew that was a lie. Once he had hold of her, all awareness of danger had left him. His responsibilities had been abandoned while he lay upon her in full view of anyone looking out of the hall, as well as the dragon. What more would he have done, if Alec hadn't called for them? Instead of guarding her, Reynold had not even protected her reputation.

He could not bear to look at her, for fear of what he might see in her face, so Reynold again headed towards the hall, silencing his squire with a dark look. And Mistress Sexton said nothing either, no doubt eager to escape to her chamber.

Although he could not like them, Reynold understood his own failings. But why had Mistress Sexton responded, instead of flinching from him as she had in the past? Perhaps she had been driven by a different kind of need, he thought, with a scowl, the same striving to keep her home that had made her beg a stranger for help.

But it hadn't felt like that. Reynold knew what it was like to be kissed out of obligation, for payment rendered. His few encounters with women had been hurried joinings far from his home, where he had not revealed either his leg or his name. He had not wanted any talk about himself, or, worse yet, any comparison to his brothers, to reach Campion.

Although no coin had changed hands today, had Mistress Sexton's kisses been bartered for his duty? Reynold frowned, searching for a more palatable answer. Perhaps the peril of the moment and their close proximity had seized them both, he thought.

But no matter what excuse he gave her, Reynold knew it was already too late for him. Against his better judgement, against all the reasoning that had served him well over the years, he was becoming as besotted as his own squire.

Sabina made her way to her chair in the hall, trying to keep her composure while her mind raced and her heart pounded. She would have sought the sanctuary of her room, but she didn't want to raise any questions, and, in truth, she didn't know if her shaky legs could take her that far. She had been so caught up in the moment that she hadn't considered what she was doing, but now the ramifications of her actions hit her, stealing her breath.

Finding her chair, she sat down and let Adele put food before her. She took out her knife to cut a piece of apple, but her hands moved by rote while her thoughts were in a turmoil. There was no need to panic, Sabina told herself. It had been but a kiss, that's all, and not her first. Yet 'twas the most important, the only one that moved her, shook her, and threatened to alter her very world.

Although the kiss had surprised her, her own reaction did not. It had been coming on for some time, Sabina realised. And why not? A handsome stranger, a knight and a lord, tall, dark and confident, vowed to protect them all and slay a dragon for her. Even Ursula was soon taken with him. And the more time Sabina spent with him, learning his quiet strength, his gentleness, his far-ranging knowledge, the way he squinted his eyes when he was thinking… Well, only a stone would be unmoved.

Of all the men in the wide world, why did it have to be Lord de Burgh? Sabina almost choked back a laugh, for no one had ever affected her except this one, who held her hopes, her future, her life in his sword hand. And yet perhaps it was best, for what she had asked from him was too much for anyone, and only now did she see that.

Sabina's hand trembled and she nicked her finger. The tiny drop of blood set her heart pounding again, and she felt light-headed. How could she go on as before? But what about her home? Her legacy? What of Grim's End?

'You've cut yourself!' Ursula's voice seemed to come out of nowhere, and Sabina saw her attendant take her hand and dab it with a piece of linen.

''Tis nothing,' Sabina murmured. For it was noth-ing, nothing to the blood that had been spilled here in the village and might yet be spilled. *His* blood. Her breath caught.

'I think I know what ails you.' Alarmed at Ursula's words, Sabina looked up to see her attendant wearing a sly grin. She leaned close.

'When Adele told me you had gone out riding with

Lord de Burgh, I was beside myself,' Ursula whispered. 'That is until I looked out the window to see him kissing you!' She straightened, a triumphant expression on her face, but Sabina shook her head in confusion.

'You are dazed to be sure, and who can blame you? A handsome man like that…' Ursula raised her other hand to fan her flushed cheeks before leaning close again. 'But do not take too long to recover your wits, for you would be wise to plan what you would do and say now.'

Sabina could only gape at her attendant, uncomprehending.

'See? All your worries were for naught. And lest you still harbour any, I spoke with Peregrine, questioning the boy subtly, mind you, and he said that Lord de Burgh has no children, no wife, no betrothed, no sweetheart. So he would make an excellent match! Indeed, the boy claims the family is very wealthy. Isn't that wonderful news?'

Sabina shook her head, for she had no desire for riches. She had only wanted one thing, but now…

As usual, Ursula could not understand her hesitation. 'Surely you do not think him the type to take liberties?' the older woman asked. 'I would not believe him capable of compromising a gentlewoman and abandoning her. Still, perhaps we should put some pressure upon him to offer for you as soon as possible.'

'No!' Sabina finally roused herself to respond. 'I cannot allow it.'

'Why?' Ursula asked, frowning in disapproval. 'Do you intend to let him kiss you and let it go, as if you were a dairymaid and he the blacksmith's son?'

Sabina shuddered, as though Ursula had doused her

still-heated form in ice water. 'He is not the black-smith's son.'

'I know, dear,' Ursula whispered. 'I am sorry. I didn't mean—'

Sabina did not let her finish, but took Ursula's hands in her own. 'You will do say nothing of this, and you will do nothing.'

'What? Why?'

''Tis impossible,' Sabina said.

'I don't understand why—'

Sabina cut her off. 'You must believe me, Ursula, for you don't know all. There's something I haven't told you.'

'What is it?' Ursula asked, her expression stark.

But Sabina only shook her head again. There were things she hadn't told anyone, things she didn't dare. About the dragon. About herself. They might not have mattered before, but now everything took on a new significance. What had once seemed simple had become painfully complicated.

Worst of all, her vow, which had once been so crystal clear, was growing murky, clouded with other concerns.

Chapter Nine

Mistress Sexton had something on her mind, and Reynold had a feeling he wasn't going to like it. He could tell by the set of her chin and the glint of her blue eyes that it was probably not pleasant. In fact, she looked like someone who was heading to the gallows.

And since she hadn't spoken more than a few words since yesterday, Reynold didn't need a genius like his brother Geoff to guess that she wasn't too happy about what had happened, although she seemed to enjoy it at the time. Or had she? After a long, restless night, Reynold had begun to wonder what was real about their encounter and how much he had imagined.

She had certainly chosen her time well. The hall was empty, but for the two of them, so at least they would not be overheard. Mistress Sexton was a born leader and knew better than to chastise her minions in front of each other. Reynold, his jaw tight, would bear this humiliation in private.

'I would speak with you, my lord,' she said, stopping to stand before him, hands clasped together.

'Yes.' Reynold steeled himself against what was coming, the prodding of his old wound, suddenly fresh. But rather than wait for her attack, he launched his defence, hoping to have done with it quickly. 'If this is about the kiss, I'm sorry. It won't happen again.'

Mistress Sexton made a strangled noise, and Reynold saw her face go pale and then flush. Was the memory too distasteful for discussion? Reynold turned on his heel and walked towards the windows, muttering a curse under his breath. Wasn't this why he had left Campion, to avoid such entanglements? And yet here he was halfway across the country and worse off than he had been at home.

'I release you from your vow.'

Reynold whirled at her words. *'What?'* She looked so uncomfortable that he might have spoken more gently, but for the fact that she was telling him to go, to leave Grim's End behind. *Would she rather face the dragon than his attentions?*

'I realise now that I asked too much of you,' she said, and Reynold noticed that she could not meet his eyes. 'I cannot ask you to risk your life for me, for *us*.'

Reynold's lips curled in contempt. She had been perfectly content with the arrangement until yesterday. Did she think he would ask for more in exchange for his service? As far as he was concerned, nothing had changed, except for his own brief lapse in judgement.

'I'm afraid that my vows cannot be discarded so

easily,' Reynold said. 'What happened to your concerns for the people of this area, your claim that the worm must be vanquished so that everyone can live without fear? Surely you do not want the beast to triumph?'

'No,' she answered. 'But neither do I want you to be hurt.'

Reynold snorted. 'Have you so little faith in me, mistress? I am no coward.'

''Tis too dangerous!' she said, ignoring his question.

Reynold caught and held her gaze. The task always had been perilous, as was simply living in Grim's End. ''Tis no different a threat than it was yesterday. Why release me now?'

Mistress Sexton looked away, without answering, and Reynold grunted, his suspicions confirmed. 'Then I will keep to my vow.'

She glanced at him then, as though she might argue, but whatever speech she began was drowned out by a loud noise, a dull roar from outside. To Reynold it sounded different than the one yesterday, and he wondered if there were two worms. But he would not make the same mistake twice. He rushed to the doors, threw them open, and ran out in time to see a flash of fire streaking through the air to fall upon an abandoned hut, igniting the thatched roof.

Right hand on his sword hilt, Reynold lifted his left to shade his eyes and search the skies, but he saw nothing and heard no more until Mistress Sexton's shouts rose from behind him. He turned to see her pulling the cart that contained the pails, fearless of the beast, concerned only with putting out the blaze. And with one last check of the empty heavens, Reynold joined her, their efforts soon aided by the rest of the small band.

When the last of the flames were extinguished, Reynold surveyed the wet and weary residents of Grim's End. They had battled valiantly, and now, more than ever, he appreciated their bravery. Having never witnessed any of the previous attacks, he could understand the panic that drove the other inhabitants away. Had anyone been inside the hut, they might have been roasted alive.

Any blaze could be deadly, but this one seemed more so, though Reynold could not claim to have vast experience with fires. He gazed at the smoking remains as if to find an answer there, while something tugged at the back of his mind.

'See?' Urban asked, gesturing toward the burned building. His garments were covered with soot and ash, and there was no denying he had worked as hard as the others. Still, his tongue remained as sharp as always. 'Think you that a *chain* will protect us against this?'

'I see fire, but no dragon,' Reynold said.

'We heard it,' Alec said, his eyes wide. 'We were checking our traps.'

'Yes, I heard something, too, but our flying beast remains elusive,' Reynold said, squinting at the sky. Reynold was beginning to understand why no one had seen the creature except a madman, whose description he now discounted.

'I saw its fiery breath,' Mistress Sexton said. She looked so bedraggled that Reynold felt a sudden ache in his chest, a surge of pride at her courage and visibly flagging strength. Would that he could take her in his arms, but he knew she would not welcome his comfort.

'And you could have been killed,' Urban said to her. 'This is what comes from wandering about out of doors, making ourselves targets for the beast.' His accusing glare was not lost on Reynold.

'I will not cower in the cellar while Lord de Burgh risks his life for us,' Mistress Sexton said.

Surprised, Reynold glanced towards her and saw her lift her chin as though daring any to deny her words. Reynold's own mouth felt dry, curbing his response, but Urban might have argued had not Ursula's voice rung out loudly in the hushed silence. 'Urban, please help me back to the manor.'

At her words, the others hurried to pile the buckets into the cart, and Alec began wheeling it toward the hall. Only Peregrine and Mistress Sexton remained behind while Reynold stood staring at the ruins, as though the answers to all his questions might suddenly come to him from the ashes.

'Let us have a closer look,' he said, gesturing towards his squire.

'We did not finish our conversation.'

Mistress Sexton's soft speech again caught Reynold by surprise, but he shook his head. There was nothing to discuss, and right now he had more important things on his mind.

Still, the stubborn female persisted, stepping close to lay a hand upon his arm. 'I would not have you hurt or killed, my lord.'

Reynold's heart lurched, and once more he felt

himself weakening. He wanted to believe her, to accept the promise he thought he saw in her blue gaze. But he could not let himself. He could be imagining things, and even if he were not, her concern was misplaced.

'I don't think you need worry about the dragon doing me in,' Reynold said.

'You would leave us then,' she said, with a nod, though her expression held no joy.

Reynold shook his head, his lips curving into a grim smile. 'Unless it is invisible, I don't think a worm threatens your village.'

'But the roar,' she protested. 'You've heard it,' she added, looking bewildered.

Reynold shrugged. 'The sound could be made by anything, another beast, or, more likely, a horn or an instrument of man.' The roar yesterday had been subtly familiar, but Reynold could not identify it. And although today's was different, again he felt a tug at his memory.

'But what about its fiery breath?' Peregrine asked. 'I saw that myself, and look at what it did.'

'Now, that is something else,' Reynold said, squinting at the sky. 'The flames fly through the air, and yet we do not see their source. If you were not expecting a dragon, how would you explain it, squire?'

Peregrine looked thoughtful. 'You could send fire through the air with an arrow, especially the larger ones that are shot with a crossbow.'

Reynold nodded. 'But the smaller ones are also effective when wrapped in pitch-soaked ropes and set alight.' In fact, there had been a time in his youth when he and his brothers had tried to outdo each other in acquiring such skills, until one of them accidentally set fire to the poultry pen, causing Campion to put an end to the competition.

'I cannot believe that someone or something is shooting flaming arrows at us,' Mistress Sexton argued. ''Tis too great a distance. And what of all the animals that were attacked?'

'One thing at a time,' Reynold said. 'For now, let us consider how else a blaze might be sent from afar.'

Mistress Sexton appeared baffled, while Peregrine's face screwed up in concentration. But the squire only shook his head, for once unable to produce an answer from his seemingly vast store of learning.

Reynold was trying to tap his own store, though it was not as fresh in his mind. 'Campion Castle has never been besieged, but none the less we all learned the craft of siege warfare,' he mused aloud.

'We?' Mistress Sexton asked.

'My brothers and I,' Reynold said.

'All seven of them,' Peregrine noted.

'You have seven brothers?' Mistress Sexton echoed, with a startled expression.

'No, I am one of the seven de Burgh brothers, sons of the Earl of Campion,' Reynold said, and somehow the words caused a catch in his throat. *I am a de Burgh and proud of it.*

His lips curved at the reminder of his heritage, and suddenly Reynold recalled what had eluded him. 'My brother Geoffrey is the scholar of the family, so he would know more. But if I remember aright, he said that

Good King Richard discovered some kind of incendiary weapon abroad that he later used against his enemies at home.'

A jar that carried fire inside it, Geoffrey called it, for he was intrigued by various references in old books. Some versions could not even be doused by water, but fed upon it, Geoff claimed. And unless Reynold was mistaken, there had been talk of a loud roar accompanying the delivery.

'But how would someone send something like that through the air?' Peregrine asked.

Reynold shrugged. 'A catapult or some kind of pipe. Geoff tried both.'

'*What?*' Mistress Sexton's eyes were wide.

'We were all enlisted to help him with his experiments,' Reynold explained. 'Although some said his efforts were too much like alchemy, Geoff defended the practice as a science and declared there was nothing wrong with a search for knowledge.' And there wasn't—until someone's hair was singed, and, once more, Campion put an end to it all.

Mistress Sexton stared at him, as though dumbfounded, and Reynold smiled. 'Seven boys will get up to some mischief.'

'And your father?'

'Nothing he could not handle,' Reynold said. And he realised it was true. There was nothing Campion could not mend, except perhaps a son's leg that was not quite right. Drawing a deep breath at the reminder, Reynold bent down to inspect the remains of the hut that had burned. It was easier now that he knew what he was looking for, and, taking up a stick, he poked at a small object that glinted in the light.

'See this?' Reynold asked.

Peregrine nodded.

'It might be a piece of the jar used to carry our fire,' Reynold said.

Peregrine kneeled close to inspect the glass, then glanced up at Reynold in wonder. 'I saw bits like this elsewhere, but thought it was just a part of something that had been left in the house.'

''Tis not the first I have discovered here either,' Reynold admitted. 'But when they said they used sand to put out some of the fires, I thought perhaps the heat had worked upon it.'

Peregrine gaped at him with such a comical expression that Reynold laughed. 'I do not have my brother Geoffrey's learning, squire, but just enough to stumble along.'

At that admission, Reynold's thoughts turned sombre once more. He gave Peregrine, kneeling beside him, a sharp glance. 'Perhaps we should send a message to Geoff,' he muttered. Although he hated to call his brother away from home and family, he knew Geoff would be intrigued by the mysteries of Grim's End and possessed more of the knowledge needed to solve them.

Apparently, Peregrine did not agree. The boy shook his head and surged to his feet. 'We don't need any help. You are doing just fine. Isn't he, mistress?'

Mistress Sexton, who still appeared bewildered, nodded her head. 'Of course.'

Reynold straightened, rubbing his bad leg as he rose. It was stiff from bending and had set up a familiar dull ache, which made him speak more harshly than he intended.

'Perhaps you should reconsider, mistress. My father is a powerful earl. He can put pressure upon your liege lord to protect those who have sworn him allegiance. Or he can step in to aid you himself, with his sons and their armies behind you.'

Mistress Sexton looked stunned. 'I don't understand,' she admitted. 'Are you saying that something else, some *person*, is responsible for the attacks on the village?'

Reynold nodded. 'Person or persons—a band of outlaws, perhaps, too cowardly to face soldiers. The de Burghs can provide both infantry and mounted knights to do battle against any number.'

Mistress Sexton shook her head warily. 'And how is Grim's End to support these armies? We cannot even feed ourselves. And who or what are all these men to fight? The dragon, whether man or beast, never shows itself, attacking only to disappear for days.'

'Then a garrison could be left here,' Reynold said, spurred on by what he couldn't name. It wasn't the leg talking any more, but something else that goaded him to speak, to let Mistress Sexton know that she had only the least of his family when she could do far better with the rest.

But she continued shaking her head. 'I want no host of strangers here. You agreed to slay the dragon, and I released you from your vow. But if you are willing to help us against whatever is threatening our village, we would be grateful for it.' She paused to look him at him directly. 'You, not an army of soldiers.'

'She's right, my lord. This is your quest, no one else's,' Peregrine said.

Reynold heard the boy, but he had eyes only for Mistress Sexton, gazing at him calmly. And he had ears only for her words, which were far more welcome than any nonsense from the l'Estranges. When given the opportunity to call upon his brothers, she put her faith in him, alone, a faith that Reynold sorely needed.

The time might come when he would have to send for his family, when whatever menaced Grim's End could not be caught or fought by Reynold and his squire. And perhaps he was just postponing the inevitable. But for now, only he would try to solve the mysteries of the abandoned village, keeping Mistress Sexton to himself for a little bit longer.

With a stiff nod of acceptance, Reynold turned to head toward the manor, and Mistress Sexton and Peregrine fell in beside him. Their company was familiar and welcome, and Reynold felt his tension ease. As long as they both forgot about the kiss, perhaps things could continue on as they had before.

As they followed the old track, Peregrine pointed towards the church with its elaborate carving. 'Maybe there never was a dragon,' he said. 'Maybe the founder of the village killed some invader or had a dragon as his device.'

Mistress Sexton looked so appalled by the notion that Reynold barked out a laugh.

'Well? It could be true,' Peregrine said. 'Like Uther Pendragon, King Arthur's father!'

'You are awfully well read for a squire,' Reynold said, not for the first time.

'Thank you, my lord. The Mistresses l'Estrange have been training me up for knighthood.'

'Yes, so you've said.' Reynold slanted the boy a glance. 'I'm thinking that's not all they were training you for.'

Peregrine flashed a grin. 'I admit that they did place special emphasis on dragon lore, just to make sure I would be able to aid you in your quest.'

Reynold shook his head. He had not yet put his mind to fighting the new enemy, but he was heartily relieved not to be facing a giant winged foe.

'Who are the Mistresses l'Estrange, and what do they know of our worm?' Mistress Sexton asked.

'Not much, apparently,' Reynold said. 'Else they would not have wasted so much time training Peregrine in old legends and stories of exotic beasts.'

''Tis time I do not regret, for 'tis better to be prepared than not,' Peregrine said. He flashed another grin. 'But at least now you don't have to don those furry breeches!'

Sabina followed the two males into the hall as if in a dream. Although they seemed to be in high spirits, she felt dazed and battered by the events of the past two days. And even as she tried to sort through her thoughts, they returned to one moment in time.

Like a treasured memento to be taken out and viewed again and again, one memory came to mind. And once more, she felt the soft grass upon her back, a heavy weight above, and opened her eyes to see the incredibly handsome face of Lord de Burgh above her own. The nearness of any other man might have startled her and sent her into a panic, but not this one. She had never felt so secure, so free from fear, and yet so alive, so full of something else…

She had but a moment to savour the nearness of him, to study each cherished feature, and then he kissed her. It was a shock, unexpected since he often seemed so distant, yet Sabina had seized the moment, slipping her arms around his strong shoulders and lifting her mouth to his. She was hot and breathless and trembling, but in a good way, in a way she had never known before, in a way she wanted to last for ever.

But it was over all too soon. Sabina was still amazed that something so brief could have such enormous consequences. Lord de Burgh had been dismissive afterwards, and while that pained her, Sabina was glad, for, unlike Ursula, she knew that nothing more could come of it. Still, her conscience kept her awake that night as she struggled with the truth. The final realisation that she had come to care more about this knight, a stranger, than her own home, her people, and her father's wishes, had shaken her to the very core.

Today it had taken all of Sabina's strength for her to release him from his vow, to save him, rather than herself. She had never expected him to refuse. Nor did she understand much of what had followed: Lord de Burgh's coldness, his inexplicable behaviour and his wild claims of fire in a jar and sand that turned into glass. Of vast armies at his beck and call. And the dragon that wasn't a dragon.

Sabina sank into her chair without even changing out of her gown, still damp and dirty from the fire, and felt so weary that she wanted to slump in defeat. Ursula, seated nearby, leaned forwards with an expression of alarm.

'What is it?'

At first, Sabina simply shook her head, for there was too much to explain properly, too much she did not want to share. And when she did speak, it was not of the most private of her concerns, but the most pressing. 'There is no dragon,' she said, as if saying the words aloud would make them more convincing.

'What?' Ursula asked.

'What?' Urban moved closer, appearing even more frightened than usual. Indeed, everyone looked to her, and Sabina felt her heart pound in response.

'There is no dragon,' Lord de Burgh said. And her tension eased, bolstered by the relief that he wasn't leaving, that he was still here to lead, to protect, to do battle. For one more day, at least, Sabina could lean upon his strength, if necessary. And so she simply listened as he gave the others a short version of what he had told her, that he thought the fire was manmade and saw no evidence of a dragon.

As usual, Urban was the most sceptical. 'But what of the attacks on the animals? We saw the remains of those that had been mauled,' he said, and the others nodded.

Lord de Burgh did not seemed concerned. 'Perhaps another creature was responsible, by coincidence or design.'

'What do you mean *by design*?' Urban demanded.

'I mean that someone might have loosed a beast, such as a wolf or bear, on purpose,' Lord de Burgh said. 'Or that same someone might have killed the animals himself.'

'You mean someone like a werewolf?' Alec asked, his eyes round.

'No, someone with a knife or axe, an outlaw or a lunatic who might well call himself The Dragon.'

Everyone from Grim's End appeared dumbfounded at that. And no wonder. For months they had been living in fear of a flying monster that killed and burned with its breath, only to be informed that there was no such thing. Sabina tried to remember who first claimed a worm was to blame for the attacks, but her memory of that time was hazy, full of confusion, fright and tension. Had someone simply linked separate events? Or had someone thought of the village's founder and drawn their own conclusions?

Sabina drew in a deep breath as she realised how quickly she had fallen in with the claim. She had even suspected someone might have stirred the dragon to life, someone who had disturbed its rest…

'What will you do now?' Alec asked. Although he put the question to Lord de Burgh, not the mistress of the manor, Sabina felt no outrage, only a sense of relief.

'Well, we don't have to wait for the chain to be completed,' Lord de Burgh said. 'We can scout the area to see if we find a camp.'

'There might be more than one,' Alec said. 'There

might be a whole band of brigands trying to drive us out in order to take over the village.'

'That's certainly possible,' Lord de Burgh said.

Sabina couldn't tell whether the knight was humouring the boy or if he actually had heard of such a case. She knew little of the wide world, but she supposed that villains might want a location convenient to other villages and the main road, yet out of the way. If so, they had gone to a lot of trouble when they could have just ridden through Grim's End, wreaking havoc. But perhaps her liege lord would not ignore wanton violence as easily as he had claims of a dragon.

'Do you have any idea why anyone would want to destroy the village or see it abandoned?'

Startled by Lord de Burgh's question, Sabina glanced up to see him sombrely surveying the group. They all shook their heads, as did she. For who would desire such a thing? Surely no one in their right mind would do such a thing.

'I cannot believe that all this time we feared a monster where there is none,' Alec said in an awed tone.

Urban shook his head, as though still unconvinced, but it was Adele who spoke. 'There is a monster all right,' she said softly. 'Even if a man is responsible, that man is a monster.'

Chapter Ten

Reynold slid from Sirius and stumbled, nearly falling. With a low oath, he cursed his aching leg, which could withstand a day in the saddle better than the riding and dismounting and crouching he had done for hours today. He had gone out at first light to search for signs of a camp, alone, though Peregrine had wanted to accompany him. But the knowledge that something other than a dragon was menacing the village made Reynold leave the boy to watch the others.

His young squire might not have fared well against a winged worm, but he had been practising his sword skills and had learned to throw a dagger. Hopefully, it would be enough to keep Mistress Sexton safe, Reynold thought as he limped toward the manor. For the first time since leaving the luxuries of Campion behind, he longed for them, mainly a hot bath in which to soak his protesting body.

It was an impossibility here. Adele would be willing to heat the water, but who would carry it? Urban would probably sneer at him and tell him to go swim in the pond. Alec and Peregrine could be pressed into service, but everyone in Grim's End already had much to do, rather than wait upon his wants. And, as always, he did not want to draw any attention to himself, to his infirmity.

Lost in his thoughts, Reynold nearly ran into Mistress Sexton in the kitchens. The woman was light of foot, as well as graceful, and he had not heard her approach. But at the sight of her, Reynold drew himself up straighter, torn between his relief at finding her safe and his dismay that she would see him thus.

'What happened? Were you attacked? Are you hurt?' she asked, her face pale.

'No. I found nothing,' Reynold said. He had known the brigands wouldn't be easy to find, for he had seen no evidence of them before when scouting the outskirts of the village. Obviously, their camp was not close by, and they came and went, preying upon Grim's End as they pleased. But his lack of success today was grating.

Reynold might admit to a certain uneasiness about fighting a flying creature that spouted fire, but he thought himself more than a match for any man. There were few who could best a de Burgh, and only then through deceit. Yet, his foe remained elusive.

'But your leg,' Mistress Sexton protested.

''Tis nothing,' Reynold said. Trying even more to hide his pain, he stumbled and winced.

'It is something,' Mistress Sexton argued. Then she stepped close and slipped an arm around him, as if to help carry his warrior's weight.

Reynold had never leaned upon anyone, and he was

so shocked by the gesture that he froze, unable to move, perhaps even to breathe. No one had ever offered to help him. Indeed, any man who did so would have found himself knocked to the ground. But Mistress Sexton was not a man, and Reynold did not know how to react.

''Tis nothing,' he finally repeated, shrugging as though to throw off her touch. But she only tightened her grip. This woman dared much, and yet Reynold told himself that he did not want to hurt her, should they continue to scuffle. And so he remained where he was, unmoving, uncertain.

'Let us go to your chamber, where you will be more comfortable, and I will bring you some food,' Mistress Sexton said. And before Reynold knew what she was about, they were heading toward the hall and the stairs together, moving slowly. The ignominy might have been too much to bear, but for the feel of her slender body aligned against his, the scent of her golden hair drifting close, and the gentle strength of her touch.

Those small pleasures kept Reynold beside her, although he did not let her take any of his weight, until he realised they had an audience in the hall. 'There is no need for this,' Reynold said, pulling from her. 'I can make my own way.'

'Nonsense,' Mistress Sexton said, tugging him back. 'Everyone needs help sometimes.'

Reynold barked out a laugh. 'Not in my family.' But he let her guide him toward the steps, grimly going upwards, for he could not bring himself to push her away.

'Nonsense,' Mistress Sexton said. 'I don't believe that your six brothers are perfect.'

Reynold laughed again. 'I did not say they were perfect, only that they never need help.'

'That can't be true, for didn't you say that your one brother, Geoffrey, asked you all to help him with his experiments?'

'That's different,' Reynold said, with a frown. The young de Burghs hardly needed to be coaxed into playing with fire, and Geoff could have managed without them. Yet, something else nagged at his memory, and suddenly Reynold recalled the time Geoff's wife had been kidnapped. The most learned of the de Burghs had wept, relying on his siblings to find her. And mighty Dunstan had required his brothers to free him from his enemy's dungeon. And Robin had a problem with the courts…

'That's different,' Reynold repeated. Those were rare instances, not an ongoing situation like his own.

'Still, you gave your aid freely, did you not? And you would do so again?'

Reynold nodded, though he wanted to shake his head, for the circumstances were not the same.

'If people care for each other, they help each other, without expecting anything in exchange.'

Reynold's lips curled at the tender homily, which was easily spoken, but less easily put into practice. If his view of the world was more jaundiced than the lovely damsel's, it was justified, for when they reached the top of the winding stair, Reynold saw Urban watching them intently. He stiffened, unwilling to allow that one to see his weakness, and Mistress Sexton turned her head to follow his gaze.

'Why concern yourself with Urban's opinion when you are so obviously the stronger?' she asked, leading him towards his chamber. ''Tis only a weak man who seeks to brag and boast, making more of himself than he is.'

While Reynold knew he was the better man, there was no denying that Urban had something he did not: two good limbs. ''Tis simple for you to say, for a woman is not measured by her strength,' Reynold muttered.

'Maybe we should be, though I would be found wanting.'

Reynold eyed her up and down. Unless she was concealing some infirmity beneath that supple gown, she was more than capable. Perhaps she wasn't an Amazon like his brother Simon's wife, but she had strength where it counted, the heart to lead these people and keep her village alive.

'No one could find you wanting,' Reynold said, his voice hoarse with barely suppressed emotion. For despite all his warnings to himself, he was here, beside her, hungry for all that he could not have.

She shook her head, a blush tinting her cheeks. 'You do not know all, my lord.'

The statement simply spurred Reynold's interest, making him want to learn everything about Mistress Sexton from her fondest memories to her favourite foods, games that delighted her, people who did not. 'Tell me,' he said in a whisper.

But she only shook her head once more and thrust open the door to his chamber, pausing to survey the small space with a frown. 'Let me get Father's chair for you.'

'No,' Reynold said, annoyed by both the change in

subject and the reminder of the real reason she was here with her arm around him. *Because of his lack.* Nothing else.

'But there is nowhere for you to sit except the bed or the trunk.'

'The trunk will do.' To prove it so, Reynold eased himself on to the hard wood and stretched out his legs, leaning back against the rough wall behind him. 'I'm fine,' he said in dismissal, eager now to be left alone.

'But I shall bring your food,' she protested.

'I don't want any.'

She stepped out of the room, and Reynold grunted in annoyance, for she had not closed the door behind her. He did not want to rise again, even though his berth was not exactly comfortable. He loosed a sigh, tired and angry at her, at himself, at things he thought accepted long ago.

'Adele will bring your meal.'

Reynold looked up, startled to see that she was back. If Adele was fetching him food, why was Mistress Sexton lingering? Did she plan to eat with him? Reynold wanted to tell her to go, to leave him be, but his mouth was suddenly dry. He had never been alone in his bed-chamber with a woman and so he could only gape when she pushed up her sleeves and knelt before him.

'First, let's get your boots off,' she said. 'Then I want to take a look at that leg.'

Reynold blinked in astonishment. Surely he had not heard her aright? 'What did you say?'

'First, the boots,' she said. Lifting his good leg, she tugged at the foot covering, pulled it off and set it aside. Then she reached for his other leg, and Reynold flinched when her fingers made contact. No one touched him. *No one had ever touched him.*

'Does that hurt?' she asked, a look of concern on her lovely face.

But Reynold couldn't speak. He could only stare at her, dumbfounded, as she sat back on her heels holding his foot in her hands. *No one had ever dared touch him.*

Since he said nothing, she removed the boot, but when she put her hands on his ankle, he jerked. 'Is it sore to the touch?' she asked.

Reynold only gaped like one of slow wit. *No one had ever wanted to touch him.*

'I ask because my mother taught me the uses of herbs and poultices for healing, as well as massage,' she said. 'Is there something that you use to make it feel better?'

Reynold shook his head and finally found his voice, though it sounded rusty. 'I take nothing.' Long ago Geoff had warned him against well-meaning people offering to dose him with some concoction that could prove dangerous. 'There are too many poisonous plants and too few people with the kind of wisdom to handle them properly.'

'Your mother—' she began.

'Dead.'

'I am sorry.'

Reynold did not want to discuss that, so he kept to the subject at hand. 'Geoffrey has a little knowledge, and he always claimed that while certain plants can relieve aches and induce sleep, sometimes they cause more problems than they cure.' Reynold even refused to take wine to dull the pain, for he had seen how too much of the drink affected Stephen.

Mistress Sexton nodded. 'Yes, my mother advised to stay away from those plants that cause sleep, for that meant they could cause death, as well. But I don't think you could go wrong with a bit of willow bark.'

Willow bark? Reynold thought Geoffrey had mentioned that, so he nodded. But he found it hard to concentrate on the conversation when his leg rested in her palm.

'What about a poultice?'

Reynold had a vague memory of smelly plasters and darkened rooms, of wanting to be free to run outside with his brothers, but he said nothing.

Mistress Sexton looked down at his leg, encased in hose beyond his braies. 'However, I would need to know more about the source of your discomfort. Do you suffer from an injury?'

Reynold shook his head.

'So it has always been with you?'

Again, Reynold did not answer. It had been difficult enough to discuss his infirmity with his youthful squire, but to calmly speak of so private and painful a subject with this beautiful woman was beyond him.

'I would only know more in order to better treat you,' Mistress Sexton explained. 'There are a number of plants that can be used for wounds, whether new or old, such as pine resin, which also helps the muscles, so that might be something to consider. If your skin is sore to the touch, almond oil is known to be soothing, while waterweed is good for inflammation of the legs.'

She paused to glance up at him. 'Is it an inflammation or is it muscular?' When he did not answer, she simply continued, as though talking to herself. 'Bay would probably be helpful, for it treats bruises and certain aches. You should be soaking in a hot bath, with bay leaves or perhaps mustard seeds. They also can be made into an excellent poultice.'

Reynold was so appalled by the conversation that it took him a moment to realise that she was tugging on his hose. By the time she had his attention, his bare foot was in her lap and her hands were moving up his calf to his braies.

Astonished, he jerked, but she held his limb steady, pushing up the edge of the garment, while Reynold stared. His protest lodged in his throat, his breath seized and his heart stopped. No one had ever seen his leg, except perhaps his family long ago when he was too young to prevent it. *He never let anyone see his leg.*

Wild thoughts careened around in his head as he groped for his wits. For an instant, he considered leaping to his feet, throwing Mistress Sexton aside, and running from the room. But he was frozen, immobile upon the trunk, unable to do anything but watch in horror as she prepared to reveal the part of him that he most despised.

In size and shape, the limb was nearly the same as its twin. It was not withered or twisted or topped with a clubbed foot, as Reynold had seen in others who were lame. In fact, only he could tell that it was not quite the same length and didn't move the same way as the other one. But the flesh itself was glaringly different. Where the other thigh was firm and unmarked, this one was mottled in the manner of a burn, red and ugly, the surface alternately smooth and rough, the hair oddly sparse. *Which is why he wanted no one to look upon it.*

As Reynold stared, too aghast to move, he saw long fingers, pale and slender, move over the misshapen area, gently touching, smoothing, soothing. And then, not only did he see what was happening, he felt it, and some sort of sound escaped him. *For no one had ever touched his leg.*

'Does that hurt?' she asked.

Reynold could not answer. He had expected her to recoil in disgust, but she kept stroking his skin, speaking with the same matter-of-fact calmness. And this was no old hag of a healer, but a beautiful woman, *Mistress Sexton*. Reynold blinked as moisture suddenly pressed against his eyes, and he swallowed hard.

'Yes, I think a hot bath or a poultice of mustard would help,' she said. 'But I have noticed you rubbing it, so I suspect that massage would be the most effective.'

Reynold nearly swallowed his tongue as she lifted his foot and pressed firmly but gently against the rough skin. She rotated the appendage, then his ankle, and then her fingers closed around his leg, spreading and kneading. As her hands moved upwards, Reynold braced himself for pain, but her movements *relieved* the pain. He groaned, leaning back and relaxing, as if his aching body were liquid, supple and warm.

Reynold lost all sense of time as she probed and prodded with her fingers and thumbs, rubbed and circled and pressed and stroked until he felt like a limp rag, all dis-comfort wrung from him by the power of her touch. His foot remained in her lap, his toes touching the cloth that covered her belly, but when her hands moved upwards to the very top of his thigh, Reynold stiffened again.

His breath caught for a different reason this time. Although he realised that her actions were meant to be curative, they did more than ease his aching leg. Indeed, they set other parts of his body to aching, with a sudden joy, with a fierce hunger, with the ecstasy of lying here while her hands moved upon him.

Reynold swallowed a harsh groan, for he did not know what to do. He was loathe to put a stop to the most wonderful sensations he had ever known, but soon it would become apparent even to the innocent damsel that, while well intended, her ministrations were having another effect entirely.

Perhaps it would be better if he could not see her slender fingers doing their work, if he did not dwell upon her bent head, the golden strands of her hair falling to brush against his skin, or the way her breasts strained against her garment as she worked. Pulse pounding, Reynold shut his eyes to block out the sights of all those things, only to open them again when a loud clattering sound broke the silence.

Jerking upwards, Reynold put a hand to the hilt of his sword, wary of some new threat. But 'twas only Peregrine standing upon the threshold of the chamber, a fallen tray at his feet and his eyes wide.

'I'm, uh, forgive me, my lord,' he stammered, kneeling to pick up the wooden cup. 'I beg your pardon.'

Reynold felt disappointment wash over him like a cold bath, taking away all the heat and emotion he had felt under the hands of the woman who knelt before him. But the icy return to reality made him realise that he ought to thank the boy for recalling his wits. Mistress

Sexton had been moved by mercy, while Reynold would repay her in different coin. Hadn't he promised never to repeat the kiss? 'Twas much more than that which he desired now.

'Mistress Sexton was just leaving,' Reynold said in a hoarse voice as he collected himself. 'Pick up the food and join me, for I wish to discuss this day's work with you.'

Peregrine stared at him as if shocked before nodding grudgingly. Perhaps the boy was worried that Reynold might steal Mistress Sexton away, but nothing could be further from the truth. When lucid, Reynold had enough sense to know that the beautiful damsel would aid him as best she could, for she needed his help. That was all.

Once Grim's End was restored to her, no one would ever touch him again.

Sabina hurried to the small room off the kitchens, eager to avoid the questioning glances of the others, especially Urban or Ursula. Once there, she shut the door behind her, leaned against it and loosed a long, low breath. She kept her store of herbs and plants in the small space, and its quiet and privacy was welcome, for she needed a moment to collect her thoughts. Yet she struggled against the urge to hurry to complete her task, so she could return…to him.

When had she become so greedy?

Sabina had been cautious in treating Lord de Burgh's leg because he often seemed leery of her touch. But she could not stop herself when she saw him wince in pain. And, once begun, she had continued, unheeding of his stiff posture and his silence. She had only wanted to help him, yet somehow over the course of the massage, she took such pleasure in her work that she never wanted to stop.

It was a personal thing, putting one's hands upon another, and Sabina had always assumed a certain distance those few times she had treated someone other than her father. But with Lord de Burgh, she sought closeness instead, and it was all she could do to maintain her composure, hiding her flush, her quickened breath and her pounding heart from his gaze.

These past months Sabina had struggled so hard, thinking only of doing her duty, that she could see no harm at seeking a little respite for herself. But at whose expense? Sabina frowned as she prepared the poultice. Lord de Burgh had made his stance clear, and she should abide by it, keeping only to the agreement between them.

And yet she could not sit idly by and watch him suffer. It was her duty as mistress of the manor to ease his aches while he served Grim's End, Sabina told herself as she took a pot of the plaster with her and headed back up the steps. If she enjoyed smoothing it upon his skin, 'twas only an added benefit that hurt no one.

But when she reached Lord de Burgh's chamber, the door was closed against her. Sabina knocked, expecting to be admitted, yet Peregrine barred her way, slipping out to shut the portal behind him.

'I have a poultice for Lord de Burgh,' Sabina explained.

Peregrine appeared uncomfortable as he shook his head. 'He wants his privacy.'

'But I would apply this healing unguent.'

Peregrine frowned, as though in apology, and held out a hand. 'I will take it.'

'But you are not trained in the healing arts.'

The squire cleared his throat. 'He, uh, insists that he will put it on himself.'

'But…'

Something in Peregrine's expression stopped Sabina from arguing further. 'Of course,' she said softly, handing the small container to the youth.

He opened the door a crack, but turned to look at her, shaking his head once more. 'If you ask me, you are both too strong and too silent,' he muttered.

Sabina had no idea what he meant. 'Strong? Me?' She laughed, but it was a low bitter sound. 'You are mistaken, squire.'

In the days that followed, Reynold grew impatient, with himself, with Mistress Sexton, and most of all with The Dragon. Whatever or whoever it was, the worm stayed well away. If only Mistress Sexton would do so, as well.

Instead, she seemed to be intent upon smothering him with kindness. She greeted him when he returned from scouting with a cup, presented him with more than his share of their meagre food supplies and waited upon him. And even worse, she was determined to press upon him various willow-bark tonics, plasters made of bay or mustard, hot baths and massages.

Despite himself, Reynold yearned for such pampering, for never before had anyone doted upon him. Perhaps his older brothers recalled their mother or his mother, but Reynold did not. Campion Castle was the domain of men, or at least until recently.

Reynold remembered no nurturing female presence

there except for the winter when Marion, his brother Dunstan's future wife, had lived with them. She had overseen the household and made it a brighter place, and they had come to view her as a sister. Although she obviously had affection for them all, she had not singled any of them out for special treatment. Nor had she made Reynold's heart stop with her beauty.

But Mistress Sexton did. And that is why he had refused further massages, along with any baths. Although he would never forget the feel of her hands upon him, he did not trust himself to stay still for another session.

Something, whether her kisses or her touch or the combination of both, had unleashed a hunger in Reynold such as he had never known. His innocent desire for Amice was nothing in comparison, his more heated urges for paid companions naught, as well.

And this appetite sparked to life at the very sight of Mistress Sexton, yet would not disappear when she was away. It gnawed away at his insides, each day growing stronger. And he could only try to contain it. For now, his will held, but the denial only added to his resentment.

When he trudged inside from scouting, his ill mood even kept Peregrine at a distance, but Mistress Sexton was not so easily cowed. She approached him immediately with the offer to fetch a stool on which to prop his leg.

'No, I need it not,' Reynold muttered. As always, he sank on to one of the benches by the trestle table, instead of the more comfortable berth offered by her father's chair. Frustrated with his lack of progress, he was tired and sore and so sweaty that he did not want Mistress Sexton to come close.

But ignoring his words, she brought the stool anyway, setting it close to where his legs were stretched before him. Reynold glared at her, as though daring her to touch him, an action that he both desired and denied. In fact, just looking at her made him want to seize her, take her in his arms and return her massage. But he could not. Would not.

And like a festering sore, the knowledge pricked at him, making his anger simmer. Reynold tried to remember the days when he had felt so at ease in her company. But that was before he had felt her hands upon him, before he was so aware of her, before he hungered for that which he could not have.

'Don't touch me,' he warned, as she reached for his leg.

'But you are in pain,' she protested.

Reynold looked away, unwilling to divine what was in those blue eyes, truth or lies, care or duty. 'I did well enough without your unguents, and I will do so again.'

'And yet I see you rubbing your leg, so why not let me massage it properly?' she asked. 'You know that I can rub it better than you can.'

Reynold slanted her a glance under his dark lashes. 'I am sure of it,' he said in a voice rough with innuendo. But he could see that the meaning was lost upon her.

'Then why not accept my aid instead of scowling and grunting like a spoiled child?'

'I am here. Isn't that enough? Or does my vow include bowing to your every whim like everyone else in Grim's End?' Reynold asked. 'Perhaps you are the selfish one, mistress, who would keep your people here, rather than move them to safety.'

Reynold heard Peregrine's gasp and regretted his words. Frowning, he looked at Mistress Sexton, prepared to apologise, but the sight of her stopped his mouth. Her face was white, and her hand was trembling.

'I am here because I made a vow to my father as he lay dying, a promise to keep his home and his legacy,' she said. 'And 'tis as sacred to me as yours is to you, my lord.'

Rising gracefully to her feet, she hurried away. Reynold pushed himself upwards, but his foot caught on the errant stool and he sank back down on the bench with a curse. What use to go after her anyway? The last thing he needed was to hare off after her into her bedchamber, a place where he might not be able to control himself, his tongue doing far worse than loosing a few careless words.

Turning his head away from her retreating figure, Reynold came face to face with his squire, who obviously had taken umbrage at his rudeness. 'Twas no surprise since Peregrine was Mistress Sexton's most ardent supporter.

'You are the spoiled one!' the boy said. 'How many people are blessed with what you have? Did you ever take a moment to realise that you have wealth beyond what the rest of us can imagine, a loving family to protect you and stand by you, and brothers who would die for you, if necessary?'

Reynold stared in shock as his squire continued. 'Your father is not only caring, but wise, and does not barter his sons for power, as some noble families do. He lets all of you do as you wish, while gently guiding you. I do not have a father. I don't have any brothers. The l'Estranges took my sister and I in when our mother was killed, and we are grateful every day for our rescue.'

Reynold felt a pang at the story, but the boy soon lost his sympathy with a mocking snort. 'But, oh my, you have a bad leg! Well, so what? Do you know how many of the truly lame would love to be you? How many of the poor cannot feed themselves because of their infirmities? You can get around and do nearly everything anyone else does, often better than most because you are tall and strong and have been trained as a knight.'

Reynold sat staring, enraged at the way the boy dared speak to him, and yet, even in his anger, he recognised a bitter truth.

'How many people look everywhere for love? But when you have it given to you freely, you run away from it. You fled from your family, and now you would turn from the woman who loves you. It's easier for you to believe the worst, that all women are spoiled, selfish and deceitful, than to be a man. Slay me if you will, but you're the selfish one, my lord.'

Reynold barely listened as the quaking youth finished speaking, for his attention had been caught and held by the most startling of Peregrine's claims: *the woman who loves you.*

Chapter Eleven

Reynold stared at the squire, his heart stopped in his chest. Surely, he had not heard the boy aright? And if he had, Peregrine must be mistaken. As Reynold looked into the youth's mutinous expression, all he saw was jealousy. The squire was so besotted himself, he would weave some tale to explain his own lack. That was all that lay behind his incredible claim. For Mistress Sexton did not, could not, love one such as Reynold de Burgh.

Rising to his feet, Reynold once again was tripped by the edge of the stool, and everything inside him boiled over. He lashed out, kicking the small wooden prop, a hated symbol of his infirmity, with all the strength of his confusion and frustration. It clattered across the tiles to bang up against the carved panel at the back of the hall, accomplishing nothing.

But then he heard a shriek from behind the screen. *What the devil?* Reynold took a step forwards just as Urban scurried out from the narrow passage, looking terrified. The man blinked, as though dazed, and for a moment Reynold wondered whether the stool had struck him. But it lay on its side, intact, against the edge of the screen.

'What is it? Are we under attack? What are you doing?'

'I might ask the same of you,' Reynold said. He had become used to Urban skulking about, but was the fellow actually spying on him? And what did he hope to gain by it? But Reynold had only to remember what the man had just heard to have his answer, and he felt his face heat.

'What do you behind the screen?' Reynold asked, moving closer.

'Nothing,' Urban answered. He reached up to swipe at his eyes with one hand, as though unconcerned.

But Reynold would not be so easily dismissed. 'Would you spy upon me?' he demanded. His temper, loosed once, was now barely leashed.

Urban's expression became shuttered. 'What care I what you do?' he asked, in a belligerent tone. As Reynold advanced, he frowned. 'This hall is my home, and I am free to go where I will.'

'As long as you do me no ill, Master Urban,' Reynold said, leaving no doubt as to his intent.

For a moment, Reynold thought the man would argue, but he turned and scurried away, back behind the panel to the kitchens.

Reynold stood watching until Urban disappeared, only then realising that his hand was upon the hilt of his sword, ready for battle.

'My lord?'

Reynold turned to see that Peregrine was standing beside him, wearing a puzzled expression. 'I don't think he was spying,' the boy said. 'I think he was asleep back there.'

'Asleep?' Reynold echoed with a snort. 'Doesn't he get enough rest at night that he would nod off during the day?' The words were meant to mock the useless steward, who did little to grow weary, and yet as soon as he spoke them, Reynold sucked in a harsh breath. The idea that struck him so forcefully was obvious now that he thought about it. Indeed, one of his wilier brothers would have caught on far earlier.

'What?' Peregrine asked, seeing the look on his face.

Glancing at the boy, Reynold realised that he had failed to follow his own advice. He had warned Peregrine often enough to be wary, and yet he had accepted the residents of Grim's End without question when any one of them could be unworthy of his trust. Alec or Adele or even young Peregrine, the squire who appeared out of nowhere, might have a past or present at odds with what they showed to the world. Urban, the least likeable and most difficult, would be the easiest to suspect, and for that very reason Reynold tended to discount him. And yet…

'Urban is not always with us,' Reynold said aloud. Although he did not keep an eye on the inhabitants of Grim's End at all times, there were so few that it was easy to notice when someone was missing.

Peregrine frowned, as though trying, as usual, to follow Reynold's thoughts. 'Sometimes he goes looking for game,' the boy said.

'And yet he has produced nothing,' Reynold said. At other times, he was simply gone, and Reynold had never questioned where, perhaps because Mistress Sexton's man might be cowering in the cellar, with or without pitchfork.

Reynold glanced at Peregrine, who would trust all and sundry, and saw that even the boy was frowning. 'You don't think that Urban has something to do with the…dragon, do you?' he asked. 'But he's always been the most fearful.'

It was difficult for Reynold to believe that Urban had anything to do with the attacks on the village, either, for the former steward seemed too frightened, too righteous and too inept. 'I don't know,' Reynold said slowly. 'But if he is so weary as to sleep during the day, perhaps we should see for ourselves what he is about at night.'

Reynold discovered that Urban slept in the cellar, where the Grim's End residents had often made camp in the past few months. His pallet was not far from Alec's and Adele's, but the stairs were within easy reach. Having made a show of seeking his own bed earlier this evening, Reynold let them settle in for the night before returning to the now-darkened hall, where he huddled with his squire.

'I can ask Alec if he's heard or seen anything,' Peregrine suggested in hushed tones, but Reynold shook his head.

'Let us not alert anyone to our interest.'

Peregrine's expression was one of shock. 'You don't suspect Alec of being involved in…something, do you?'

Reynold shook his head, though he wasn't about to exonerate anyone at this point except perhaps his guileless squire. 'Still, he might inadvertently give away our plans.'

Peregrine nodded, though he appeared wary. *Good.*

The boy needed a reminder not to give his trust so easily.
Then Peregrine looked down at the shadowy tiles, as if
uncomfortable. 'My lord, I'm sorry about what I said
earlier,' he whispered. 'It's not my place to—'

Reynold cut him off with a raised hand. 'Let us speak
no more of it,' he said in a tone that brooked no
argument. Reynold had no desire to return to the topic
of Mistress Sexton or his own deficiencies. Perhaps
there had been some truth in the boy's tirade, but
Reynold did not have time for such contemplation now.

Peregrine looked as though he had plenty more to
say, yet he held his tongue. And with parting nods, the
two dispersed to dark corners of the manor, Peregrine
to keep watch by the hall doors and Reynold in the
kitchens. Reynold concealed himself where he could
view both the cellar and the doors and sat back to wait.

But he could not get comfortable. Although he had
long since grown accustomed to the oddities of Grim's
End, now he was reminded of the eeriness of the place.
He had kept watch before in far more dangerous circumstances and had gone into battle fearlessly. But this was
different. Instead of a bustling manor, he was in a silent,
empty shell, the only building occupied for miles
around, and Reynold could not shake the sense of
unease that crept upon him.

The moon was casting a faint glow on to the tiles
when he heard the soft sound of movement coming
from the stairs that led below. Although he had been expecting it, still the noise was chilling. And soon a
cloaked figure emerged, passing so quietly by him that

it hardly seemed to be Urban. Indeed, if Reynold had not known that only three people occupied the cellar, he might have thought the shape was someone else.

But Reynold knew it was not Adele or Alec who slipped so furtively out the door. Leaving his hiding place, Reynold followed just as silently, yet once outside, he saw no sign of his quarry. A thick fog had rolled in from the sea, blanketing the area with white, obscuring even the most familiar landmarks, and for one long moment Reynold imagined Urban disappearing into it like a wraith.

But then he heard a sound, loud in the silence, and he whirled, as if to face some unknown foe, only to find nothing. Its direction was confusing in the mist, and Reynold hesitated. He had expected Urban to go to the stables, perhaps to steal one his mounts, or to the barn or mill, away from prying eyes.

Yet the faint noise came from the opposite direction, meaning Urban was moving away from the manor and its outbuildings toward the sloping hillside of the mound. But what would he do there? Reynold squinted into nothingness as he kept to the shadows at the rear of the Sexton home, his footsteps falling softly against the giving earth.

He had never been to the mound, for there was nowhere upon the raised earth in which to hide a beast or an outlaw camp. And although legend claimed that the village was founded by a dragon-slayer who buried his foe there, it was not a place normally visited. Grim's End had grown up nearby, but did not encroach upon it. Indeed, it seemed apart from the man-made structures, ancient and forbidding. Although sheep must have grazed here in the past, there were none to do so now, and the grass grew tall, swaying in the night breeze.

Reynold felt the hairs on the back of his neck rise, for even though he knew there was no worm menacing the village, it was hard not to imagine something stirring to life deep within the grassy tomb. Reynold remembered his earlier jest—that the dragon was invisible—and felt a sudden chill.

The sound of moving soil somewhere close by was startling in the stillness and made it seem as though something was rising up from the grave, though Reynold could see nothing. He wondered where Peregrine was, for the stout-hearted squire appeared to have advice for any situation. If here, no doubt he would recommend the use of a magic sword and might well pull one out of a nearby rock, like Arthur himself.

Magic, which Reynold oft mocked, seemed real in this most peculiar location, and he even regretted his sport of the l'Estranges, for they might do better here than he, weaving some spell to banish the mist and even the night itself.

Yet Reynold had only his wits and his sword arm, so, hand on his hilt, he crouched low, approaching the sound as best he could in the disorienting fog. Suddenly, something loomed up before him, and he drew in a harsh breath. But it was only the ruins of the old church, the worn dragon on its crumbling side leering at him through the veils of vapour.

Had he gone too far? Where was Urban? Was he inside what was left of this place? Reynold circled the remains of the building before stepping over the stones of what had been one wall. But there was nothing within, only a jumble of rocks and grass. A trick of the moonlight through the haze cast a glow upon what was left of a carving, and Reynold recognised the message that was written in the new building.

Repent and Seek Your Reward.

Reynold found himself staring at the Latin words, then jerked as he heard a sound again, the same dull thud. Crossing towards the opening, he stepped out of the old church once more, moving in the direction of the noise. It was louder now, as though whoever—or whatever—was causing it had grown careless.

Reynold began to head up the slope, but then he heard a clunk directly to his right, as though he was right upon the sound. *Or atop it.* His unease returned full measure, and he sank low to the ground, where he barely missed being hit by a shovel.

What the devil?

Reynold reached up and snatched at the handle, pulling the owner of it down with him. The frightened shriek that accompanied the flailing limbs beneath him could only belong to Urban, and Reynold rose to his feet, jerking his captive by the neck. The dark hood fell away, and Urban's pale face materialised out of the mist.

''Tis you!' the man choked out.

'Who else were you expecting?'

'No one, no one, my lord,' Urban said. 'Unhand me!'

Reynold let go, and Urban fell to his knees, clutching his throat. 'How dare you!' he croaked, lifting his head to glare at Reynold.

Ignoring the man's protests, Reynold took up a warrior's stance, hand upon his sword hilt. Although he had neither heard nor seen anyone else, he remained wary, lest someone come out of the darkness at him.

'What are you doing here?'

''Tis none of your concern,' Urban said.

'Everything here is my concern because Mistress Sexton has made it so.' As soon as the words left his mouth, Reynold felt the sharp prick of suspicion. Was Urban here upon some order from his mistress? *Were not all women spoiled, selfish and deceitful?* 'If you are on some mission, speak now.'

'I am a free man and steward to the Sextons,' Urban said. 'I need no one's permission to come and go.'

'Perhaps not, but when there are only five inhabitants, every person's movements are of interest. What do you here?' Reynold asked. Picking up the shovel, he crouched low to the ground, where even the thick fog could not hide evidence of Master Urban's activities. He had been digging. But for what? And why here? And why now?

'I do not answer to you.'

Reynold slanted him a hard glance. 'And yet I will have an answer.' Sweeping a hand into the small hole, Reynold felt nothing except earth. Was this the first time Urban had been out digging or would he would find the soil disturbed elsewhere, should he look in the morning light?

Obviously, the man would not be here at this hour, if he did not want to hide his actions. But what, if anything, had they to do with the plague upon Grim's End? Sitting back on his haunches, Reynold eyed the slumped figure carefully. 'What are you looking for?'

'Game.'

'And what is it that lives underground?'

'Moles. Mice. Rabbits. I thought to build a trap.'

'In the dead of night,' Reynold said, rising to his feet. 'Methinks I have never seen you so ambitious during the day.' Slowly, Reynold circled the area, but there was only Urban and his shovel and this small hole. Was he looking for something, or burying it?

Before Urban could tell what he was about, Reynold snatched at the man's cloak and searched his person. Despite Urban's squeaks of protests, Reynold found only a sack, which he had either emptied or intended to fill. But with what?

Further questioning did no good. Surprisingly, the man who always appeared most afraid did not waver in the face of Reynold's grim queries, but claimed that he was the one suffering injury.

'I have every right to conduct my own business, without interference from you, a stranger who has no power here,' Urban declared.

'And what business might that be?' Reynold asked, tempted to show the scrawny fellow just how much power he wielded with his sword arm.

'I have already told you.'

'Ah, yes, the hunt for moles,' Reynold said, his voice laden with disdain. But he had no desire to linger here upon the slope that housed the dead, especially when it was cloaked with a mist that sent sounds awry and made even a grown man lose his bearings.

'Very well, let us have Mistress Sexton's opinion,' Reynold finally said. For a long moment, he thought

Urban might even refuse to accompany him back to the manor, but at last they made their way to the hall.

The noise of their entrance brought Alec and a wary Adele up from the cellar. Leaving the indignant Urban there with them and Peregrine, Reynold marched up to Mistress Sexton's bedchamber. He knew which one it was, of course, for he had been guarding her for some time. But he had never begged entrance before, and, as he faced the portal, he wondered why he had not sent his squire on this errand.

It was too late now, so Reynold knocked upon the worn wood. He heard Ursula's nervous query and announced himself upon an urgent errand. He could have left then, but something held him at the door even as Ursula opened it.

'I need to speak with your mistress,' Reynold said, his voice suddenly low and hoarse. He had said little to Mistress Sexton since his rude behaviour earlier in the day, and he wondered, wildly, whether he should take the opportunity to apologise. But then he remembered Peregrine's tirade that had followed. Had Urban listened and reported all to his mistress? Reynold's lips tightened into a thin line as he recalled his purpose here involved nothing personal.

But Ursula obviously thought otherwise, for she slipped away, as though to give him privacy. Reynold would have called her back, but the door swung open, and Mistress Sexton stood in the entrance.

She had thrown some sort of heavy robe over her nightclothes, and behind her lay a bed, its linens disordered, from which she had so recently risen. Reynold quickly glanced away from the sight that made his heart pound. But 'twas no easier to look at Mistress Sexton herself, for the moonlight glowed on her golden hair, giving her an ethereal look, as though she was not of this earth. But hadn't she always been too beautiful, too perfect, for mere mortals, for Reynold de Burgh?

'What is it, my lord?' she asked, her lovely features tense with anxiety.

Reynold cleared his suddenly thick throat. 'There is no danger,' he assured her. And he had to stop himself from stepping over the threshold to take her into his arms, intending comfort, but seeking more…

''Tis Urban,' he said.

Mistress Sexton's gaze flew to his. 'Is he hurt?'

Reynold shook his head, jealous of her concern for the man. 'Not yet,' he muttered. He drew a deep breath, trying to concentrate on the matter at hand, rather than the sweet scent of her, stronger here in the darkness, in the closeness…

'I found him sneaking out of the manor long after the rest of you were abed,' Reynold said. 'I followed him into the mist and found him digging a hole at the edge of the hill where you claim the dragon is buried.'

Mistress Sexton's eyes grew so wide in her pale face that Reynold feared she might faint, though he had never seen her show any signs of weakness. Still, it was the middle of the night and she recently roused from bed, so he reached for her, simply to steady her upon her feet. But she stepped back, away from him, shaking her head vehemently.

And before Reynold knew what she was about, he was staring at the door, shut firmly in his face.

At first light, Reynold looked down at the hole in the ground, unseeing. He flexed his hands, trying to deny the urge to hit something with his fists. What was the matter with him? That was the sort of thing his brother Simon would do—punch away angrily at anything. It was Simon who had the temper, not Reynold, who had learned long ago to keep everything to himself. So why was he suddenly boiling over with rage and frustration that he had thought well tamed?

He blamed a sleepless night, as well as Mistress Sexton. If she hadn't waylaid him, begged him to do her bidding, and then dismissed him like the basest villein... If she weren't so beautiful. And if she hadn't made him believe, hope, want...

'My lord?' Peregrine's voice pierced the darkness of his mood, recalling him to the matter at hand, a pile of soil and the place where it had once been. Reynold already had searched the slope for signs of other disturbances, but found nothing.

'Unless Urban filled in any previous area, replacing even the grasses, this is the only spot,' Reynold said. He wished now that he had thought to follow Urban before, that he had trusted none of them, not even Mistress Sexton.

Peregrine studied the hole, then glanced beyond it to where the ground gently sloped upwards. 'And this is where the dragon is buried?' he asked quietly.

'According to Mistress Sexton,' Reynold said, though he was beginning to wonder what—and who—to be-

lieve. Yet, as Peregrine pointed out, Urban's hole was
close to the mound, and Reynold felt a nagging at the
back of his mind. He searched his memory again, for
something that would explain Urban's actions. And the
answer came to him so swiftly that he wondered why
he had not considered it earlier. Startled, he glanced at
his squire, only to see the same enlightenment reflected
on the boy's face.

'Wasn't Beowulf's dragon guarding a treasure?'
Peregrine asked, softly.

'Exactly,' Reynold said. There were other tales, too,
in which a frightening creature, such as a worm, guarded
a grave that held precious burial goods. 'The dragon
shall be on the mound, old, exultant in treasure,' he said,
quoting an old proverb.

'But I thought there was no dragon,' Peregrine said.

'There isn't a beast with wings, but there's something, or, more likely, someone,' Reynold said. He
squinted into the distance, cursing himself for his slow
wit. 'It's so obvious, why didn't I think of it before?'

'But no one said anything about a treasure.'

'Oh, yes, they did,' Reynold muttered, frowning.
'Didn't Mistress Sexton mention a hoard of coins?'

Peregrine's brow furrowed. 'Yes, but that didn't have
anything to do with the dragon,' he said. 'And, anyway,
I thought that was just a story.'

*Like so many that whirled around Grim's End, weaving
in and out of its past and present*, Reynold thought. And
who could tell which were authentic? Geoff claimed that
even the most outlandish tale was based upon a small
grain of truth. So where was Reynold to find that nugget?

'Weren't there a couple of accounts of a human turning into a dragon because of a curse or his own lust for the worm's treasure?' Peregrine asked. His eyes grew wide. 'You don't think Urban can turn into a dragon, do you?'

Reynold snorted. 'No. I think he's barely a man, let alone a beast.'

Peregrine appeared relieved, but then he lowered his voice. 'Besides beasts, there are stories of ghosts appearing at the mounds that hide valuables. You didn't see any, did you?' he asked, warily.

Reynold shook his head. If there were any ghosts, last night would have been the time for them to appear, for he'd never faced an eerier evening. But now, without the darkness and the mists and the strange sounds, the area appeared benign, simply a formation of the earth, where tall grasses swayed gently.

Reynold poked thoughtfully at the soil with the tip of his boot. 'Perhaps we should see if there is anything buried here.'

Peregrine gasped. 'Dig up something's grave?'

Reynold shrugged. Was this really a tomb or only a peculiar hill? Reynold knew of only one way to find out. 'I would like to know what Urban is seeking.'

'But look at what happened to Beowulf,' Peregrine protested, obviously appalled by the suggestion. 'Isn't that sort of treasure cursed?'

Reynold shook his head. Unlike his squire, he feared no such blights, perhaps because, deep down inside, he felt cursed already.

Chapter Twelve

Sabina was surprised to find the hall empty, despite the early hour, and as she walked towards her chair, she tried not to think the worst. She had slept little, tossing and turning and wondering whether she had dreamed of Lord de Burgh's visit to her room. But his absence this morning was telling, and she feared that he had gone, even though she could not blame him. Resting her hands upon the back of her chair, she took a deep breath in an effort to steady herself for whatever lay ahead.

And then the doors were thrown open, and his tall, dark figure strode across the threshold. He looked a lord, master of this hall and any other, Sabina thought, and she gripped the hard wood, lest she run across the room to throw herself into his arms. The action would not be welcome, she guessed, and one glance at his cold expression only confirmed her suspicions.

'My lord,' she said, bowing her head.

'Mistress Sexton.' His tone was clipped, his expression forbidding as he took his usual seat. The other residents of Grim's End, alerted by the sound of the doors, began appearing, and Sabina knew she had little time for private speech.

'I would beg your pardon for my abruptness last night,' she said. 'It was late, and I was indisposed.'

Although he nodded, the brusque movement held no forgiveness, and Sabina sank into her chair, her body tense. She would have said more, but the sound of Urban's hail echoed across the hall.

'Mistress Sexton!' The steward headed directly towards her, and he looked no more pleased than Lord de Burgh.

'Yes, Urban, what is it?' Sabina asked, though she had little patience for the man. Obviously, she had not imagined Lord de Burgh's visit to her room. Had she recalled his words correctly, as well?

'I told you when you invited this man into your home that he was dangerous,' Urban said, pointing to Lord de Burgh. 'Now he is accosting those who live here, though he has no right. I am the Sexton steward, and this man holds no sway over me.' He looked to Sabina as though expecting her to confirm his words, but she said nothing. She still wasn't sure what had happened last night.

'I am doing as you bid, trying to find out what is menacing Grim's End and put a stop to it. Since we know there is no dragon, we must look to other causes,' Lord de Burgh said, with a pointed look at Urban.

Sabina blinked in confusion. 'You think Urban is responsible?' she asked. The very notion was laughable, and she could see why such a claim would have raised the steward's hackles, for he had proven his worth many times over in the past months.

'Obviously, he cannot send fire through the air when he is here in the village,' Lord de Burgh said. 'But I would know why he is sneaking out in the dead of night to dig holes in the mound. Is he trying to poke the dragon to life?'

Sabina sucked in a sharp breath at the words, for they too closely echoed her own fears. But if there was no dragon, how had anyone reawakened it?

'Or is there something you haven't told me about the legends of Grim's End?' Lord de Burgh asked, fixing her with a hard look.

There were things she hadn't told him, but they didn't really pertain to any legends, Sabina thought. Still, she flushed and glanced away to where Urban stood, his stance not quite as righteous. Indeed, he appeared uncomfortable now, as though Lord de Burgh's taunt had struck home.

'What were you doing?' Sabina asked the steward, for she could find no reasonable explanations for his actions, nothing that made sense to her anyway.

Urban drew himself up. 'You would listen to this stranger when I have served the Sextons faithfully? You charged him to slay the dragon, and yet he has not done so, but continues to exert more and more influence over you and explain his lack by denying there is such a beast.'

'There is no such beast,' Lord de Burgh confirmed. 'There are people—or perhaps only one man—responsible for killing your animals, scaring your residents and setting fire to your fields and your buildings. He's learned how to send flames through the sky, probably because of a visit to the east, maybe a crusade, or contact with some foreign traveler—'

His speech was cut off by the clatter of something crashing to the floor. The distraction allowed Sabina to draw in the breath that had caught in her throat as Ursula bent to pick up the cup she had dropped on her way in from the kitchens.

'Excuse me, my lord,' the older woman muttered, her face ashen. But Lord de Burgh paid Ursula no heed. He was glaring at Urban, and Sabina gripped the arms of her chair, struggling against the panic that threatened. *It was a coincidence, nothing more*, Sabina told herself.

She looked to Ursula, but the woman had ducked her head. Surely her attendant could not believe…? And yet, Ursula did not know all, Sabina realised. Still, she shook her head, unable to take such a leap of logic.

''Tis nonsense!' Urban said. He looked pale, as well, but he didn't know, couldn't know… He whirled towards Sabina. 'Mistress, you can vouch that I have done none of those things, but have always served you well.'

Sabina nodded, for, in truth, how could Urban had done anything when he was with them most of the time?

The steward appeared relieved. 'And I am always serving you, mistress. Even last night I was working on your behalf.' He paused, as though still hesitant to explain himself, then hurried on. 'If you must know, I was so desperate to rid ourselves of this interloper,' he said, glaring at Lord de Burgh, 'that I would find some way to pay a real dragon-slayer.'

Sabina eyed him curiously.

'I refer to the legend, not of the dragon, but of the Sexton hoard,' Urban explained. 'After you mentioned it, I began thinking about it and realised that it could be the answer to all our problems.'

Sabina could only shake her head at such folly.

But Urban licked his lips, as if in glee. 'And I decided to begin looking for it at night, to avoid the prying eyes of those who might steal it from me.'

Sabina dared not look at Lord de Burgh, for she could not imagine him taking anything, even an imaginary hoard of coins.

'But he spied upon me!' Urban said. 'Mistress, call him off, for I have a right to do all that I can for you and Grim's End without his interference.'

Sabina frowned. She understood why Urban felt threatened, but the knight was only doing his duty, and Urban's nocturnal doings were peculiar, at best. Sabina did not like the idea of anyone wandering about alone, especially at night, if only for their own protection.

'Peregrine and I have come up with a solution,' Lord de Burgh said, though a glance at his squire told Sabina the boy was not very enthusiastic. 'We shall begin digging ourselves to see what can be found.'

'What?' Sabina asked, startled. And she was not alone, for all the residents of Grim's End appeared dismayed by such a suggestion.

'We will start where Urban was working,' Lord de Burgh said, turning towards the steward.

Everyone looked at Urban, who was sputtering a protest, as if horrified, though perhaps not for the same reasons as the rest of them.

'If your coins are there, then all to the good,' Lord de Burgh said to Sabina. 'If not, then there is no harm done.'

'But I think there will be harm,' Sabina protested. 'That hill holds our history, and 'tis shameful to defile a grave, whether a dragon is buried there or not.' The words rang in her ears, so similar to those she had spoken once before that she felt a sudden chill.

''Tis all nonsense!' Sabina insisted. 'Urban knows I have no hidden stash of gold, that the Sextons have always lived simply.'

'And yet, he sneaks out at night to look for it,' Lord de Burgh said. 'Perhaps Urban is not the only one who believes the legend. Does anyone else know of it?'

''Tis hardly a legend, my lord, just an old rumour, rarely mentioned,' Sabina said. 'Urban, did you speak of this with anyone else?'

He shook his head, and Sabina chose to believe him, rather than give in to her growing sense of dread.

'What of the rest of you?' Lord de Burgh asked, glancing at the other faces in the hall. 'What have you heard of this treasure?'

Sabina flinched at the word. 'There is no treasure!'

'Gamel told us lots of stories,' Alec said. 'I can't remember any about the Sextons, though. Most involved his ancestors and some king, Cyneric the Grim, who was buried with riches.'

'In the mound,' Lord de Burgh said, smugly.

'I, too, heard my kinsman's accounts, and I might have repeated some of them to one of the villagers,' Ursula admitted. 'But he is dead.'

She looked at Sabina, her face bleak, and Sabina blanched. She told herself it was all a coincidence, random bits and pieces of old gossip and happenings that were not connected. Yet her heart began to pound wildly as the old fears rushed back under a new guise. She had thought nothing more frightening than a dragon, attacking from the skies, but there were other evils, less deadly perhaps, but more personal and just as horrifying.

'Will you join me, Mistress Sexton?'

Sabina was sunk so deeply in her own tortured thoughts that she started at the mention of her name. She looked up to see that Lord de Burgh had risen from his seat and was awaiting her reply. Although she would go nearly anywhere with this man and do almost anything for him, she shook her head. What he planned to do struck too close to home, to the very heart of Grim's End.

Lord de Burgh showed not a flicker of reaction to her refusal, but turned towards Urban, his dark brows lifted in question. 'And you?'

'I might not be able to stop you, but I will not watch you steal from Sexton property,' Urban said.

His words surprised Sabina. 'How do you know 'tis Sexton property?' she asked.

Urban appeared stunned by her question. 'Why, I just assumed…' he began, then he frowned. ''Tis Sexton land from the Marking Stone to the church.'

'The old church,' Sabina said.

Urban licked his lips. 'But I thought… The Sextons have always tended the mound.'

'I don't think anyone could actually own it, for 'tis a landmark that stands for the beginning of Grim's End, its very founding,' Sabina said. As she spoke, she glanced towards Lord de Burgh, but he was already turning away, ignoring her protests.

'I'll come,' Alex said, but Adele shushed him.

So Lord de Burgh went alone, while the rest of the villagers remained in the hall, with Peregrine awkwardly keeping them company—or 'spying' upon them, as Urban claimed. It was just the first of his many rants.

'Your father would be horrified to see you relinquish your authority to a stranger, handing over Grim's End as though 'tis but a trifle,' the steward said, nearly as soon as the doors had shut.

Sabina did not comment, for she suspected that her father would have approved very much of Lord de Burgh and might have ceded more to the knight, perhaps even his daughter. But that was before, Sabina thought, frowning. Now she would make no man a wife.

'You cannot let him take away our very liberty,' Urban continued. 'You must make a stand and tell him that he has no authority over us.'

Sabina shook her head. 'I begged this man to help us, and that is what he is doing.'

Urban scoffed. 'Helping himself is more likely,' he muttered.

'The de Burghs have more wealth than you can imagine,' Peregrine said, glaring at the steward. 'Lord Reynold has no need of the dragon's treasure!'

Stunned by his words, Sabina sucked in a sharp breath and glanced at the boy, who coloured and turned away. *The dragon's treasure?* How had an old rumour of coins become something else entirely? Sabina wondered, her dread returning.

Urban, too, appeared dismayed. But then his expression turned sour once more. 'Well, I, for one, won't stand for it.'

Sabina eyed him scornfully. She didn't know how the older man expected to hold sway over Lord de Burgh, and she grew weary of his constant complaints. He had brought all this upon himself. Indeed, there had been no talk of treasure until his ill-fated venture under the moon. 'Perhaps if you would stay in at night, you could go about as you pleased.'

'I will not be dictated to!'

Astonished, Sabina turned to face him. Urban had always been dictated to, by her or her father or others as he achieved each new position. It was only after the population of Grim's End dwindled that he began to act as though he *was* her father, owner of the manor and most of the village, as well.

'I will tell you what I've told everyone here often enough,' Sabina said, meeting his gaze directly. 'You are free to go at any time.'

An expression of shock crossed his face, to be replaced quickly by entreaty. 'Let us all go, at last,' he said. 'Then that petty lord will have no reason to stay, either.'

Sabina shook her head. She was not going to abandon Lord de Burgh when he was here at her behest, doing what she had begged him to do. And it would be hard enough to part with him eventually; she would not hasten that pain. And for what? There was nothing waiting for her elsewhere.

Sabina didn't know what Urban saw when he looked at her, but he backed away, shaking his head angrily. Then he turned and headed towards the cellar, sending a sharp glance at Peregrine, as though daring the boy to follow.

Sabina watched the steward with a heavy heart, for he had served the Sextons well, and at one time he was all that had held their small band together. But now it seemed that their world was falling apart, unravelling like a fallen skein of thread upon the hard tiles.

Reynold paused to lean upon his shovel. Wearily, he stretched his aching leg and wondered whether to abandon his work. At first the labour had been a welcome way to ease his frustrations, and he had thrust the implement into the ground with increasing force. Alone with his thoughts, he had kept at it, not even returning to the manor for dinner.

But as the day dragged and the soil did not yield up anything, Reynold had begun to tire of the chore. His leg pained him, his other muscles protested, and he questioned his purpose. As with the dragon itself, what had seemed so sensible earlier now appeared fanciful, with about as much substance as a pair of fur breeches soaked in tar.

If local legends had put a fortune here, someone would have looked for it long ago, Reynold reasoned. And, if anything had been found, that, too, would have passed into legend. Instead, the residents viewed the spot as the dragon's resting place, nothing else. And who would imperil himself by poking around the beast's tomb?

Reynold frowned. And yet, such a warning would do much to keep the villagers at bay. And perhaps the Sextons not only watched the church, but the mound, as well, to prevent any exploration of the area. Mistress Sexton certainly seemed outraged at the idea of plundering the ground. But she had not forbade him, either. Reynold shook his head. Now he was arguing with himself and imagining enough to fill a tale.

Tired and hungry, Reynold threw the shovel over his shoulder and limped back to the manor. The small building, tucked among some trees, was a welcome sight as he approached. He realised, with some dismay, that it had come to represent home for him. *Only for now*, he told himself. *Perhaps only for a small while longer*, he thought, then stifled a pang. Perversely, despite the door that had been slammed in his face, he yearned to remain.

Frowning at the thought, Reynold flung open the doors and dragged the dirty shovel with him, lest it disappear from his sight. He would have to send Peregrine to see what other tools could be found in the stables and outbuildings, for he had no desire to travel to another village for such an implement.

At his entrance, Mistress Sexton rose, a look of concern upon her beautiful face. Was it for what he had done or what she feared he might find? Reynold wondered.

'Let me get you a willow-bark tisane,' she said, as she hurried towards him. 'Adele, heat some water for Lord de Burgh.'

Something inside Reynold eased at the knowledge that her concern was for him. Even though he knew it sprang from his service, not himself, he yearned for her nurturing, like a plant craved the sun. Yet he told himself it was the offer of a bath that was most welcome, and he grunted at the thought of a long soak. He would haul the buckets himself, rather than go without, just this once.

While Reynold ate, a metal tub, too small for his tall frame, but big enough to sit in, was found and dragged to the kitchens, where it would be easier to fill. And when the water was heated, he and the residents of Grim's End, well trained in handling buckets, made short work of the chore.

Soon Reynold stood before a full tub, eager to remove his filthy clothes, especially the hard mail that he had been wearing every day since he left Campion. The others drifted from the kitchens until, finally, he was alone with Mistress Sexton. The sun was sinking low outside, and she stood in the gathering gloom, more beautiful than ever when lit by the soft glow of the fire.

'Do you want me to…' Her words trailed off, and she looked away, only to draw a breath and return her gaze to his. 'Shall I help?'

Reynold felt as though he had been struck by a lance, hard in his chest and belly and below. As so often before when facing Mistress Sexton's charms, his wits seemed to flee, for he did not bother to wonder why she would make such an offer. He only yearned to agree, to let her strip the garments from his body and wash his aching flesh with her gentle hands.

For a long moment, they stood a few feet apart, the steaming water on one side, the fire on the other, and the very air cracked with the tension between them. Desire rose up so fierce as to nearly overcome Reynold, and he could have sworn it was reflected in Mistress

Sexton's pale face. He had only to nod to set something in motion that he had only imagined, something far beyond his wildest dreams.

'My lord!'

The sound of Peregrine's anguished shout broke the spell. Mistress Sexton's expression turned to one of alarm, and Reynold put his hand upon the hilt of his sword, the long moment of temptation forgotten in the face of some new threat.

'I—I think he's gone,' Peregrine said, appearing at the top of the stairs that led below.

'What? Who?' Mistress Sexton asked, but Reynold knew immediately. He waited, scowling, as his squire hurried to explain.

'Urban,' Peregrine said. 'I— He went to the cellars earlier, and since there is no other way out of them except the stairs, I did not…' Peregrine paused to draw a deep breath. 'I did not keep good watch.'

'How long?' Reynold asked, his fingers tightening on the hilt.

'I don't know, my lord,' Peregrine answered. 'When we finished filling the tub, I remembered he was down there. And I didn't want him to interrupt—er, come upon you in your bath, so I sought him out, but he is not there.'

Ignoring the weariness that weighed heavily upon him, Reynold drew a deep breath. 'Saddle Sirius, and I will see if I can find him. He can't have gone too far on foot.' But even as he spoke, a sudden, sharp fear spurred his anger. *'Unless he stole the horses.'*

Peregrine ran for the doors, but Reynold was halted

by a hand upon his arm. 'He did not join us for dinner,' Mistress Sexton said. 'But I thought he was still sulking.'

She looked more sad than alarmed, and Reynold reached out to close his fingers around her wrist, his temper barely leashed as he asked that which was uppermost in his mind. 'Was this bath designed to distract me while he fled?' he demanded in a low voice. 'What else would you have done to keep me here?'

Mistress Sexton's gaze flew to his, and Reynold saw only dismay and confusion in the blue depths. 'I don't understand. I have offered you baths often enough and was glad, for your sake, that you finally accepted. 'Twill grow cold soon, so you had best make use of it.'

'And let your man go?'

'Of course! I told him he could leave, as I often had before, though I did not believe he would do so.'

Reynold shook his head, his anger still simmering far too close to the surface. 'Did it ever occur to you that Urban might be up to more than digging for coins?'

'What do you mean?' Mistress Sexton asked, her expression clouded.

'He didn't take the horses, my lord,' Peregrine said, appearing at the doors. 'But it is nigh on full dark, and since I don't know how long he's been gone…'

Reynold loosed Mistress Sexton's wrist and swore under his breath. 'So he is gone for good and whatever secrets he might have are gone with him.'

'Secrets? What secrets?' Mistress Sexton asked.

Still cursing, Reynold turned towards her. 'Perhaps Urban was not digging for himself, but on someone else's instructions,' he muttered. Perhaps whoever was

attacking the village grew impatient for the treasure…
Reynold drew a deep breath. 'Perhaps Urban has been
in league with the dragon all along.'

'What?' Mistress Sexton gasped. 'How can you say
that?'

Easily enough, Reynold thought. Though the suspicion had just come to him, it made sense. 'Who bid you
hide in the cellars? Who fostered your fears in the guise
of protecting you?'

Mistress Sexton blanched. 'But he kept us safe! He
kept us together! Without Urban, we could never have
survived. Why would he help us remain here, if he really
wanted us to leave?'

'I don't know,' Reynold said. 'But who better to
inform upon your activities, your whereabouts, your
plans, your very state of mind?'

Shaking her head, Mistress Sexton backed away as
though to run from Reynold's claims. 'I don't believe
he's a traitor. I don't believe you.'

'Then you won't mind if we search the manor, will
you?' Reynold asked.

Peregrine made a sound, as if of protest, but Reynold
held up his hand to stop the boy from further speech.
Tired and angry and frustrated at every turn, he glared
at Mistress Sexton, daring her to refuse him.

But she only shuddered and turned from him. 'Do
what you will.'

If only I could, Reynold thought bitterly as he
watched her retreating figure. His hands flexed at his
sides, as if to reach for her, but he held himself in check.

Beside him, Peregrine stood silent, and the tub they

had worked so hard to fill waited, its water cooling as surely as Reynold's blood. Mistress Sexton's offer to bathe him seemed but a dream now, a figment of his fevered imaginings, destroyed, as always, by the harsh realities that lay between them.

If only I could.

Chapter Thirteen

Sabina sat alone in her chair in the hall, blinking in the near darkness. Ursula had sought her bed after Lord de Burgh had finished searching their room, but Sabina refused to join her. She was fearful of the conversation that might ensue, fearful of the way everything seemed to be falling apart.

Despite Lord de Burgh's accusations, Sabina refused to believe that Urban had done anything wrong except give in to his temper. As Ursula had predicted, the faithful steward grew resentful of Lord de Burgh and fled rather than cede his power. Although Sabina understood, she felt his loss as the latest, most disheartening, in a long line of abandonments.

Nearly everyone was gone now. There were only four residents left in Grim's End, three women and a boy, all of them at the mercy of a knight who was held here only by obligation. But wasn't that what held the others here, as well? Sabina didn't want to acknowledge the truth, but after Urban's defection, how could she deny it?

She watched blankly as Peregrine took his pallet to the cellar, no doubt to keep an eye upon Adele and Alec. Then a tall shadow fell over her as Lord de Burgh approached the trestle table where she was seated.

'You can go to your chamber now,' he said.

Yes, Sabina supposed she could, for Ursula would be asleep. There was no danger of her attendant saying things that Sabina didn't want to hear or posing questions that she did not want to answer.

'You were right about me,' she said softly.

'What makes you say that?' Lord de Burgh asked in a rough voice, as though impatient to seek his rest.

'I am selfish,' Sabina admitted. 'I wanted to keep my home and my heritage and gave no thought to anyone else, endangering the lives of those closest to me, rewarding loyalty with fear and peril.'

Sabina heard Lord de Burgh snort, but she did not look at him. 'I am a coward, too. I told myself that I was keeping my vow to my father, but I was afraid to go, afraid to leave behind everything that I loved, every place, every memory, every person to be lost for good.'

'You are not a coward.'

'You don't know,' Sabina muttered, clasping her hands together tightly. 'You don't know.'

'Then tell me,' he said. His voice was deeper and held a new urgency, but Sabina simply shook her head, unable even to glance his way.

She heard him swear under his breath and turn aside, only to swing back towards her. 'I think you are grieving over a man who was no friend to you.'

Sabina shook her head. 'I am grieving over my life because there is nothing left of what I knew. I might as well leave and have done with it.'

'I won't let you go.' The words, spoken in his low, raspy drawl, made Sabina's head jerk up, and she finally gazed at the dark man looming over her. Perhaps she had hoped to see something in his face, but, as usual, his expression told her nothing.

'I am not handing over Grim's End to whoever is behind these attacks, and I won't let you do it, either,' he said.

Sabina swallowed her disappointment at his explanation, for he was only doing what she had begged him to do. And she was a fool for wanting anything more. But just how long could this continue? *What was to become of them?* Sabina knew better than to let such thoughts cross her mind, but they did, and her breath caught.

She felt hot and dizzy, and her heart began pounding with familiar dread. Even as she tried to will it away, Sabina knew she could not wait. She had to act quickly, yet without undue haste that would draw Lord de Burgh's attention. The thought of his presence only increased her panic, and it took all of her strength simply to rise to her feet and nod to him, as though in goodnight.

Sabina dared not look at him or try to speak, lest she give herself away, but concentrated only upon reaching the stairs and the privacy of her room. He would not leave the candles burning, so she might be able to get away without him following close behind.

So she hurried upwards, escaping before he discovered that she was not the woman he thought her.

The next morning Reynold headed back to the mound, for want of other options. The search of the manor had revealed nothing, no hidden stash of jewels among Urban's things or directives secreted about the place. He had not even found any cherished love notes among Mistress Sexton's things or personal records that might reveal more about her.

Yet Reynold couldn't shake the suspicion that the beautiful damsel was hiding something, especially after the events of yesterday. Perhaps the bath was just as it seemed, an offer made many times that he finally accepted. But there was the odd conversation that followed, in which she appeared eager to abandon Grim's End after weeks of insisting otherwise, then left the hall without another word.

And, like Urban, Mistress Sexton sometimes disappeared, not for great lengths of time, but long enough for Reynold to notice. There were slammed doors and extended visits to the garderobe, when she refused to speak. Initially, Reynold had been too smitten by her charms to mistrust her, or, indeed, any of the villagers. But now, after Urban's flight, he began to wonder about each and every one of them.

Especially Mistress Sexton.

After all, it was her entreaty that had halted his journey, her presence that kept him here, and her company that he could not go without… With a grunt, Reynold pushed aside such thoughts to focus on the hole he had dug yesterday. The sight was discouraging, but what else was he to do? He could rove further and further from Grim's End, searching for some signs of a camp while leaving the others unprotected. Or he could continue where Urban had left off.

But just how deep should he go? Sticking the shovel to stand upright in the dirt, Reynold walked around the mound, surveying it more closely. He had no idea why Urban had chosen this spot in which to dig, but it was on the very edge of the hill's slope. If he had not come across Urban's work and was intent upon exploring the site, Reynold would have chosen a more direct route. Either he would go straight down from the top or make a trench across, so as not to miss anything that might be found on the periphery.

Without knowing what he was searching for, Reynold decided on the trench, and after selecting a new location, he began to dig with more interest, cutting across the surface of the hill. Still, his shovel struck nothing but earth and stones, and finally, he set it aside to lean on it. A fresh breeze came in off the sea, with a hint of a chill, which served his heated body well now, but was a harbinger of worse to come.

Veering away from that train of thought, Reynold scanned the area for signs of movement. But he saw nothing except stray birds until his gaze swept the mound and lit upon the glint of metal.

Reynold was surprised to notice something shiny in the newly excavated dirt. Since his shovel had struck nothing, he had continued on, but now he leaned over to pluck the thing from the pile of soil. It looked like a metal bolt, worn and discoloured. Reynold supposed that such things were often to be found in the ground, tossed aside long ago or part of some forgotten ruin that had decayed into nothing.

Still, Reynold blamed himself for not paying more attention as he worked. He had been expecting to hit a purse or a chest of coins, rather than loose objects scattered among the stones. But now he would dig more carefully, lest he miss something. The bolt had been uncovered recently, so Reynold set to work in the same general area, keeping an eye out for small objects.

Reynold took his time, yet it wasn't long before he spied another piece of metal, this one in the ground below, rather than the excavated soil. Reaching down, he brushed the dirt from the surface and saw that it was again a bolt, but the way it was lodged in the earth at an angle made it seem as though it were holding something together. He shook his head, for it touched nothing, and yet, he hesitated to remove it.

Leaving the find where it was, Reynold continued on until he located another, evenly spaced from the earlier one, and in the same sort of odd position. This was not random, Reynold thought, but what did it mean? Leaving the two bolts in the ground, he took the loose one with him as he headed back to the manor for a meal, and, hopefully, some answers.

The few remaining residents of Grim's End were in the hall, and Reynold propped his shovel by the doors and stalked across the tiles to join them.

'What do you think of this?' he asked, laying his discovery upon the trestle table. The group gathered round, but Reynold saw no signs of recognition on their faces.

'What is it?' Alec asked, leaning forwards.

''Tis obviously man-made,' Peregrine said, picking up the bolt and turning it in his fingers. 'It looks like something used in building, but what? And how did it get there?'

'Perhaps it is part of something the dragon ate, remnants from its belly,' Alec suggested.

'Is this all you found?' Mistress Sexton asked, frowning. 'You did not disturb the dragon's remains?'

'No,' Reynold said. 'I found no bones, grim or otherwise, only bolts. But they are lying in the ground in a pattern, as though part of some larger whole.'

'There's more than this one?' Peregrine asked.

'I left the others where I found them,' Reynold explained. Although the piece of iron did not constitute a treasure by any means, it aroused the curiosity of the boys, at least.

'Can I help you dig?' Alec asked.

'Yes, me, too,' Peregrine said. 'The more hands there are to do the work, the more quickly we will find the treasure.'

'There is no treasure,' Mistress Sexton said, looking exasperated. But Ursula, standing behind her, did not appear as certain.

'I could use some help with the earth that I'm removing,' Reynold said. 'The piles are becoming too big.'

'We could all help, passing buckets,' Alec offered. 'It would be like putting out the fires.'

'I would not leave the ladies unprotected,' Reynold said, which caused Peregrine to look an entreaty at Mistress Sexton. She frowned in disapproval, but did not gainsay them as they made plans to return to the very heart of Grim's End.

Whatever misgivings the villagers had about excavating their mound seemed forgotten once they shared in the search itself. Peregrine rigged up a tent to protect the hole from the worst of the squalls that sometimes blew through Grim's End, yet the weather favoured them. And they followed the line of bolts until they came across something else, wider and longer. It curved downwards, buried deep.

'Is that part of the dragon's spine?' Mistress Sexton called from above.

Reynold shook his head. 'Not unless its spine was made of wood,' he said as he pointed out the decaying matter. It was not the first wood they had found, but the most intact. They had also come across bits of old pottery and pieces of iron, but no cache of treasure.

Still, Reynold continued digging, as though the ground would yield up answers to all that plagued him. And keeping at the task made him feel as though he was accomplishing something, while staving off the future. Indeed, if there was a certain desperation to their efforts as the days grew cooler, the small band were all aware that their lives at Grim's End were coming to a close.

And so they dug until they could predict a bolt's position by the colour of the sand, and the so-called spine of the dragon began to take on a monstrous shape.

But it wasn't until Peregrine began digging on the other side of the mound, deeper in the original trench, that they began to realise the bolts and wood probably encircled the mound.

'It's like stepping into a giant bowl,' Alec said, obviously awed by the discovery. 'Perhaps the people of Grim's End built a coffin big enough to house the worm.'

As a village resident, the boy was reluctant to dismiss the legend of its founding, but Peregrine was not so biased. 'If so, wouldn't we have found its bones, huge ones that would be impossible to overlook?' the squire asked.

'It's not a coffin,' Reynold said from his stance within the wide hole. Turning around, he looked at the half that was uncovered and what appeared to be its mirror image, though mostly buried. 'Nor is it a bowl,' he said, as recognition dawned. 'It's a ship.'

'But how would such a thing be buried here? We are too far from the coast,' Mistress Sexton said, coming to stand at the edge of the site to see for herself.

'Perhaps a big storm blew it ashore,' Alec said.

Reynold was thinking the same thing, but surely such a tempest would have destroyed the craft, not interred it so perfectly. Perhaps they would find a missing portion which would give evidence of its foundering, yet how had the earth risen up around it?

'It must be more than forty feet long, too big to have been tossed over the cliffs to reach this place,' Peregrine said. 'But why would anyone bury a boat?'

The question, like so much to do with Grim's End, simply hung in the air, unanswerable.

'A ship,' Mistress Sexton said, shaking her head.

'Well, at least now I hope you are all convinced that there is no hoard of coins hidden here.'

And yet they did find coins when they dug deeper, a shiny one that Ursula spotted from the top of the slope, and another that Reynold discovered later on. Both were old, with odd markings, and made of gold.

'Perhaps an ancestor of yours found one of these in the soil, and thence the legend grew,' Reynold said, holding the piece up for Mistress Sexton to see.

On this day, he was deep in the belly of the ship, the cut earth towering over him on one side, the skeleton of wood and bolts spread before him on the other. Although Reynold knew little of ships except what he had read in Geoffrey's books, he guessed they must be nearing the bottom.

Perhaps, in his eagerness, he moved too quickly or grew careless. Or perhaps the sandy soil they had carved so relentlessly could take no more. But one minute Reynold was holding the coin high, and the next he was knocked to the ground, swallowed up by the earth.

Standing at the opposite edge of the pit, Sabina screamed a warning, but it was too late. The ground, seemingly sturdy, suddenly gave way, sliding on to Lord de Burgh. At the sight of his body twisting beneath the onslaught, Sabina's breath caught, and she choked back another cry, unable to speak or move. But she would not stand by and watch him die, and struggling against a paralysing fear, she lurched forwards, only to fall to the ground.

'Careful! Don't cause any more movement,' Peregrine warned. Although not much older than Alec, Lord de Burgh's squire took charge, directing everyone to stay away from the collapsing side of the hole, while he scrambled over the open area to reach Lord de Burgh, half-covered in dirt and stones.

The knight's head was free of debris, but his eyes were closed, as though he had been knocked unconscious. *Or was he dead?* Sabina could only watch in horror as Peregrine reached under the fallen man's arms and struggled to drag him out from under the soil into the open area.

Once he was well away from the crumbling wall of earth, Peregrine leaned close, speaking to him and touching his limbs as though searching for crushed or broken bones. Would the man who spent a lifetime ignoring his bad leg now face worse injury?

Sabina felt a hand upon her shoulder and realised that she was still crouched upon the grass where she had fallen. 'There, there, mistress, he will be well. It would take more than a little dirt to stop Lord de Burgh.'

Sabina nodded, even though she could hear the strain in Ursula's voice. She lifted her head and saw a bleak scene. Adele and Alec were staring helplessly into the pit, for what could they do? Only Sabina had any knowledge of healing, and even as she tried to think of what she must do, fear and panic pressed down on her, keeping her still.

What would they do if they lost him? What would *she* do, if she lost him? The pain of their eventual parting had been easy to put off until tomorrow and the next day. But suddenly Sabina was faced with the fact that the man she loved might already be gone.

It was too much. Her breath seized, and Sabina began to tremble, but through the haze of her own misery she heard Peregrine calling out to her. And though no longer in control of herself, she obeyed, rising to her feet and clambering down into the huge hole, past the bolts and rotten wood that marked the shape of a ship, to where Lord de Burgh lay.

'I can't find any blood or anything…broken,' Peregrine said in a whisper. 'But he won't wake up.' The boy seemed one step away from tears, and perhaps that was what gave Sabina her strength as she turned to the prone form.

Lord de Burgh was breathing, that much she could tell by the rise and fall of his great chest. She ran her own hands over him, looking for anything unusual, bumps or twisted limbs, but all seemed straight and strong. Yet she knew that sometimes victims of injury were hurt inside, and there was nothing anyone could do.

Sabina swallowed hard. 'Wet a cloth or a piece of clothing, if nothing else,' she said to Peregrine. She heard him scramble away, but she had attention only for Lord de Burgh, his strong face somehow more relaxed than she had ever seen it. There were no lines of tension, no grim set to his handsome features.

Blinking against the tears that threatened, Sabina took his hands in hers. Big and calloused and warm, they were both strong and gentle, as was he, for Lord de Burgh was everything that a man should be. Not only a knight, a hero who held to his oaths, he was a flesh-and-blood being with sometimes maddening habits that just made her love him all the more.

'You can wake up now, my lord,' Sabina whispered. But he did not stir.

Sabina loosed a deep, shuddering sigh, and then Peregrine was at her side, handing her a damp cloth. Brushing back Lord de Burgh's dark hair with one hand, she wiped the dirt from his forehead and stroked one cheek.

'There, that's better,' she said aloud, more for herself and Peregrine than for Lord de Burgh. But as if the moisture had wakened him, the knight opened his eyes. Suddenly, he was looking at her, and Sabina cried out with relief.

'My lord, are you all right?' Peregrine asked.

He blinked, as though dazed, and then rose on to an elbow. 'What happened?'

'Part of the earthen wall there caved in upon you,' Peregrine said. He paused, as though reluctant to continue. 'Can you, uh, move your legs?'

The question was met by a scowl, and Sabina scooted back as Lord de Burgh heaved himself to his feet, the soil that clung to him flying in all directions. Peregrine quickly moved under one arm and Sabina the other, but as she looked at the sides of the pit, she felt her heart sink.

'Perhaps you should just rest here a while longer,' Sabina suggested. But she should have known better. Just as Peregrine's words had roused Lord de Burgh from the ground, hers spurred him onwards, as though he must prove to the world that he was completely unaffected by the fall, the weight of the earth and his slip into unconsciousness.

Stubborn fool, Sabina thought, but she said nothing

as the three of them struggled upwards, her own climb made more difficult by the drag of her long skirts. By the time they made it to the surface, she was hot and breathless.

'Let us rest here,' Sabina said when they reached the grass.

'I need no rest,' Reynold argued.

'I want to take a better look at your leg.'

'There is nothing wrong with my leg.'

Tired, sore, and still shaking with the effects of the harrowing experience, Sabina felt her temper snap. 'None the less, I am mistress here, and I would make sure that all within my household are well.'

Through the corner of her eye, Sabina saw Peregrine shepherding the others well away, perhaps even back to the manor. But she paid them no heed. Her attention was focused solely on the man who could have been killed, yet was now shaking his head at her as though she were his enemy.

''Tis my responsibility,' Sabina said.

'*'Tis my leg,*' he countered. Then his knees buckled, and he lurched forwards. Sabina caught him as best she could, helping him to the grass even as he swore at her and tried to push her away.

'Why can't you accept some help?' she demanded.

'And why can't you mind your own business?' he practically snarled at her. 'You with your perfect body and your perfect beauty, you know nothing of—'

Sabina cut him off with a gasp. 'You think I'm whole?' she asked, her voice rising. 'I'm afflicted with something far worse.'

He glanced at her sharply, as though he didn't believe her. 'That's nonsense.'

'Is it?' Sabina asked, but she could no longer face him. Heart pounding, she turned away, ashamed to admit that which plagued her. She had spoken in anger, yet now she had no choice. She took a deep breath and said aloud that which she had hidden from everyone for so long. 'I have a madness.'

'What are you talking about?'

Sabina felt Lord de Burgh's hands close about her shoulders, but she could not look at him. 'Fits. Frights,' she muttered. 'It started after my father died. I thought at first that something in the foul dragon breath was affecting me, perhaps because I'm a Sexton.'

'What makes you say that?'

Sabina shook her head. 'It might be the madness, but I had begun to think that the dragon was after me, more than anyone else. And you say I am no coward,' she said, bitterly.

'You aren't a coward,' he said.

'And you don't know all,' Sabina insisted. 'The truth, my lord, is that I am assailed by fears. Then I begin trembling and my heart is beating too fast and I can't breathe. I'm hot and cold and dizzy and faint, useless when I most need to be strong, starting at nothing while my people suffer in silence, brave beyond measure.'

Unwilling to see his reaction, Sabina tried to pull away from his grasp, but he held her fast. 'I have heard that madness can sometimes be cured,' she murmured. 'So I thought to go to Bury St Edmunds, but I could not, for I was too afraid.'

Sabina would have fled if she could have mustered the strength, but Lord de Burgh pulled her towards him. Ignoring her protests, he took her in his arms, enclosing her with his strength and his warmth. One big hand came up to cup her head, stroking her hair, and Sabina finally gave in to the lure of his comfort.

She buried her face against his chest, and even the hard links of his mail shirt were a reassurance that nothing could harm her here. At last she was safe, secure, and untroubled by fears.

Lord de Burgh murmured something unintelligible, soft words meant to soothe her, and Sabina wanted to respond in kind. *I love you*, she thought, but she dared not speak the words aloud, and she had just told him why.

Chapter Fourteen

It took Reynold a full day to convince the others that he was unhurt, though battered and bruised, and able to return to digging. Mistress Sexton, especially, claimed the task too dangerous. They had been lucky this time, she said, and that was true enough. Reynold knew that his brother Simon had been trapped by falling earth when undermining, and the most stubborn of the de Burghs had nearly been killed.

But when Mistress Sexton said they tempted fate if they continued defiling a grave, Reynold could not agree. The mound held a ship, not any remains, and they had come too far to abandon their search. He might have wished for Simon's or Geoffrey's expertise in shoring up the walls of the hole, but he would do his best.

For what else was there? Their days at Grim's End were numbered, but Reynold was not ready to think about the future, especially that of Mistress Sexton. Although he didn't fully understand what ailed her, she was not mad, Reynold was sure of that. She had been hiding something from him, as he suspected, but it had nothing to do with the dragon, a realisation that did much to ease the tension between them.

Although she called herself a coward, Reynold thought her even more courageous to lead her people, fight fires and face dragons. Strong, brave, nurturing, kind, beautiful and yet struggling with a problem of her own, Mistress Sexton threatened to make Reynold abandon his old precepts where women were concerned. *Maybe, just maybe, this one was different.*

'Look, the soil is an unusual colour there,' Peregrine said, drawing Reynold from his thoughts. Perched upon the bank, Peregrine pointed to an area at the very bottom of the cavity that Reynold had recently uncovered. Moving closer, Reynold knelt down to see for himself. Deep in the belly of the ship, he might not have noticed what Peregrine saw so clearly from above, yet he realised this spot *was* distinctive, the dissimilar ground forming a square.

Reynold glanced up at Peregrine and nodded. The boy scrambled back into the hole, and they set to dig in what seemed to be the very heart of the ship. Here Reynold wielded a smaller shovel and his hands, searching for anything out of the ordinary, the smooth surface of a chest or the thin contour of a piece of gold.

After all the work they had done, all the ground they had moved, all the time they had spent within the mound, Reynold was astonished when his fingers touched something almost immediately. Until now, they had found nothing beyond the two coins, bits of pottery and cloth, blackened wood and loose stone. Had they finally come upon the dragon's treasure?

Sucking in a sharp breath, Reynold felt along the edge of the object, with a sense of disappointment. Smooth and long, it was probably a bone, which would draw Mistress Sexton's wrath down upon them.

But Reynold had come too far to leave it be. After he had fallen, Adele gave him a small broom to brush off the dirt, and now Reynold used that to carefully dust away the soil. Rough usage, such as pulling the item from its berth, might very well cause damage. And Reynold did not care to admit to Mistress Sexton should he break any remains buried here.

When he finally was able to lift it out of the ground, Reynold realised that what he held in his hand was too strangely shaped for a human bone. Wide at one end, it tapered to a point at the other. Beside him, Peregrine crowded in to take a closer look.

'It's a horn,' the boy whispered.

'What have you found? What is it?' sharp-eyed Ursula called from above.

'A horn,' Peregrine called back.

'Is it one of the dragon's horns?' from beside Ursula Alec's voice rose with awe and curiosity.

Reynold shot a glance at his squire. In their many discussions of worms, he could recall no mention of horns. And if there ever had been a dragon, where was the rest of it?

'Perhaps this was used to call the beast or emulate its sound,' Peregrine said.

Something certainly had been used recently to create a roar, but Reynold doubted that it was this worn instrument, buried so far beneath the ground. Still, he fingered the end, and when he found no hole, he gently shook out the dirt that filled the opening.

'Or perhaps it holds not noise, but ale,' Reynold said, drily.

'A drinking horn?' Peregrine asked. 'I've heard of them, but never seen one.'

Reynold had seen them, though he could not understand their appeal, then or now.

'How do you even set it down?' Peregrine asked.

'Maybe the point is not to,' Reynold said, with a wry twist of his lips.

Peregrine flashed him a grin, but then turned pensive. 'But what is it doing in the bowels of the ship?'

Reynold shook his head. What was the ship even doing here? His quest for answers about Grim's End only seemed to yield up more mysteries.

Peregrine frowned. 'Perhaps long ago "grim" was a word for ship?'

'Perhaps,' Reynold said, for the explanation was as good as any other. 'Better take this up to Ursula,' he added, and he stood watching as the boy scrambling up the banked earth.

Mistress Sexton's attendant had insisted on dragging a chest to the site, presumably to fill with the treasure she had hoped was hidden here, but Reynold didn't think an old drinking horn was what the woman had in mind.

But perhaps that was not all, Reynold thought, and he returned to his task. Using mostly his hands, it was slow going, and often he would get excited by the feel of something, only to discover a piece of fur or bits of material that had disintegrated in the earth. But, finally, his fingers closed around something smooth again, and he worked steadily until an object protruded from the earth.

'It's only another old piece of wood,' Peregrine said, his disappointment apparent.

Still, Reynold slowly followed the shaft into the earth, where he glimpsed a glint of metal, and eventually they uncovered a cudgel that stood on end as if thrown here long ago.

'An axe!' Peregrine said, obviously more impressed by the weapon than by the horn.

'Careful, it looks as though it might fall apart,' Reynold said as Peregrine hoisted it in his arms to deliver to Ursula and her mistress. Reynold wondered what Mistress Sexton would make of such a thing, but he did not stop his work to find out.

Although he no longer eyed the damsel with suspicion, Reynold kept his distance, for with no obstacles standing between him and temptation, he didn't know how long his will would hold. And he was well aware that the comfort he gave when she wept in his arms could have turned into something else had they not been upon the grassy slope by the mound, where all could see.

'My lord?' Peregrine's voice once again drew Reynold from his thoughts, and they continued their search. Not far from the axe, Reynold felt something else smooth and hard, but thinner and curved. It proved to be a piece of iron that had been worked into its shape, but to what purpose, he did not know.

'What is it?' Ursula called.

'Just a piece of metal,' Peregrine answered.

'Not jewellery?'

Reynold snorted. Mistress Sexton's attendant must be growing impatient, for what they had pulled from the earth so far was no treasure by any reckoning.

'No, we don't know what it is,' Peregrine answered. He turned the piece over and over in his hands, studying it thoughtfully, before glancing up at Reynold in surprise. 'I think it's part of a helmet.'

Reynold shook his head, for 'twas like none he had ever seen. He watched, fascinated, as Peregrine fitted the thing over his head to hang over his face. ''Twould seem to be backwards to me,' Reynold muttered.

But a helm would go with the axe, Reynold reasoned, with a sense of foreboding. Not only had they come across no cache of coins to please Ursula, but what they were finding were personal objects—the kind that might be found upon a dead man.

When Reynold returned his hands to the soil, it was with some reluctance, lest he come upon the owner of the items that Ursula so zealously inspected. However, when his fingers closed, once more, upon something smooth, it was not the shape of a skull, but of small circles, obviously crafted by man. Although Reynold suspected what he held in his hands, he said nothing, leaving Peregrine to recognise the object after a part of it was uncovered.

''Tis a mail coat,' the squire whispered in awe.

But 'twas an old one, strangely crafted, and they struggled for a long time to release the entire thing from the earth's grip. As Peregrine carried it up to the waiting women, Reynold shuddered at the thought of what was left below. Yet he set to his task until he came upon them, not the solid bones of someone recently deceased, but bits and pieces, as if they, too, were disintegrating in the sandy soil.

'Twas not a welcome discovery. Reynold had faced down armed enemies without flinching, yet he was uncomfortable squatting among the remains. Perhaps he would not have felt such dismay had he simply stumbled over a grave, but these bones lay at the very core of Grim's End, a village steeped in curious legends and abandoned by all except a handful of the living.

'So it is a burial place,' Peregrine said, softly, as he stared down at the evidence. He glanced up at Reynold. 'But why are these other things here?'

'Personal possessions,' Reynold said. 'Considering the axe, the fellow might have fallen in some primitive battle.'

'Remember what happened to Beowulf?' Peregrine said quietly. 'He was buried in a broad high tumulus.'

'A mound,' Reynold said.

'But that was after battling a dragon that was guarding its treasure,' Peregrine noted. 'And here in Grim's End, there's no dragon or treasure, just a ship.'

Reynold could only shake his head. Who knew what the ancestors of these villagers had done and why? Some pagan rituals and strange rites were not even to be found in Geoffrey's books. Perhaps what happened here was lost to history except for a thread of rumour that survived, changing over the years into something unrecognisable, making the mound into the tomb, not of a ship, but of a dragon.

With a frown, Reynold continued his search of the

square chamber, but the bones appeared to be all that remained.

'What is it? What are you setting aside down there?' Ursula called, as if she expected Reynold and his squire to keep hidden valuables for themselves. Reynold shook his head at Peregrine in warning, but it was too late. His squire was already calling out the truth.

As Reynold suspected, Mistress Sexton soon appeared at the top of the pit, a horrified expression on her face. 'Bones? You found *bones*?' she accused, as though by unearthing the remains Reynold had called down some ancient curse upon Grim's End.

But perhaps that was her fears talking. Dusting off his hands, Reynold made his way towards the sloped side in order to climb out, lest she be stricken with her malady. And, indeed, when he made it to the bank, she was pale and stiff.

'You desecrated a grave,' she said, with a gasp, and Reynold reached out to take her hands. He held her gaze, too, never wavering, as she drew one deep breath and then another.

'What do you fear?' he asked.

'Nothing,' she muttered, glancing away. 'Everything.'

'But this can't be all that is hidden there,' Ursula protested. She stared at the objects she had laid in the chest with a look of dismay that appeared to have little to do with the discovery of the bones.

'What did you expect, the fabled Sexton hoard?' Mistress Sexton asked, her scorn evident.

Although Reynold could not blame Mistress Sexton for her distress, he shared Ursula's disappointment. The villagers had gone to a lot of work, expending all their energy and time on a huge undertaking that had yielded little. Reynold was not sure what he had hoped to find, but some riches would have helped Mistress Sexton and her people establish themselves elsewhere. Yet, like so much associated with Grim's End, it seemed that the rumoured hoard was as insubstantial as the dragon itself.

'But treasure lies below the grim,' Ursula insisted. 'That's what your grandfather said.'

'What?' Mistress Sexton blanched and turned towards her attendant.

Ursula blinked, as though only now realising what she had just said. ''Tis nothing, mistress, just another story.'

'One you heard from my grandfather?'

Ursula took a step backwards and began wringing her hands. ''Twas something I overheard, mistress, probably just the ranting of a sick man.'

'Sick? When was my grandfather sick, except when he lay dying…?' Mistress Sexton's expression grew fierce. 'Ursula, you helped tend to him. What did you do?'

'Nothing, mistress, I swear,' Ursula said, obviously agitated. 'Your mother bid me sit with him and to fetch her, if need be.' Ursula paused to eye Mistress Sexton with entreaty. 'He mumbled to himself. Most of it I could not understand, and I paid no heed, unless he asked for your mother. But one time, I was unsure, so I leaned close. He must have thought I was her, for he grabbed my arm with surprising strength.

'"Remember the treasure is under the grim," he said very clearly as he looked me right in the eye.' Ursula shivered. 'Then he fell back and I ran to get your mother.'

'Why did you never tell me this?' Mistress Sexton asked.

'In truth, mistress, I forgot all about it,' Ursula said. 'When I found your mother, I told her, and she brushed it aside. She claimed that he said lots of things from the past that gave him comfort, but that I was not to worry. And so I dismissed it from my mind. It wasn't until recently that I remembered it.'

'So you are responsible for this,' Mistress Sexton said, sweeping an arm to encompass the vast chasm that had been the mound.

'No, mistress! I would never speak to Urban of such things,' she said, with a sniff.

'But you did tell someone.' Mistress Sexton persisted.

'Yes, but that was just in the course of relating old tales, after the fashion of my kinsman Gamel. His stories were mentioned, and I added this one, never thinking…' Ursula trailed off, as though unable to go on. 'But, then it doesn't matter because that one is…dead.'

Mistress Sexton blanched again, and Reynold wondered whether this conversation was too much for her. And what was the point of it? No matter who told what to whom, the legends were just as fanciful as the dragon purported to be buried here, and the precious store of gold was nothing but a couple of coins possessed by the dead.

'Peregrine, why don't you take the women back to the hall, so that they can rest out of the sun?' Reynold suggested.

The boy nodded, but Mistress Sexton reached out to touch Reynold's arm. 'You will rebury the bones, won't you? And all that went with them?'

Her expression was so stark that Reynold was tempted to take her back to the manor himself. But he no longer trusted himself with her comfort, so he merely nodded. As Peregrine led the women away, Reynold stood watching until their figures disappeared behind a copse of trees.

Then he turned his attention to the gaping hole before him, one square sunk even deeper into the bowels of the skeleton of a ship, and he shook his head. It was the end of the road, for the hopes of the villagers, for the work that had kept them occupied, and for the time that they would spend in Grim's End.

'What are you going to do now?' young Alec asked.

What else was there to do? Reynold frowned as he gazed out over the scarred earth. 'We return everything to the ground, and then we fill it all in.'

Sabina slipped into her room, shut the door behind her and slumped against it. Weary and overwhelmed, she was eager for a few moments to herself. Ursula remained in the hall, which was just as well, for Sabina was not sure how she felt about her attendant's revelation.

She could see that Lord de Burgh thought it nonsense, but he did not know all, and Sabina wondered whether she should tell him. Reluctant to disclose her father's dying words to everyone, she had said nothing out by the mound. And what could it possibly matter? They had looked under the grim and found only the bones of the dead.

Sabina shivered. She tried not to dwell on the fact that they had desecrated a grave, but she couldn't help it. Old fears returned, childhood notions that to disturb the mound was to rouse the dragon. Even though now Sabina knew that there was no worm and that no action had stirred it back to life, their troubles had started not long after someone else had wanted to defile the mound.

Sabina told herself that she should be glad that the dark suspicions she had refused to consider had at last been proven wrong. And yet, even now she hesitated to remember the moment she had tried so hard to forget—when her betrothed had returned.

Shaking, Sabina made her way to the room's sole chair and sank down upon it, stifling a sob at all that had happened since. She dipped her head low, eager to bury her face in her hands, but a noise within the room made her look up. And as though her very thoughts had conjured him from the air, Julian Fabre stepped out of the shadows.

Sabina half-rose from her chair, a cry upon her lips, certain she had seen a ghost or some figment of her imagination that meant she was truly going mad.

'Greetings, my love,' he said, flashing a set of white teeth that anyone would envy. He had always been the handsomest man in the village, with his shock of dark hair and startling green eyes, and he had made the most of that beauty, using it to seduce and charm, to turn attention away from the ugliness hidden inside.

'Struck speechless, are we? That has to be a first,' Julian said, as he stepped closer. 'Unlike most women, little Sabina always had her opinions and voiced them far too often.'

Sabina's breath caught, and she felt panic press down

upon her. *Not now*, she thought. *Not now*, when she needed all her wits about her. Staring at him, unblinking, she thought of Lord de Burgh and how he had steadied her only a little while ago.

'Not much to say? Well, that's fine because, for once, I'll do the talking.' Julian walked around the small space as though it couldn't contain him, his intensity making him unrecognisable to her as the boy she had once known.

'I thought you lost your precious knight when the mound caved in,' he said. He picked up her silver hairbrush as if it were suddenly of great interest to him, then glanced at her under his long lashes. 'Thought I'd have to swoop in and take over.'

Sabina gasped.

'Surprised? Oh, I keep an eye on what is mine—or I make sure Urban does.'

'Urban!' Sabina whispered, still unable to believe that her father's loyal steward would work against the Sextons.

'Yes. He is practically worthless, but I needed him to keep me informed while I remained out of sight,' Julian said, as he roamed the chamber. 'It was very accommodating of you to do all my work for me, though I don't know if I should be insulted by your sudden change of heart. Why would you refuse to let me dig up the mound, only to help a stranger do so?'

Julian shook his head at her, as if in reproach. 'I can only imagine that you have become more desperate over the past few months, for he cannot be more persuasive than I.'

Sabina simply stared at him, uncomprehending. He looked the same as he had when she'd last seen him all those months ago, but his clothes, obviously once fine, were frayed and worn, his hair too long and ragged.

'Still quiet, I see. But now I really do need you to speak, for I see that your precious knight is filling in the mound,' Julian said. He eyed her intently. 'So where is the treasure?'

'There is no treasure,' Sabina said wearily. 'Just as I told you before. There was nothing in that mound but a dead man.'

'Really? That would be most unfortunate.'

Blinking at him, Sabina finally recovered herself. This was no ghost or vision, but a real man, the man she had once thought the embodiment of her girlhood dreams. Yet he had broken all vows and abandoned all honour, and now he had set Urban to spy upon her? 'Why are you here, Julian? What do you want?'

'I would think that's a bit obvious, Sabina, but then you were never one to think the worst of people, were you? Trusting little Sabina. Naïve. Honest to a fault. Full of righteous goodness.' He moved close to her and reached out to lift her chin with one long finger, which Sabina slapped away.

Far from offending him, the action seemed to please the man Julian had become. 'At first I just wanted to get rid of everyone, but you proved far too stubborn. Foolish, stubborn Sabina, clinging to her visions of honourable knights and worthy wars. But then I began to think you might be useful.'

'What are you talking about?' Sabina asked, her heart in her throat. 'What are you saying?'

'Why, that I am *The Dragon.*' Julian threw the words

over his shoulder as he resumed his pacing. 'Since you refused to let me dig into the mound after I asked you so nicely, I had to find some way to have it to myself. And it was a clever scheme, you must admit, even though you refused to go. When you would not leave, I thought perhaps it was fate, throwing us together again. I began to think we might resume our relationship, after I had found the riches, of course, and became worthy of you.'

'What?' Sabina surged to her feet. 'You think that wealth would make you *worthy*? You come in here, acting as if you've done nothing wrong, when you attacked my village, scattered my people and killed my father?'

'I didn't kill your—'

'You killed my father!' Sabina screamed. She saw the alarm on Julian's face, but she couldn't stop. Her heart pounded, yet with anger, not fear. 'And then you think you can *marry* me, take to your bed and your life the woman you most wronged in the world? What sort of a monster are you? You are most assuredly a worm, but the kind that crawls upon the ground and slithers through faeces, hiding in the dirt.'

The words had barely left Sabina's mouth when she heard a faint sound, as though of the beast itself, yet it came from the skies outside, not from the man standing before her. 'If you are The Dragon, then what is that?' she asked, eyes narrowed.

Julian cocked his head to one side. 'It appears that I am needed elsewhere. But, first, tell me where the treasure is,' he said, advancing on her.

'There is no treasure,' Sabina shouted. For a moment,

all was quiet as she stood facing him, and then she heard a knock upon her door.

Turning, Sabina hastened with the bolt, for fear Julian might prevent her from escaping. But it swung open, revealing young Peregrine, with his sword drawn. Fearing for the boy, Sabina was reluctant to let him in, yet when she turned, the room was empty.

Julian had disappeared, just as surely as the last time he had been here.

Reynold put the bones and all else back into the square hole that marked the very bottom of the mound and was filling it in with the different-coloured soil when he heard something eerily familiar. It was not the sound of flying fire, but that of the dragon's roar none the less, and Reynold climbed out of the pit as quickly as possible, a wary eye upon the skies.

'Did you see anything?' Reynold asked Alec, the only other person left at the mound.

The boy shook his head; loathe to leave him alone, Reynold took him along as they hurried to the manor. Even though he knew no worm hovered above them, Reynold crouched low to the ground as he ran, keeping to the tall grass as much as possible before racing to the copse of trees at the rear of the building.

There they halted beneath the cloaking greenery, Reynold holding up a hand to silence Alec. Although he expected no trouble, in the past days and weeks Reynold had grown lax, and now he cursed himself for sending the women back to the hall without his protection.

His glance through the leaves was one of caution

only, an automatic gesture, so he bit back a grunt of surprise when he saw a dark figure climbing down the side of the stone structure. As Reynold gaped, the figure turned, revealing itself to be a man, slender and agile, with a face so handsome as to bring Reynold's brother Stephen to mind.

Reynold's initial fear that a passing thief had attacked the last of the villagers turned into something else entirely, especially since the man was coming from above—where Mistress Sexton's window lay.

'That looks like Julian Fabre, the blacksmith's son,' Alec whispered. He turned to Reynold, his eyes wide. 'Mistress Sexton's betrothed.'

The hushed words rang in Reynold's head like a shout, and he reeled as though the boy had struck him. The pain that lanced through him was far worse than any ache in his leg, and he could hardly bring himself to speak, lest he howl his anguish to the skies. 'You go inside,' he managed to whisper. 'I'm going to follow him.'

Reynold had no idea what the figure was up to, but he was not about to allow the man Mistress Sexton had claimed was dead wander in and out of Grim's End at will. Were the two of them lovers? Reynold's hurt was joined by anger and frustration, and he felt a fool to have thought Mistress Sexton different. He wondered just how far her deceit went, but he could spare no thoughts for her perfidy now when he needed all his wits about him.

With a bitter twist of his mouth, he acknowledged his fate: to be betrayed by the woman he loved.

Chapter Fifteen

Sabina hurried down the stairs, Peregrine close behind her. Although she wanted to hide in her bedchamber, it was no longer a haven. Indeed, the only place where Sabina felt secure now was with Lord de Burgh. *By his side. In his arms.* But as she rushed to the hall, anger, fear and worry for him dogged her footsteps. What if Julian came upon Lord de Burgh in the pit and buried him, for good this time…? Sabina stopped at the bottom of the steps, her breath lodged in her throat.

'Are you all right?' Ursula asked, her own face pale and drawn. 'We heard the dragon's roar and didn't know what to do. What happened?'

Sabina shook her head as she tried to breath. *Not now*, she thought, desperately. *Not when Lord de Burgh might be in danger.* She focused on him, on his tall form and his beloved face, while she grasped Ursula's arm.

'Julian. Julian was in my room,' she finally managed. 'Julian Fabre.'

'*What?*' Ursula's voice rang with shock, and Sabina could hear Adele's gasp.

'But I thought he was dead,' Adele said, an expression of terror on her face. 'Was it *his* remains that were disturbed in the mound?'

'No, he is no ghost,' Sabina said. 'He is alive and well.' *Too well.* She paused to draw a deep breath as Alec raced into the hall.

'Did you see Julian?' the boy asked, his eyes wide.

Even as Sabina nodded, she looked past the boy for a familiar figure, but Alec was alone. 'Where is Lord de Burgh?' she asked. 'I thought you were with him.'

'Lord de Burgh went after Julian,' Alec said. 'We saw him sneaking from the manor, and Lord de Burgh set out to follow him.'

Sabina felt her heart contract with fear. Although she had faith in Lord de Burgh, in his skill and his strength, Julian held to no knightly code. He was dangerous and devious. And what if he were not alone?

'Come, sit down,' Peregrine said, as if divining her thoughts. Taking her arm, he led her to her chair and Sabina sank into it, while Peregrine gathered the remaining residents of Grim's End around the trestle table.

'For the moment, let us all stay here, for I don't think Lord de Burgh would want us to separate. If need be, we can go to the cellars or the roofs—'

Ursula interrupted him with a gasp. 'Are you saying we will be attacked?'

Peregrine shook his head, and his calm authority was so like his master's that Sabina felt her tension ease.

'No, but I would have us be prepared, so please

follow my direction, if necessary. For now, we will await Lord de Burgh's return, and perhaps you can tell me what I need to know about our enemy.'

'Is Julian our *enemy*? Surely not—' Ursula began, but Peregrine held up a hand in the manner of his master and turned to Sabina. 'Who is Julian Fabre?'

Sabina hesitated to answer simply because she was unsure what to say, but Peregrine's steady demeanour helped her gather her thoughts. Ignoring Ursula's sputtering, she focused on the squire. 'Julian is the son of the village blacksmith. He was always clever and ambitious, and well favoured among the villagers,' she said, with a glance toward her attendant.

'At first, he planned to follow in his father's footsteps, but to work only upon armour. It was more prestigious to cater to knights, he claimed, but then that was not enough and he wanted to become a knight himself. And so he planned to join Edward's crusade in the Holy Land.'

Sabina paused, looking down at the fingers entwined in her lap. 'It was then that Julian asked my father for my hand. We were both very young, but he agreed we could marry upon his return.' It was an agreement Sabina now rued, but the Sextons saw few knights in Grim's End and were impressed by the qualities required to join that select fraternity. Sabina, especially, was dazzled by the image of such a noble character, strong and dashing and honourable.

But Julian Fabre had turned out to be none of those things. Perhaps he never had been and had hidden his true nature behind vaunted objectives, a glib tongue and a sheen of dazzling charm. And far away from Grim's End in the wretched heat of foreign climes, he revealed himself.

'But he did not return,' Sabina simply said. 'At first, his father claimed that he was missing, and we waited, but as the years went by, we lost hope.' Sabina's mouth twisted at the word. 'And other stories began to trickle into Grim's End that told, not of noble deeds, but of a newly sworn knight who fled, deserting his countrymen in the midst of battle.'

But still Sabina held fast, refusing to believe such things about the man to whom she was pledged until one night he appeared in her bedchamber, hiding from his father, from her father, and from any who would call him traitor. 'And then early this year, he came back,' Sabina said.

'When?' Ursula asked. 'You said nothing!'

'And why would I speak of it?' Sabina asked. 'Offering no apology for his long silence, he dismissed the accusations against him with his usual ease and charm, focusing instead upon a gold coin he had found while hiding in the ruins near the mound. I told him that it could have been dropped by any passer-by, but he insisted it was just as the old stories said: the treasure lies beneath the grim.'

Ursula ducked her head, obviously embarrassed by whatever part she had played, while Sabina continued. 'I told him we had no fortune, that he of all people should know that. And when I refused to help him defile the dragon's burial place or speak to my father about such a plan, he simply…disappeared.'

Afterwards, Sabina tried to forget his very existence, especially since she neither heard nor saw any more of him. 'As far as I know, he never approached his family, and his father began to say he was dead, for that was preferable to the rumours. I, too, declared him dead, rather than face the curiosity of the villagers.'

Sabina had even forbade Ursula, who doted on Julian, to speak of him, but she shook her head now at such folly. 'I might have convinced myself he was gone, but he stayed nearby, wreaking havoc on his own family, on the people he once called neighbors.'

At Ursula's curious look, Sabina spread her arm toward the steps. 'Just now, upstairs, he called himself *The Dragon*! He is to blame for all this, the attacks on the people, the animals, my father…' Sabina could not continue, while the residents of Grim's End exclaimed in horror.

Peregrine, alone, seemed unsurprised by her revelations. 'He must have learned to send fire through the air in the Holy Land, just as Lord de Burgh guessed. And the other sound… You said he was a blacksmith? Perhaps that was the sound of a bellows.'

'Surely not,' Ursula protested.

'It would have to be a large one, specially made,' Alec said. 'But, yes, that is what it sounded like sometimes, the roar of a bellows!'

'He used the old legend against you, taking advantage of people's fears,' Peregrine said.

Sabina nodded. 'He thought we would all go, but when I did not, he set Urban to spy upon us.'

'Urban! That coward,' Ursula said, with a sniff of disgust. 'I never liked him.'

'Do you suppose this Dragon set Urban to digging on purpose, with the hope that we might do his searching for him?' Peregrine asked.

'Perhaps,' Sabina said. 'He bragged about us doing his work.'

'Or else Urban grew impatient with the waiting and decided to have a look himself,' Ursula said.

'But if he knows we found nothing, why did he come here and accost you?' Peregrine asked.

Sabina shook her head. 'He kept asking me where the treasure was even though I told him we had found nothing.'

For a long moment, there was silence in the hall, then Peregrine spoke, his expression thoughtful. 'He must think you know something.'

'About what?' Sabina asked.

'About this legend of treasure or hoard of coins,' Peregrine said. 'That's probably why he's let you stay, in case he might need you to provide him with some secret information or lead him to it.'

'To *what*?' Sabina asked, exasperated. 'We've already looked under the grim. Whether that means the dragon or Cyneric the Grim or some ancient ship, there still was nothing there. I don't know anything else.'

'Perhaps you do,' Peregrine said. 'Think.'

Sabina shook her head, but she searched her memory, repeating again what they had already discussed. 'As Ursula said, the treasure lies under the grim. That's what she heard my grandfather say, and that's what my father told me.'

'What did your father say?' Ursula asked, leaning forwards. 'When was this?'

'When he lay dying before his own manor, stricken by the man he would have taken in as a son…' Sabina's throat constricted, and she took a moment to compose herself. 'He made me swear to hold the village together, to keep his home and his heritage. And he said, *"If you have a need…look under the old grim."*'

'The old grim,' Peregrine repeated. He gave her a speculative glance. 'You are certain he said old?'

Sabina nodded, though she was impatient with such nonsense. 'What is the difference? Of course the grim is old. Grim's End was founded years and years ago.'

Peregrine looked pensive. 'Yes, but what if there are two dragons, one old and one new?'

'There is only one mound,' Alec said.

'Yes, but the mound is not specified, just the word *grim*, which has been passed down by the Sextons throughout generations,' Peregrine noted. 'Where might there be another grim?'

It was the mention of the Sextons that made Sabina draw in a sharp breath. 'The church,' she said. 'The Sextons have always tended the churches, and the dragon decorated the side of both, the new church and the old one.'

Ursula was on her feet in an instant. 'It must be buried beneath the ruins, where Julian found his coin.'

Alec, too, had risen and was headed toward the extra implements that they kept in the hall for working the mound. 'Let's go see!'

Sabina glanced at Peregrine, unwilling to do anything without Lord de Burgh. 'But you told us to remain here,' she said.

Unlike his master, who was always decisive, Peregrine appeared uncertain. 'We can wait, or we could look now, while we know that your betrothed is well away.'

'*He is not my betrothed,*' Sabina said, rising from her chair. She wished now that she had kept her father's message to herself, for she saw no point in any further digging. Whatever words had been repeated over the years were just that, words meant to comfort the living in the throes of grief, tales as fanciful as Gamel's ramblings.

But Ursula was already headed toward the doors, and Peregrine, though much to be admired, was still enough of a boy to want to join Alec in the search. Sabina, alone, seemed reluctant, dreading the prospect of uncovering even more remains, this time in holy ground.

'What about Lord de Burgh?' Sabina asked. What if he returned to find them gone, or, worse yet, needed their help?

Peregrine obviously did not share her concern, for he smiled in grim assurance. 'Lord de Burgh can take care of himself.'

Still, Sabina kept a watchful eye on the area as they left the manor. The others, except for Adele, seemed too eager, while each step towards the old church filled Sabina with a sense of doom. She might have halted them, but she didn't know whether it was the fears that made her uneasy or legitimate worries. She had been stricken too often when faced with nothing to trust her instincts any longer.

So she simply followed behind as Alec led the way, hopping over the crumbling side of one old wall with ease. He combed the inside, pushing aside tall grasses and pieces of old tiles, while wondering aloud about the best place to dig.

'The dragon is over here, on the outside,' Ursula said, pointing to the only wall that still stood mostly intact.

Sabina shivered. Was there some significance to that fact? She had often thought that everything in Grim's End might fall to dust, but the dragon would remain. Yet, there was no dragon, only an old ship and the bones of a dead man.

'There's a grim inside, too,' Alec said, but Peregrine was already standing before the smaller carving.

'*Repent and Seek Your Reward,*' the squire read aloud. He turned to Sabina, as though the words held a meaning that only she could divine. 'Perhaps this indicates where the treasure is hidden.'

Sabina shook her head at what she had always viewed as sound religious advice. And yet, even to her, the word *reward* now seemed fraught with import. She drew in a sharp breath, and Peregrine, seeing her response, turned and began to dig below where the message was carved.

Distancing herself from the others, Sabina sat upon an old stump, away from the ruins, and tried to contain her growing sense of dread. If only Lord de Burgh would return… But such thoughts invariably choked her, so Sabina concentrated only on the forms of the two boys, Peregrine and Alec, digging below the church wall.

How long would they work before everyone agreed that there was no hoard of gold hidden in Grim's End? Or would they simply move on to another spot? Sabina frowned, for surely they would decide the Marking Stone was next, full of some subtle meaning beyond denoting boundaries.

Sabina distracted herself with such thoughts for a while, but it seemed that hardly any time had gone by when Alec gave a shout. Ursula and Adele crowded round Peregrine, and Sabina heard their gasps, yet was afraid to join them, for fear 'twas someone's grave they had disturbed.

But then they parted, looking to her as one, and Sabina finally rose and walked to where they all stood. She saw nothing upon the ground, but when she reached Peregrine, he held out a piece of jewellery, gold with some kind of gemstone blinking in the light of the lowering sun.

Peregrine handed it to her, and Sabina clutched it tightly, her knees weak. She said nothing, but sank upon a fallen stone nearby to study the precious item more closely. It looked none the worst for having been entombed, and for how long? But Sabina knew that one piece of jewellery did not constitute a hoard. The item could have been lost here or gifted to the old church, though she knew of no one in Grim's End who had ever possessed such a thing.

'Twas not worth a fortune, but enough to help repay Lord de Burgh for all he had done for them, Sabina thought, as well as provide some money for the villagers. Now that she knew Julian had deliberately destroyed Grim's End, Sabina did not know whether she could ever revive it. Even if she could, it would never be the same. *She* would never be the same…

A shout from Alec dragged Sabina from her gloomy thoughts, but she had barely risen from her makeshift seat when he gave out another. And another. And soon there was no denying that they had found more than one valuable. In fact, the enormity of the discovery stole her breath.

While Sabina watched, stunned, Peregrine spread the bounty upon the grass: other pieces of exotic jewellery, a purse containing the fabled gold coins, gold buckles, a set of silver dishes the like of which Sabina had never seen, a loose coin, a gold finger ring, a golden sceptre fit for a king, a lyre, and clasps of silver and gold. 'Twas indeed a treasure beyond anyone's imagining.

'But what is this? Why is it here?' Sabina asked.

Everyone looked down at the priceless hoard, as though struck dumb, but finally Alec spoke. 'Gamel used to tell us tales of a great king, buried with all his wealth, so maybe this was all his.'

'Buried beneath the church?' Sabina asked, with a shudder.

'Buried within the mound,' Peregrine said. 'I would guess that these are the king's riches, but they were moved long ago, perhaps before they were even covered with earth.'

'Are you saying my ancestors were grave robbers?' Sabina asked, shocked.

'I doubt a true thief would rebury these things and leave such record of his work,' Peregrine said. 'Perhaps the first church sexton did not approve of a pagan burial and put these valuables away for the future people of Grim's End.'

'Isn't that a lovely tale?'

At the sound of Julian's voice, Sabina jerked, dropping the piece of jewellery she held in her hand. Turning, she saw him step out from behind a falling corner of the ruined building, his sword drawn.

'It absolves the Sextons from any wrongdoing, while

allowing those few residents left to claim all,' Julian said, with a sneer. 'But I'm afraid that I'll be taking it, so you won't have to worry over the question of ownership. Come, Sabina, and perhaps I'll let you have some of your family's ill-gotten gains. After all, you've waited long enough for them.'

'I'm not going anywhere with you,' Sabina said. 'You are dead to me!'

'Harsh words from my betrothed,' Julian said. ''Twas only my wits that saved me from certain death in places you can't even pronounce.'

'They served you ill, then,' Sabina said. 'Better that you had died a noble death in the Holy Land, befitting a great knight, than break all your oaths and vows to honour none but yourself.'

While Sabina spoke, Peregrine moved as if to draw his sword, but Julian stepped forwards with a warning for the squire. 'Don't provoke me, boy,' he said. 'I'm still smarting from your poke in my leg.'

Peregrine's mouth fell open. 'You! You're the one who attacked us on the road.'

'And, if you remember, I'm not one to be trifled with,' Julian said smugly.

'My recollection is different, for I remember that Lord de Burgh routed you easily,' Peregrine said, his expression one of contempt.

'I could argue, but why bother?' Julian asked, with a smirk. 'Your precious knight isn't here, is he?'

'Oh, but you are mistaken.'

Sabina swayed upon her feet as Lord de Burgh stepped out of the shadows of the wall that still stood, putting himself neatly between them and Julian. Still, Sabina had enough sense to pull at the others, backing away from Julian, lest he try to seize them to save himself.

Once he saw what she was about, Peregrine urged them to shelter behind the low crumbling portion of one wall, while Julian and Lord de Burgh circled one another, swords drawn.

'So we meet again,' Julian said. 'Let me introduce myself. I am *The Dragon*.'

If he thought mere words would daunt his opponent, Julian was mistaken for Lord de Burgh showed not a flicker of surprise on his grim countenance.

'And I am the wolf,' Lord de Burgh said. 'The dragon is showy and full of hot air, while the wolf is silent and deadly, an enemy to be reckoned with.'

Sabina glanced at Peregrine.

'The wolf is the de Burgh device,' the boy whispered.

Julian laughed, as though amused by Lord de Burgh's speech. 'I have no quarrel with you.'

'But I have a quarrel with you, for you are responsible for the abandonment of Grim's End,' Lord de Burgh said.

Julian nodded, as if in acknowledgement of praise. 'I was hiding in the ruins for a few days, assessing my future, when it shone brightly before me in the form of a gold coin. Unfortunately, while borrowing some goods from the village, I ran into Urban. But the poor steward, discontented with his lot, was greedy enough…er, eager to share in the promised riches.'

Sabina could see Julian slowly changing position while talking, and she wanted to shout an alarm to Lord

de Burgh, but Peregrine squeezed her arm in warning.
For Lord de Burgh was moving as well, unaffected by
Julian's chatter.

'At first I used a bellows to scare them, easily enough
for me to construct with materials borrowed from my
father,' Julian said. 'Perhaps Sabina remembers when he
complained of thievery, for I did not bother to make
myself known.'

And for good reason, Sabina thought, for John
Fabre was a decent man. Hearing rumours was one
thing, but facing the truth about his son would have
broken his spirit.

'I killed the animals or drove them off, with the help
of Urban, who conveniently opened gates or alerted me
to any unwelcome attention and whispered of the worm,
urging all to hide. It was simple, really. The fools were
easily led. Just a few choice words, a few grisly animal
slayings, and they fled.'

'But sooner or later, they would realise that no one
had seen the beast,' Lord de Burgh said.

'Not really,' Julian said. 'There are always those
who will lay claim to special knowledge—even a
dragon sighting—in order to gain attention. But some
people were tenacious, and that's when I had to get
creative. Luckily, I had learned something from my
travels and was able to concoct some dragon fire to
scare off the rest.'

'You could have burned down the whole village,'
Lord de Burgh said, still matching his movements to
Julian's slow circling.

'That might have been simpler.'

'But there was something else you wanted,' Lord de Burgh said.

'Not something, but someone. The longer Sabina lingered, the more I began to think I might have use of her,' Julian said, and he suddenly lunged forwards.

But Lord de Burgh easily deflected his sword, and Julian backed away, smiling. 'I see that little Sabina has found her knight, at last, after long years of pining after a hero from the romances, someone full of nobility and honour. In short, a creature that has nothing to do with real men and real battles.'

'Perhaps 'tis you who has little to do with what makes a man,' Lord de Burgh suggested.

Julian's mouth twisted. 'Yes, I see that she has her knight,' he said. 'Too bad he's a cripple.'

Sabina gasped as Julian swung his sword, but Lord de Burgh did not waver, deflecting the blow while seeking an opening, intent solely upon his enemy.

Again the swords clashed, a horrible sound in the stillness of early evening, and Sabina realised that Julian, though slighter, was more agile, quick and clever, spitting out taunts to distract his opponent. But Lord de Burgh was larger, steadier and implacable. He had the greater strength…as long as his leg held.

The thought made Sabina's breath catch, and she blinked in horror. *Not now*, she thought. *Not when Lord de Burgh might be killed.* She tried to concentrate on his tall form, but when Julian's blade sliced too close, it was too much for her.

She began to tremble and shiver, both hot and cold, and as the fear overwhelmed her, she couldn't breath.

Faint now, she hunched upon the grass, seeking great gulps of air, while Peregrine and Ursula clutched at her, trying to help. But there was nothing anyone could do, except Lord de Burgh, and the thought of him only worsened her state until the painful sounds of her gasping must have reached the fighting men.

'What's the matter, Sabina?' Julian called. 'Afraid I'm going to hurt your noble knight?'

While Lord de Burgh had paid no heed to Julian's earlier taunts, he flicked a glance towards her now. It lasted only an instant, but that was long enough for Julian to lift his sword with both hands, swinging hard at Lord de Burgh's neck, trying to decapitate him.

As Sabina froze in horror, Lord de Burgh danced out of the way, but Julian's blade sliced through his tunic, revealing a crimson stain. His shoulder was cut.

Sabina blinked, her vision so blurred that she was not sure what was happening. She only heard Julian gloating, already proclaiming his victory as the swords clanged again. And then Julian, with the cunning Sabina had expected, thrust out a foot, as though to kick Lord de Burgh's bad leg out from underneath him. But somehow Lord de Burgh managed to use the action against his opponent. The blow meant to knock him from his feet caught Julian off balance, and he fell on to his back in the grass.

Before Sabina realised what had happened, Lord de Burgh had his foot upon Julian's wrist and his sword at Julian's throat, demanding surrender. At the thought that the battle was over, Sabina began to breathe again. But then she saw the glint of metal as Julian's left hand produced a blade. And 'twas not any blade, but a devious device, one he had crafted himself or obtained in foreign lands. Although Sabina could not see it closely, even she could tell that the narrow weapon was intended to slip through chain mail.

A cry lodged in Sabina's throat as Julian thrust it upwards, but at the last minute Lord de Burgh twisted his body. And instead of plunging into his gut, the knife sliced through a pouch that hung from Lord de Burgh's belt, spilling its contents into the air. From where Sabina knelt, the setting sun's rays caught tiny bits of what looked like powder, yet when they drifted on to Julian, who lay below, he began screaming.

'What is it, lye?' Alec asked, his voice cracking with horror.

'I don't know,' Peregrine said in hushed tones. ''Twas something given to him by the l'Estranges, so it could be magic.'

Whether simple lye or some enchanted dust, it must have burned Julian, for his arms flailed, as if to brush it off. Then he clutched at his eyes and writhed upwards, effectively cutting his own throat. Still, he was able to heave himself forwards, knocking Lord de Burgh to the ground, and they struggled, blood flowing over them.

Too stricken to watch, Sabina turned her head away only to see Urban charging at the residents of Grim's End, pitchfork in hand. He was coming directly towards her, and Sabina, dazed and weary, could only stare as certain death approached. But then she was rolled aside, and it was Peregrine that was struck by the weapon.

The sight of Lord de Burgh's young squire prone, maybe even dead, gave Sabina new strength. She leapt at the pitchfork, but it danced around wildly. A glance told her that Alec had thrown himself upon Urban's back.

'Get off me!' Urban muttered. 'We must take what we can before the rest of them come. That's why I used the bellows to alert you all.'

'To alert Julian,' Ursula said, and she and Adele hurled chunks of stone at the steward until he lost his footing and Alec jumped free. Urban fell, striking his head on one of the heavy stones with a final gasp.

Sabina drew in a long, shuddering breath, unable to do aught else for one long moment. But then she was roused by a new sound and turned to see a group of men on horseback veer off the road towards where the last residents of Grim's End waited.

''Tis the rest of them that Urban mentioned,' Alec said, his eyes wide.

Sabina could only stare, as well. There were so many of them, all dark and mailed and heavily armed, that she knew that there would be no fending off Julian's companions with pieces of the crumbling church.

But the first man's massive horse did not even pause in its gait as it went by them, as if both they and the treasure itself were insignificant. Instead, the beast stopped where Lord de Burgh lay, covered in blood, a lifeless Julian by his side.

'Ho, brother, we have come to aid you,' the man on the horse said. Lifting his helm, he revealed a handsome face that bore no little resemblance to Lord de Burgh. 'What say you?' he asked.

Sabina had no breath left to gasp as Lord de Burgh rose on one elbow, clutching his shoulder, to grunt in answer, 'Your timing could have been better.'

Chapter Sixteen

Reynold smiled as he looked out over Sexton manor's hall, which was no longer empty, but full of the residents of Grim's End, members of the de Burgh train and his brothers. Surely, he had never seen such a welcome sight as Dunstan looming over him, offering aid as he lay wounded. At first, Reynold had thought himself dreaming, and, indeed, after answering his brother, he had promptly lost consciousness.

But now he was awake and whole and seated on a bench at the trestle table, while Mistress Sexton stood beside him, tending to his shoulder. And after weeks spent isolated in an abandoned village, he was eager for the things he once had decried: people, talk, *family*.

They were all here. They said that Campion had been against everyone travelling together, but no one wanted to be left behind. As eldest, Dunstan had led the train, which meant that either Simon had mellowed since his marriage or the two were at loggerheads throughout the journey.

'But how did you know where to find me?' Reynold

asked. He threw the question into the buzz of chatter, and at the sound of his voice, those around him quieted.

'You should know better than to start something with the locals,' Simon said, with a snort.

'What? But there is no one here except Mistress Sexton and a handful of residents,' Reynold said. 'They are all who are left of Grim's End.'

Stephen shuddered as though the very idea made his skin crawl. 'Well, yes, but you had to complain to Cyppe about it.'

Cyppe? For a moment Reynold was at a loss. Then he remembered his visit to Baderton, where he had commissioned the dragon's chain and tried to speak to those who held the manor there. 'But I didn't even talk to anyone. I was turned away at the door.'

'A de Burgh turned away,' Robin muttered.

'Fools!' Dunstan said.

'He didn't know who he was dealing with,' Simon said, his lips curling.

'What? Slow down,' Reynold said.

'Whoever turned you away at the door must have sent a report to Lord Cyppe, who then sent a message to Campion telling Father to keep his nose out of his business,' Geoff explained.

'*What?*' Reynold barked out a laugh.

'Yes, he was just asking for trouble,' Nicholas said, with a grin.

'Naturally, Father was curious,' Geoffrey said.

'*Naturally,*' Reynold repeated, his lips curving.

'And he contacted his friend Welsham.'

'Welsham, as in the Earl of Welsham?' Reynold asked.

Geoffrey nodded. 'He just happened to be Cyppe's liege lord, so Welsham did a little investigating of his own and found out that his estates were being woefully mismanaged.'

'Imagine his disgust,' Stephen said. 'Welsham's away at war in Wales, fighting for his country, while Cyppe is neglecting his duties, playing at court and spending his liege lord's fortune.'

'So Welsham stripped Cyppe of his lands,' Dunstan said, with a slow smile. 'And all thanks to you, brother.'

'Well, if it brings his attention to the situation here, then I am glad of it,' Reynold said, but as he spoke, he felt Mistress Sexton's fingers falter in their bandaging. And he realised that with the dragon dead, there was no reason for him to remain here. His brothers would expect him to return with them…home to Campion.

Reynold knew he should say something, but what? And already Dunstan was barrelling ahead. 'If we are to have a feast, we will need more supplies than those we brought with us,' the eldest de Burgh said. He ate like a horse and probably could have consumed all of the village's provisions single-handedly. 'Perhaps I should make a trip to this Baderton tomorrow.'

Several of his brothers volunteered to go along on the journey, leaving Reynold free to stay here, at least for one more day… 'Good idea,' Reynold said. 'I have a commission at the blacksmith's that you can pick up for me, as well.'

Again, Mistress Sexton's fingers faltered, but she said nothing, while Dunstan nodded, oblivious to the undercurrents between them.

'Thank you, brother,' Reynold said. 'Oh, and you'd better take a cart with you.'

* * *

'What ails Dunstan?' Nicholas asked. Although he had not gone on the journey to Baderton, the youngest de Burgh had been restless all day and now stood watching at the windows of the hall for the others to return.

Professing ignorance, Reynold rose to join him at the window, where he saw that Dunstan had halted the train in front of the manor and was now leaping to the ground as though pricked by his saddle.

Biting back a smile, Reynold moved to the doors and went outside, followed by Nicholas and the others who had remained behind. There they met a scowling Dunstan, who stopped before Reynold, elbows akimbo.

'Well, I've got it, but I don't know what the hell you're going to do with it,' he said.

Reynold burst out laughing, while everyone crowded around the cart that held a chain so large it could have no possible use. Reynold only wished Peregrine was here to see the end result of all their discussions of worm lore.

'Perhaps you should hang it over your doors as a warning to all who would enter,' Nicholas suggested, glancing at the manor.

'Likely 'twould fall and kill someone,' Stephen said, drily.

But Reynold frowned, puzzled over the reference to his doors. Did they expect him to cart the chain back to Campion? His mood having soured, he said nothing, but returned to the hall, where the supplies Dunstan had brought were soon put to good use.

When the food was prepared and the table piled high, Reynold called everyone into the hall, even those who would serve the feast, while Peregrine was carried down from his bed to be given the seat of honour. He looked curious, but pleased as he was settled into the chair that had belonged to Mistress Sexton's father, a seat that had long stood vacant.

Then Reynold stood back to address those who filled the room. 'Residents of Grim's End, my brothers, and all who would travel with them, I would have you witness this momentous occasion,' Reynold called out. 'As a de Burgh, son of Fawke, Earl of Campion, and a knight, I am here to commend my squire, Peregine l'Estrange, for bravery in battle, for intelligence and strength and skill in weaponry, but most of all for his great heart.'

Peregrine glanced at him in surprise, and Reynold smiled, his throat suddenly thick as he drew his sword. 'Thus, I would raise him to knighthood.'

Peregrine's expression of shock made Reynold bite back a smile as he faced the youth soberly. 'Will you follow these commandments, to obey God's laws and to commit no treason or agree to false judgement? And to honour all women and be prepared to help any in need?'

Peregrine flashed a grin, and Reynold knew he was thinking of their efforts to aid the resident damsel in distress, Mistress Sexton. 'I will,' the boy said.

'Then I dub you Sir Peregrine, a member of the knighthood of chivalry, which is without villainy.'

Peregrine rose unsteadily to his feet, aided by Alec, his ever-present companion now, and the hall erupted in cheers. When at last they had died down, Mistress Sexton stepped forwards and raised her cup.

'Let the feast begin,' she said.

Reynold took his place on one of the benches near the head of the table and watched the gathering in the hall as proudly as if it were his own. And if the residents of Grim's End stuffed themselves far more than was polite, they were to be excused. Reynold was all the more pleased for it, but he ate little, leaving Simon the lion's share of the trencher they shared.

'Feeling a little poorly, are you?' Simon asked, with a knowing smirk. 'Unable to eat or sleep?'

'No, I am fine,' Reynold said, though his shoulder still burned like fire.

Simon glanced to where Mistress Sexton sat beside Peregrine at the head of the table, and he kept smirking. 'Right,' he muttered.

Having no desire to get into a lengthy discussion with the least sensitive of the de Burghs, Reynold soon rose to check upon Peregrine, who looked sated, but weary and in pain. Although Mistress Sexton said he was healing nicely, Reynold still worried.

'I'll have one of my brothers carry you up,' Reynold said, wincing at the shoulder he did not trust yet with such a precious burden.

'You must take back your bed, my lord,' Peregrine said. 'I would have my pallet once more.'

'Nonsense,' Reynold said. 'I am more comfortable bedding down in the hall with my brothers.' And it was true. *The further he was away from Mistress Sexton, the better.*

'Thank *you*, my lord,' Peregrine said. 'And thank

you for this.' Peregrine's short sword lay upon his lap, a symbol of his new station.

'Thank you,' Reynold said, and he meant it. For if not for his squire's quick thinking and selfless action, Mistress Sexton might be dead. It was something Reynold could not bear to think about, along with the awful suspicions he'd had when he followed Julian Fabre back to the manor. He was ashamed of them now, for Mistress Sexton had proven herself many times over to be a woman worthy of his love. *If only he were worthy of her...*

As if to reassure himself that she was alive and whole, Reynold's gaze drifted towards where she sat, back straight, her hair glinting in the candlelight more brightly than any treasure. Was it any wonder that he had fallen under her spell, along with everyone else? The thought made him turn towards Peregrine, another of her conquests.

'Now that you are a knight, you can more easily pursue the lady you hold dear,' Reynold teased.

But the youth's reaction was not what Reynold expected. Indeed, his expression of denial was almost comical. Was he shocked that others should divine a devotion he thought well hidden?

'She's not—' Peregrine began. 'I mean, Mistress Sexton is very nice, but she is old and not even as pretty as Celia, the dairy maid at my home manor.'

'What?' Reynold asked. 'But I thought... You were most concerned with her for someone who professes no interest.'

Peregrine's look told Reynold plainly that he thought

his former master a dunce. 'I was interested in her because I knew she was meant for you,' the boy said. 'I've always known she was for you because that was part of the quest, winning the hand of the damsel in distress.'

Reynold frowned at the reminder of that nonsense. He gave no credence to the l'Estranges' predictions even though their gift of a bag of lye had probably saved his skin. And as for Mistress Sexton… 'She deserves better,' Reynold muttered.

'That's what she says of you, that you should not be burdened with someone who is afflicted as she is, though I don't know what she's talking about,' Peregrine said, shaking his head.

He glanced up at Reynold, seemingly more mystified than by any arcane dragon lore. 'What a pair you are to think neither one is good enough for the other!'

Long after the celebration was over and the residents of Grim's End and members of the visitors' train had settled upon their pallets in the cellars, the de Burgh brothers still lingered at the table, cups of ale scattered atop the worn surface.

They had talked for hours, and Reynold had listened quietly as they shared the joys of their lives, their wives, their children, their lands. But the conversation had died down, as though there was a subject none wanted to broach.

Finally, Dunstan as the eldest, spoke. 'The feast 'twas well done, Reynold, but I don't think the provisions here can feed us for long,' he said. 'Now that we are assured you are well, we must take that news to Father and on to our own homes.'

'Yes, Marion will be worried, as will Elene,' Geoff said.

Reynold nodded as he absently rubbed his bad leg. He had known it was coming, of course. There wasn't enough here to supply even a small train for long, and it would take some time to sort out the sale of the treasure that Mistress Sexton would split among her faithful few.

Reynold glanced around the table, where six dark heads were bent, and he guessed his brothers were reluctant to leave so soon. But all except Nicholas had families to return to, responsibilities that they could not ignore indefinitely. Reynold didn't know how they had all managed to come, scattered as they were, yet they had come, and he was grateful to them.

Now it was time for him to go home, too.

'When do we leave?' he asked. He looked down at the rough fingers that did not massage his aches as well as a certain mistress. The future that he had long avoided was here, and no more would he have to refuse her ministrations, deny his feelings, fight temptation. Yet, he felt no relief at the prospect.

'What do you mean, *we*?' Dunstan asked, in a low growl.

''Tis time I returned home, as well, to Campion,' Reynold said, even though the words stuck in his throat. Even though Campion no longer seemed home to him. Even though he felt like he belonged here, master of this hall and of the small band that had become like family to him.

'Why would you come with us?' Geoff asked.

'We've all seen the way you look at Mistress Sexton and the way she looks at you—'

Reynold cut him off, for he'd had a bellyful of stories and fancies. 'You know why.'

In the ensuing silence, Reynold realised they were all staring at him, as though bewildered. Annoyed, he was no longer willing to pretend, so he spat out the truth. 'Because of my leg.' *There*, he'd said it. It was out in the open, something they could not ignore. Let them flinch from him now.

But they still looked bewildered.

'What does it have to do with anything?' Nicholas asked.

Reynold could not believe that they would still attempt to overlook what he had struggled with all of his life. 'It may have escaped your notice, but I was born with a bad leg. And all your years of ignoring it have not made it go away!'

He had spoken so loudly that they all appeared startled. Unlike volatile Simon, Reynold never raised his voice. He didn't lose his temper. He just slunk away, hiding himself. But he wasn't going to hide himself any more just to make their lives easier.

'Whoa,' Stephen said. 'We are all fully aware that you were born with a bad leg. We were there, remember? Well, all except Nicholas.'

'Well, you have certainly tried your best to disregard it ever since,' Reynold said, glaring at them all.

Again, they seemed startled, and Simon lurched to his feet as though to take a swing at him. For once,

Reynold welcomed the fight, and he rose, too, despite his painful shoulder. But Geoffrey put a hand on Simon's arm, and he sank back down upon the bench as the moment, fraught with tension, passed.

'Rey, I never ignored it,' Nicholas said. 'I just, well, forgot about it.'

'You're as capable as anyone else, so why would we treat you any differently?' Simon asked, scowling.

'And you hated being fussed over,' Stephen said. He turned to Geoff. 'Remember when Father brought in that old woman to look after him?'

Geoff nodded. 'After our mother died.'

'Three years old, with a bad leg, and he knocked her down and ran away,' Stephen drawled, and his brothers laughed.

For a moment, Reynold was nonplussed. Then the memory, locked away with so much from his early childhood, returned with astonishing clarity. It wasn't the old woman he hated, but the coddling, the idea that he was to lie down in a darkened room while his brothers were out playing, that his leg would keep him from running with them…

'You wouldn't hold still for any treatments, which Father was wary of anyway,' Geoffrey said. 'He'd read some Arabic texts on medicine and had a jaundiced view of the kind of care offered to you.'

'Didn't they want to rub his leg with the fat of a criminal, just executed?' Simon asked, with a snort.

'Yes, and I remember that Father wouldn't let them bleed you, either,' Dunstan said.

'You know Father,' Geoff said. 'He said, *"The damage*

is done, and we cannot expect to undo it. Reynold must learn to live with it."'

Reynold could only gape at his brothers in astonishment as they blithely discussed what he had never heard before or else had long forgotten.

'We could all see you didn't like being treated differently,' Robin said, with a shrug of apology. 'So we didn't.'

And with those simple words, Reynold was faced with the jarring realisation that all these years he had resented something that he brought on himself. He had deemed them all thoughtless, when they were trying to be thoughtful.

'Hell, it's not like it stops you from doing anything,' Simon said, with a grunt. 'Dunstan's probably got more aches and pains from the beatings he received from Fitzhugh's minions.'

Simon's look plainly told Reynold to stop whining, and Reynold felt his resentment return, for it was easy for his whole-and-hale brother to talk. But then Simon lifted one shoulder, grimacing as he moved it gingerly. 'And my shoulder hasn't been right since that mine caved in on me.'

'I know Father's joints bother him,' Geoffrey said. 'Joy has made him some unguent. You should ask her to make you some, as well.'

'God knows I won't get any unguents from Bethia,' Simon said, with a snort, and several of the de Burghs laughed. 'Though she has other virtues that more than make up for any lack,' Simon added quickly, his lips curving.

And just that easily, Reynold's anger was gone, burned away like the tops of the fields at Grim's End, scrubbed clean even of its ash. His family accepted him as he was, and he had been a fool to think otherwise.

'We all have our problems,' Robin said. 'Poor Dunstan had to have suffered as the eldest of this brood.'

'Nay, he was born full grown with a sword in his hand,' Simon said.

'And Simon was born to compete with him,' Stephen noted, and they all looked at Simon, who scowled at the insight.

'And poor Geoffrey could have been a great scholar, if he'd just been born into another clan,' Stephen said.

'I am still a great scholar,' Geoff said, and they all laughed.

None dared look at Stephen, only now coming into his own after years of swilling wine kept him sharp-tongued and dull-witted. And perhaps that had been more of a burden than his own, Reynold realised.

'Well, my only handicap has been trying to get you oafs to laugh once in a while,' Robin said, drawing more laughter.

And what of Nick? Reynold wondered. But when his brothers looked at him, the youngest de Burgh simply smiled and shook his head.

It seemed that they had all made peace with their place in the family, and Reynold was glad of it, but his brothers were accepting in a way that others were not. And it was that harsh truth that kept him determined to leave on the morrow.

'Perhaps you saw no difference in me,' Reynold said

slowly, reaching for his cup to drink the last bitter dregs. 'But what of Amice?'

'Who?' Nicholas asked. As the youngest, Nick might not remember, but Reynold was puzzled when his other brothers all eyed him curiously.

'Amice Fauchet,' Reynold said, impatiently.

'One of Lord Fauchet's daughters?' Geoff asked.

'Is he talking about when we all stayed there?' Robin asked, turning towards Geoffrey.

'Reynold was taken with her,' Stephen drawled.

'And she wasn't taken with him?' Robin asked.

'No,' Reynold said. 'She stated very plainly that she did not want the *lame one*.'

'What a bitch,' Stephen said.

'I saw her once at court, and believe me, she has not improved,' Dunstan said. 'She has her husband by the short hairs, demanding furs and jewels and trinkets, lest she complain to her father.'

'Her sisters are no better,' Geoff said.

'Cease your gossiping like fishwives,' Simon said. 'What is the point of this prattle?'

'The point is that she rejected me!' Reynold said.

'And thank God for it,' Stephen observed drily. Then he slanted a sharp glance at Reynold. 'Surely you are not still disturbed by that? You were only a boy and she a ninny.'

Reynold felt his resentment return. ''Tis easy for you to say when you are all whole! No woman has ever looked at me.' *There*. Now this fact, too, was out, though even Reynold wanted to cringe from it. Sullenly, he glanced around the table, but the reaction was not what he expected. In fact, Dunstan threw back his head and laughed, followed by the rest of them.

'What is so funny?' Reynold demanded, half-rising from his seat.

'Settle down,' Dunstan said, with a grunt. 'If I wanted two Simons, I would have begged Campion for twins.'

'And if I had known you were the least bit interested in the opposite gender, I could have sent many fine specimens your way,' Stephen said.

While Reynold sat gaping, they all named women who had asked them about him, who had been interested in the brooding de Burgh, who looks so intense. It was all too incredible to believe. Indeed, Reynold might have suspected them of hoaxing him, but they would not lie just to make him feel better.

And in that moment, he realised that what Peregrine had said just might be true. He had grown up wealthy and free from want in a household such as few would know. He had not been fostered out to strangers, deprived of comforts or companionship. He had been surrounded by a family who loved him enough to see him as an equal, with no limits to what he could do. How many, even those born whole, could say that?

Yet Reynold had run from those who cared about him, afraid that he would not measure up, uncomfortable in his own skin. Now it would seem that the only thing holding him back was his own perceptions. Yet, acknowledging these truths was far easier than acting upon them. He squinted into the shadows of the hall.

'I'm still not good enough for Mistress Sexton,' he muttered. 'I've always thought the worst of her, for it was easier than to trust her. Jealousy consumed me only a day ago.'

'Well, hell, we're all jealous,' Dunstan said.

'I am tempted to kill anyone who looks at Bethia,' Simon stated baldly.

Reynold felt a glimmer of hope in the darkness that he had lived with for so long. 'Perhaps if I begged her forgiveness…'

'What? You're not going to tell her you thought the worst? Are you mad?' Robin turned to Simon. 'He's mad.'

'I always thought so,' Simon said.

'Why would you tell her?' Geoffrey asked. 'It might make you feel better, but 'twill only hurt her.'

'Mayhap he wants her to send him away,' Stephen said, with the startling insight he sometimes revealed.

Reynold frowned at his brother's words and shook his head, yet he felt the coward Peregrine had once accused him of being. If he was running from love, it was because of the risks involved, ones far more dangerous than any battle. For, in the end, the weapons of man could only wound his body, while Mistress Sexton wielded a deadlier power.

She could break his heart.

Sabina hurried down to the hall. After the huge feast of the night before, she had slept far too late, yet she blinked in surprise when she reached the bottom of the stairs only to find the room vacant. Had the de Burghs left without even saying goodbye? They had said nothing of their plans, but why else would they all be gone?

Sabina halted, stricken, as she wondered at the inevitable. *Had Reynold left, too?* Her breath caught, and a cry rose to her lips, but it went unspoken when she realised that the hall was not empty. Someone was seated in her father's chair.

Sabina's panic eased, for only one of the de Burghs or their train would sit there. Reynold had studiously avoided taking a seat that might proclaim him master of the hall, her father's heir, her partner…

Composing herself, Sabina walked slowly towards the great carved piece. All she could see was a dark head of hair, which could belong to any of the brothers, though there were subtle differences in shade. But as she neared the figure her heart started beating wildly, as if it knew something she didn't. And when, at last, she reached the head of the table, she turned to find Reynold de Burgh in the seat she had always imagined him.

Without thinking, Sabina threw herself at him, and he caught her easily, taking her upon his lap. But she would not stop there. If this was goodbye, Sabina was determined to seize what she could of him before he departed from her life for ever. Lifting her hands to his face, more beloved to her now than any other, she leaned forwards and kissed him.

Half-expecting him to push her away, as he so often had before, Sabina held his head in her hands, as if to prevent him from escaping. But when her lips touched his, it was clear that he had no intention of backing away. His mouth opened upon hers as though something inside him had been unleashed, and Sabina met his wild hunger with her own.

Finally, when he did break away, it was to cup her

face in his hands and look at her, his often grim features softened by desire. His eyes were bright with it, as well, or was it something else that shone there? Sabina's already-racing heart slammed in her chest.

'Is this goodbye?' she asked.

He shook his head. 'I've a mind to sit here for ever, if you'll let me take your father's seat…and your hand.'

Sabina's hopes soared only to fall once more, and she ducked her head. 'No, my lord,' she said, though they were the most difficult words she had ever uttered. 'For I would not have you burdened with a wife who may be…mad.'

'You are not mad,' he said softly, yet firmly. 'And I would not have you saddled with a husband who is…lame.'

Sabina's head jerked up. 'You are not lame—'

Lord Reynold stopped her protest with a finger to her lips. 'Say yea, then, that you will be my wife, and we will struggle through whatever awaits us, rebuilding Grim's End, holding your heritage, and making a family here. But whatever happens, we will face it together.'

It might have been the longest speech he had ever made to her. Sabina knew it was the most heartrending. And how could she refuse when all she wanted was to remain in this man's arms for the rest of her life?

Sabina nodded, her vision blurred not with fear, but with tears of joy, and she buried her face against his chest, seeking the warm haven that would now never be denied her. Already some of the tenseness within was easing, for if anyone could help her get better, *be* better, it was this man.

'I love you, my lord,' Sabina whispered.

'Reynold,' he said, and she felt him smile against her hair. 'And I love you. 'Tis a risk giving my heart into your keeping, but I must—I will—trust you not to break it.'

Sabina lifted her head and would have answered with a promise, but just then the doors of the manor were flung open, and Nicholas de Burgh hurried into the hall, followed by his brothers.

'Ho, Reynold,' Nicholas called. 'We intercepted a messenger with news for you!'

'For me?' Reynold asked in a tone of surprise, and Sabina was so startled that she did not move from her place.

'It seems that Welsham was so grateful for your help that he has rewarded you with Cyppe's holdings, including much of this area, except for Mistress Sexton's lands, which he graciously continues to grant to her,' Dunstan said. 'And he wishes you to use whatever means necessary to revive Grim's End and the villages within your fiefs.'

Sabina heard Reynold draw in a sharp breath, and she blinked in astonishment, as well.

'So I guess you'll be staying right where you are,' Simon said, bringing up the rear.

'From the looks of him,' Stephen said, as he glanced to where Sabina still sat atop Reynold's lap, her face flaming, 'I'd say he was already planning on it.'

* * * * *

*Celebrate Harlequin's 60th anniversary
with Harlequin® Superromance®
and the* DIAMOND LEGACY *miniseries!*

*Follow the stories of four cousins as they
come to terms with the complications of love and
what it means to be a family. Discover with
them the sixty-year-old secret that rocks not one
but two families in...
A DAUGHTER'S TRUST by Tara Taylor Quinn.*

*Available in September 2009
from Harlequin® Superromance®*

RICK'S APPOINTMENT with his attorney early Wednesday morning went only moderately better than his meeting with social services the day before. The prognosis wasn't great—but at least his attorney was going to file a motion for DNA testing. Just so Rick could petition to see the child…his sister's baby. The sister he didn't know he had until it was too late.

The rest of what his attorney said had been downhill from there.

Cell phone in hand before he'd even reached his Nitro, Rick punched in the speed dial number he'd programmed the day before.

Maybe foster parent Sue Bookman hadn't received his message. Or had lost his number. Maybe she didn't want to talk to him. At this point he didn't much care what she wanted.

"Hello?" She answered before the first ring was complete. And sounded breathless.

Young and breathless.

"Ms. Bookman?"

"Yes. This is Rick Kraynick, right?"

"Yes, ma'am."

"I recognized your number on caller ID," she said, her voice uneven, as though she was still engaged in whatever physical activity had her so breathless to begin with. "I'm sorry I didn't get back to you. I've been a little…distracted."

The words came in more disjointed spurts. Was she jogging?

"No problem," he said, when, in fact, he'd spent the better part of the night before watching his phone. And fretting. "Did I get you at a bad time?"

"No worse than usual," she said, adding, "Better than some. So, how can I help?"

God, if only this could be so easy. He'd ask. She'd help. And life could go well. At least for one little person in his family.

It would be a first.

"Mr. Kraynick?"

"Yes. Sorry. I was…are you sure there isn't a better time to call?"

"I'm bouncing a baby, Mr. Kraynick. It's what I do."

"Is it Carrie?" he asked quickly, his pulse racing.

"How do you know Carrie?" She sounded defensive, which wouldn't do him any good.

"I'm her uncle," he explained, "her mother's— Christy's—older brother, and I know you have her."

"I can neither confirm nor deny your allegations, Mr. Kraynick. Please call social services." She rattled off the number.

"Wait!" he said, unable to hide his urgency. "Please," he said more calmly. "Just hear me out."

"How did you find me?"

"A friend of Christy's."

"I'm sorry I can't help you, Mr. Kraynick," she said softly. "This conversation is over."

"I grew up in foster care," he said, as though that gave him some special privilege. Some insider's edge.

"Then you know you shouldn't be calling me at all."

"Yes… But Carrie is my niece," he said. "I need to see her. To know that she's okay."

"You'll have to go through social services to arrange that."

"I'm sure you know it's not as easy as it sounds. I'm a single man with no real ties and I've no intention of petitioning for custody. They aren't real eager to give me the time of day. I never even knew Carrie's mother. For all intents and purposes, our mother didn't raise either one of us. All I have going for me is half a set of genes. My lawyer's on it, but it could be weeks— months—before this is sorted out. Carrie could be adopted by then. Which would be fine, great for her, but then I'd have lost my chance. I don't want to take her. I won't hurt her. I just have to see her."

"I'm sorry, Mr. Kraynick, but…"

* * * * *

*Find out if Rick Kraynick will ever
have a chance to meet his niece.
Look for A DAUGHTER'S TRUST
by Tara Taylor Quinn,
available in September 2009.*

We'll be spotlighting a different series
every month throughout 2009
to celebrate our 60th anniversary.

Look for Harlequin® Superromance®
in September!

*Celebrate with
The Diamond Legacy
miniseries!*

Follow the stories of four cousins as they come to terms
with the complications of love and what it means to
be a family. Discover with them the sixty-year-old secret
that rocks not one but two families.

A DAUGHTER'S TRUST by *Tara Taylor Quinn*
September

FOR THE LOVE OF FAMILY by *Kathleen O'Brien*
October

LIKE FATHER, LIKE SON by *Karina Bliss*
November

A MOTHER'S SECRET by *Janice Kay Johnson*
December

Available wherever books are sold.

THBPA0108

REQUEST YOUR FREE BOOKS!

Harlequin® Historical
Historical Romantic Adventure!

2 FREE NOVELS PLUS 2 **FREE GIFTS!**

YES! Please send me 2 FREE Harlequin® Historical novels and my 2 FREE gifts (gifts are worth about $10). After receiving them, if I don't wish to receive any more books, I can return the shipping statement marked "cancel". If I don't cancel, I will receive 6 brand-new novels every month and be billed just $4.94 per book in the U.S. or $5.49 per book in Canada. That's a savings of 20% off the cover price! It's quite a bargain! Shipping and handling is just 50¢ per book.* I understand that accepting the 2 free books and gifts places me under no obligation to buy anything. I can always return a shipment and cancel at any time. Even if I never buy another book, the two free books and gifts are mine to keep forever.

246 HDN EYS3 349 HDN EYTF

Name	(PLEASE PRINT)	
Address		Apt. #
City	State/Prov.	Zip/Postal Code

Signature (if under 18, a parent or guardian must sign)

Mail to the **Harlequin Reader Service:**
IN U.S.A.: P.O. Box 1867, Buffalo, NY 14240-1867
IN CANADA: P.O. Box 609, Fort Erie, Ontario L2A 5X3

Not valid to current subscribers of Harlequin Historical books.

Want to try two free books from another line?
Call 1-800-873-8635 or visit www.morefreebooks.com.

* Terms and prices subject to change without notice. Prices do not include applicable taxes. Sales tax applicable in N.Y. Canadian residents will be charged applicable provincial taxes and GST. Offer not valid in Quebec. This offer is limited to one order per household. All orders subject to approval. Credit or debit balances in a customer's account(s) may be offset by any other outstanding balance owed by or to the customer. Please allow 4 to 6 weeks for delivery. Offer available while quantities last.

Your Privacy: Harlequin Books is committed to protecting your privacy. Our Privacy Policy is available online at www.eHarlequin.com or upon request from the Reader Service. From time to time we make our lists of customers available to reputable third parties who may have a product or service of interest to you. If you would prefer we not share your name and address, please check here. ☐

HH09R

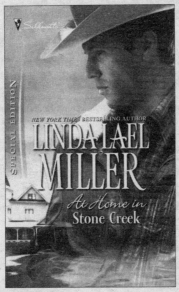

COMING NEXT MONTH FROM
HARLEQUIN®
HISTORICAL

Available August 25, 2009

• **THE PIRATICAL MISS RAVENHURST**
by **Louise Allen**
(Regency)
Forced to flee Jamaica disguised as a boy, Clemence Ravenhurst falls
straight into the clutches of one of the most dangerous pirates in the
Caribbean! Nathan Stanier, disgraced undercover naval officer, protects
her on their perilous journey. But who can protect his carefully guarded
heart from her?
The final installment of Louise Allen's Those Scandalous Ravenhursts
miniseries!

• **THE DUKE'S CINDERELLA BRIDE**
by **Carole Mortimer**
(Regency)
The Duke of Stourbridge thought Jane Smith a servant girl, so when
Miss Jane is wrongly turned out of her home for inappropriate behavior
after their encounter, the Duke takes her in as his ward. Jane knows she
cannot fall for his devastating charm. Their marriage would be forbidden—
especially if he were to discover her shameful secret....
The first in Carole Mortimer's The Notorious St. Claires *miniseries*

• **TEXAS WEDDING FOR THEIR BABY'S SAKE**
by **Kathryn Albright**
(Western)
Caroline Benet thought she'd never see soldier Brandon Dumont again—but
the shocking discovery that she is carrying his child forces her to find
him.... Darkly brooding Brandon feels his injuries hinder him from being
the man Caroline deserves, so he will marry her in name only. It takes a
threat on Caroline's life to make him see he could never let her or their
unborn child out of his sight again....
The Soldier and the Socialite

• **IN THE MASTER'S BED**
by **Blythe Gifford**
(Medieval)
To live the life of independence she craves, Jane has to disguise herself as
a young man! She will allow no one to take away her freedom. But she
doesn't foresee her attraction to Duncan—who stirs unknown but delightful
sensations in her highly receptive, very feminine body.
He would teach her the art of sensuality!